PRAISE FOR TIM PRATT & HIS WORK

"Tim Pratt is in the vanguard of the next generation of master American fantasists. His delightfully loopy vision, lateral thinking and exquisite sense of style combine to provide fiction which infuses the reader like a fine Napa Valley wine, leaving behind aftershocks that go on for days, weeks, even months."
— Jay Lake, author of *Trial of Flowers*, and *Rocket Science*

"Every generation, there are writers who emerge who seem to get it a little better than the rest of us. They're the ones who understand myth....They see the world through their vision of that world in astonish is one recent example
— Jason Erik Lundberg

"Pratt is aware of all the clichés that he might fall into, and doesn't just avoid them, he plays with them before he rips them apart and gives them new shape, usually as a tight and skillful transition."
— *Tangent Online*

"Pratt keeps his story note-perfect, balancing a love for the pulps with a careful deconstruction of them."
— Jonathan Strahan, *The Coode Street Review of Science Fiction*

"Ah, no, it's that Pratt guy. L
—Jay Caselberg, aut

"...you'll find that Pratt man
conceits and imag
— Ric

"Pratt refuses to allow real-

"A genuine t

"...a gif

HART & BOOT

& OTHER STORIES

Other books by Tim Pratt

Little Gods
The Strange Adventures of Rangergirl
If There Were Wolves
Blood Engines (forthcoming)
Ferocious Dreamers (forthcoming)

HART & BOOT

& OTHER STORIES

TIM PRATT

NIGHT SHADE BOOKS
SAN FRANCISCO

5·08 Amazon 15

For Scott and Lynne

CONTENTS

HART AND BOOT

The man's head and torso emerged from a hole in the ground, just a few feet from the rock where Pearl Hart sat smoking her last cigarette. His appearance surprised her, and she cussed him at some length. The man stared at her during the outpouring of profanity, his mild face smeared with dirt, his body still half-submerged. Pearl stopped cussing and squinted at him in the fading sunlight. He didn't have on a shirt, and Pearl, being Pearl, wondered immediately if he was wearing pants.

"Who the hell are you?" she demanded. She'd been sitting for hours here on the outskirts of a Kansas mining town, waiting for dark, so she could find a bar and a man to buy her drinks. She was in a foul mood lately, as her plans for a life of riotous adventure had thus far come to nothing. She'd fled a teenage marriage in Canada after seeing a Wild West show, complete with savage Indians and lady sharpshooters, and come west to seek her fortune among such fierce characters. Her career as an outlaw was not going well so far. The problem, of course, was men. The problem was *always* men, and the fact that she enjoyed many male qualities didn't change that fact. Seeing a man now, uninvited and inter-rupting her brooding, made her angry enough to spit in a sidewinder's eye. "What're you doing in the ground?"

"I'm not sure," the man said.

Pearl couldn't place his accent. New England, maybe? "What the hell's that mean? How'd you end up in a damn hole without knowing how you got there?"

He considered that for a moment, then said, "You swear a lot, for a woman."

Pearl dropped the remains of her cigarette to the ground. "I swear a lot for anybody. Are you a miner or something?" She couldn't think of any other reason a man would be underground, popping up like a prairie dog—and even that didn't make much sense, not when you thought past the surface.

"A miner?" He chewed his lip. "Could be."

"You have any money?" Pearl said. She didn't have any more bullets, but she could hit him on the head with her gun, if he had something worth stealing.

"I don't think so."

She sighed. "Get out of that hole. I'm getting a crick in my neck, looking down at you."

He climbed out and stood before her, covered in dirt from head to toe, naked except for a pair of better-than-average boots. Hardly standard uniform for a miner, but she didn't get flustered. She'd seen her share of naked men during her eighteen years on earth, and she had to admit he was one of the nicest she'd seen, dirt and all, with those broad shoulders. Back in Canada (after seeing the Wild West show, but before deciding to leave her husband) she'd had several dreams about a tall, faceless man coming toward her bed, naked except for cowboy boots.

Apart from the dirt, and the lack of a bed, and her not being asleep and all, this was just like the dream.

She finally looked at his face. He seemed uncomfortable, like a man afraid of making a fool of himself, half-afraid he already has. "Nice boots," she said. "What'd you say your name was?"

"Uh." He looked down at his feet, then back at her face. "Boot?"

"I'll just call you John," she said. This could work out. A handsome man, big enough to look threatening, and clearly addle-brained. Just what she needed. "John Boot. I'm Pearl Hart." She stood and extended her hand. After a moment's hesitation, he shook. Soft hands, like a baby's. No way he was a miner. That was all right. Whatever he was, he'd have a new trade soon enough. He'd be a stagecoach robber, just like in the Wild West show.

"Not on my account, honey," she said, dropping a hand below his waist and smiling when he gasped, "but we ought to find you some clothes. If I lured a fella about your size out behind a bar, you think you could hit him on the head hard enough to knock him out?"

"I suppose so, Pearl," he said, as her experienced hand moved up and down on him. "I'll do whatever you want, as long as you keep doing that."

Hart and Boot robbed their way west. Pearl had tried to hold up a stagecoach once on her own, without success. She'd stepped into the road, gun in hand, and shouted for the driver to stop. He slowed down, peered at her from his high seat, and burst out laughing. He snapped the reins and the horses nearly ran Pearl down, forcing her out of the road. A woman poked her head out the window as the stage passed, her face doughy, her mouth gaping. Pearl shot at her, irritated. The recoil stung her hand, and she missed by a mile.

Clearly, she was not a natural lady sharpshooter. She needed a man, the right *kind* of man, one who could be tough and do the necessary, but *also* do as he was told, a man for the look of the thing, so people would take her seriously, and it would be best if he was a man she liked to fuck. She didn't believe such a man existed, except in her dreams.

Until she met John Boot.

They had a simple, and, to Pearl's mind, amusing method of robbing coaches. Pearl would stand weeping and wailing in the road wearing a tore-up dirty dress. There wasn't a stagecoach driver in the West who'd drive past a woman in need, and when they stopped, John Boot would emerge from cover, guns in hand. Pearl would pull her own weapons, and they'd relieve the coach of baggage, money, and mail. John Boot was always very polite, but what with Pearl's cussing, the bewildered victims seldom noticed.

Despite her insistence that John Boot always pull out, Pearl got pregnant once during those wild months. She didn't even realize she'd caught pregnant until the miscarriage. After she'd passed it all she just kicked dirt over the mess, glad to have avoided motherhood. John Boot wept when he found out about it, though, and Pearl, disturbed, left him to his tears. John Boot had depths she didn't care to explore. He mostly did whatever she told him, and didn't argue back, which was all she wanted, but it was hard to think of him in terms of his simple usefulness when he cried.

One night after Pearl came back from pissing behind a rock, she found John Boot staring up at the stars. Pearl sat with him, drunk a touch on whiskey, feeling good. She liked the stars, the big Western sky, the first man in her life who wasn't more trouble than he was worth.

"We have to stop robbing coaches," Boot said.

This display of personal opinion irritated Pearl. "Why's that?"

"They're on to us anyway," he said, not looking at her. "There's not a coach left that'll stop for a woman in distress anymore."

"Hasn't failed us yet."

"Next time." He paused. "I know. They'll come in shooting, next time."

Pearl considered. John Boot didn't talk much. Most men talked all the time and didn't know shit. Maybe with John Boot the reverse was true. "Damn," she said at last. "Well, it couldn't last forever. But we don't have to *stop*, just change our style."

After that they robbed coaches in the traditional manner, stepping from cover with guns drawn. That worked pretty well.

One night in Arizona, Pearl had trouble sleeping. Seemed like every way she rolled a rock stuck in her back or side, and the coyotes kept howling, and the big moon made everything too bright. She figured a good roll with John Boot might tire her out, so she went to wake him up. No man liked getting roused in the middle of the night, but when they got sex in return, they kept their complaints to a minimum.

Pearl didn't believe in ghosts, but when she saw John Boot lying on his bedroll, she thought he'd died and become one. He held his familiar shape, but she could see the ground right through him, as if he were made of smoke and starlight.

Pearl didn't faint away. She said, "John Boot, stop this goddamn nonsense *now!*"

His solidity returned as he opened his eyes. "Pearl," he said blearily. "What—"

"You're going like a ghost on me, John Boot, and I don't appreciate it."

His eyes took on a familiar pained, guarded look—the expression of a dog being scolded for reasons far beyond its comprehension. "Sorry, Pearl," he said, which was about the only consistently safe response in their conversations.

"I *need* you," she said.

"And I need you, Pearl." He sat up. "More than you know. Sometimes, when you aren't paying attention to me, or you're not nearby, I get so tired, and everything gets dim, kind of smoky..." He shook his head. "I don't understand it. It's like I'm not even strong enough to be real on my own. I want to stay for you, I think I have to, but I get so damn *tired.*"

John Boot almost never cussed. Pearl took his hand. "Don't you dare go away from me, John Boot."

"Do you love me, Pearl?" he asked, looking at her hand in his.

Most men, she'd have said yes just to keep them quiet. But after these past months, she owed John Boot more than that. "I don't know that I love you, but I wouldn't want you gone."

He nodded. "How long do you intend to live like this?"

"As long as it's fun," she said.

"When it stops being fun, Pearl... will you let me go? Let me be tired, and just... see what happens to me then?"

Pearl sighed. "Help me get these clothes off, John Boot. We'll figure this out later. All this talking makes me want to do something else."

He smiled, and a little of the sadness and weariness receded from his eyes.

The next day a posse caught up with them, and once Pearl and John Boot were relieved of their weapons it became clear that they were being charged with stagecoach robberies *and* murders. Someone was killing lone travelers in the area, and Hart and Boot were convenient to take the blame for that, though they had nothing to do with it. Pearl declared their innocence of all crimes, but she'd taken a pearl-handled gun in the last robbery, a distinctive weapon, and when the posse found that, it settled all questions in their minds.

Pearl and John Boot never robbed another coach, and neither did anyone else. Stagecoaches and stagecoach robbers, like lady outlaws and wild Indians, were dying breeds. Hart and Boot were the last of their kind.

The lovers were taken to Pima County jail in Florence, Arizona, a depressingly dusty place with no accommodations for women. For propriety's sake the authorities decided to leave John Boot in Florence and take Pearl to a county jail in Tucson. She argued against that course with a blue streak of profanity, but they took her away all the same, and Pearl was separated from John Boot for the first time since he'd crawled out of the ground in Kansas.

Pearl sat in her cell, looking at the rough wooden partition that divided the "women's quarters" from the other half of the cell. She was wishing for a cigarette and thinking about John Boot. What if he just went to smoke and starlight again, and disappeared?

She wanted him with her, wanted him fiercely, and around midnight a knife point poked through the thin wooden partition. Pearl watched with interest as the knife made a ragged circular opening, and a familiar head poked through.

"John Boot," she said, not without admiration. "How'd you get out? And how'd you get here all the way from Florence?"

"I'm not sure," he said. "You wanted me, and I came... but it made me awfully tired. Can we go?"

Pearl crawled through the hole. The adjoining cell was unoccupied, the door unlocked, and they walked out together as if they had every right in the world to leave. *We can be caught but we can't be kept*, she thought, elated, as they stepped into the starry night.

They stole horses and rode farther southwest, because they hadn't been that way yet.

A week later they blundered into a posse in New Mexico. The men were looking for cattle rustlers, but they settled for Hart and Boot. Pearl offered the men sexual favors in exchange for freedom, and called them every nasty name she could think of when they refused. John Boot just stood unresisting, as if the strength had been sapped out of him, as if he'd seen all this coming and knew how it would end.

The lovers were taken back to Florence (Pearl was beginning to hate that place), where they were put on trial immediately. The officers didn't want to keep them overnight and give them a chance to escape again.

The judge, a bald man with pince-nez glasses, sentenced John Boot to thirty years in the Arizona Territorial Penitentiary, a place famed for its snakepit of a dungeon, tiny cells, and ruthless guards. John Boot listened to the sentence with his usual calm, nodding to show he understood.

Then the judge looked at Pearl and frowned, clearly undecided about how to deal with her.

I'm young, she thought, *and a woman, so he thinks I got railroaded into this, that I'm John Boot's bedwarmer, a little girl led astray.*

Pearl couldn't abide that. "What the hell are you waiting for, you silly old bastard?" she asked.

John Boot winced. The judge reddened, then said, "I sentence you to five years in the same place!" He banged his gavel, and Pearl blew him a kiss.

She'd never been to prison before. She figured she wouldn't like it, but she didn't expect to be there for very long.

She was right on the first count, but sadly wrong on the second.

Pearl and John Boot weren't separated during the long ride through the desert, and Pearl vented her fury at him as they bounced along in the back of the wagon, under armed guard. "Thirty years he gave you, and me five. They think five years will knock the piss and wildcat out of me?"

"How do you stay so energetic all the time?" John Boot asked. "You've got enough strength of will for any two people. I'm surprised fire and lightning don't come shooting out your ears sometimes!"

Pearl rode silently for a long time, thinking on that. "You reckon that's how you came to be?" she asked, looking down at her knees. "Some of that fire and lightning I've got too much of spilled out, and made you?"

They'd never really talked about this before, about where John Boot came from, where he might someday return, and Pearl looked up in irritation when he didn't reply.

He was sleeping, head leaning back against the side of the cart.

Pearl sighed. At least she couldn't see the boards through his head this time. He hadn't gone to smoke and starlight. She let him be.

Pearl and John Boot climbed out of the wagon and stood in the rocky prison yard. The landscape outside was ugly, just flat desert and the dark water of the Colorado river, but the prison impressed her. Pearl had never seen a building so big. It seemed more a natural part of the landscape than something man-made. Like a palace for a scorpion queen.

"Put out that cigarette," the warden snapped. His wife stared at Pearl sternly. The warden looked tough, Pearl thought, and his stringy wife in her colorless dress looked even tougher.

Pearl flashed a smile. She took a last drag off her cigarette and flicked it away.

John Boot looked from Pearl to the warden to the warden's wife like a man watching a snake stalking a rat.

"Welcome to the Arizona Territorial Penitentiary," the warden said.

His boots aren't nearly as nice as John's, Pearl thought.

"I hear you two are escape artists," the warden said. "Well, you can forget about that nonsense here." He began to pace, hands knotted behind him. "Back the way you came there's fifty miles of desert crawling with scorpions, snakes, and Indians. The Indians get a reward for bringing back escapees, fifty dollars a head, and we don't care how banged up the prisoners get on the way. They'd love to catch a woman out there, Hart. We'd get you back, but you wouldn't be the same, and I truly don't want that to happen to you, no matter how bad you are."

"I bet I could teach them Indians a few things," Pearl said.

The warden paused in his pacing, then resumed. "Keep your tongue in your mouth, girl. Besides the desert, there's two branches of the Colorado River bordering this prison, moving fast enough that you can't swim across. Then there's the charming town of Yuma." He pointed west. "You try to go that way, and the folks in town will shoot you. They're not real friendly." He turned smartly on his bootheel and paced the other way. "That's not real important, though, because you won't get outside. The cells are carved into solid granite, so you can't cut your way out with a pocketknife." He pointed to a tower at one corner of the wall. "That's a Gatling gun on a turret up there—it can sweep the whole yard. There was an attempted prison break not long ago, and my *wife* manned the gun. Cut those convicts down."

"Ladylike," Pearl said. "Mighty Christian, too."

The wife stiffened and crossed her arms.

"I'm not happy about having you here, Hart," the warden said, putting his face close to hers, exhaling meat-and-tobacco-laden breath. "I had to tear out six bunks to make a ladies-only cell for you, and we had to hire a seamstress to make a special uniform."

"Shit, you dumb bastard," she said. "I'll sleep anywhere, and I'd just as soon go naked as wear whatever burlap sack you've got for me."

John Boot groaned.

"We're gonna clean that backtalk out of you, Hart," the warden said. He turned to the guards. "Get this man to his cell," he said, pointing at John Boot. "My wife and I will escort Miss Hart to her quarters."

The guards led John Boot away. The warden later wrote that Boot looked distinctly relieved to be leaving his lover.

Pearl went with the warden and his wife through an archway into a cramped corridor. Iron bars filled every opening, and the low ceiling made her want to duck, even though her head cleared it by a good margin. The hall smelled like sweat and urine.

"Did you enjoy shooting those boys, Mrs. Warden? Feeling that big gun jump and buck in your hands?"

"That's enough, Hart," the warden said. "Get in." He pointed to an open cell door. Pearl could see the boltholes on the wall where the bunks had been removed. A curtain hung from the ceiling, blocking the open-pit latrine from view. She'd expected open-faced cells, like at the county jail, but these cells had real doors.

"Cozy," Pearl said, and sauntered in. Men hollered unintelligibly down the corridor.

"We're going to make every effort to guard your modesty," the warden said. "You'll never be alone with a man. My wife or a female attendant will accompany me and the guards if we ever need to see you privately."

"Doesn't sound like much fun," Pearl said. "Maybe just one man alone with me every couple days? You could hold a lottery, maybe." She showed her teeth.

The warden shut the door without a word.

Pearl sat on the bunk for a while, thinking. The cell was tiny, with a narrow window set high in one rock wall. She'd roast all day and freeze all night, she knew. John Boot had better get her out soon.

She got bored, and after a while she went to the door, looking out the iron grille set in the wood. "Hey boys!" she yelled. "I'm your new neighbor, Pearl!" Hoots and whistles came down the hall. "I bet you get lonely in here! How'd you like to pass some time with me?" She went on to talk as dirty as she knew how, which was considerable. She wondered if John Boot was in earshot. He liked it when she talked like this, though he always blushed.

The men howled like coyotes, and the guards came shouting. Pearl sat down on the bunk again. She'd wait until the men quieted down, then start yelling again. That should get under the warden's skin, and pass the time until John Boot came to set her free.

Pearl woke when John Boot touched her shoulder. She sat up, brushing her hair away from her face. John Boot looked tense and dusty.

"Are we on our way, then?" Pearl asked.

He shook his head, sitting down beside her. "I don't think I can get us out, Pearl."

"What do you mean? You got into my cell, so you can get us out."

"I can get myself out, sure." He laughed forlornly. "Walls don't take much notice of me, sometimes. But you're different. Back in Tucson I had to cut you an opening." He thumped his fist on the granite wall. "I can't do that here."

"You could steal keys," Pearl said, thinking furiously. "Take a guard prisoner, and..." She trailed off. There was the Gatling gun to think of, and fifty miles of desert, if they somehow did make it out. "What are we going to do?"

"You've only got five years," he said, "and you being a woman, if you behaved yourself—"

"No! They ain't winning. Or if they do win, I'll make them miserable, so they can't enjoy it. You keep looking, John Boot. Every place has holes. You find one we can slip out of, hear?"

"I'll try Pearl, but..." He shook his head. "Don't expect too much."

"Long as you're here," Pearl said, unbuttoning her shirt.

"No," he said. "It's tiring, Pearl, going in and out like this. It's not hard to get dim, but it's hard to come *back*. Look at me." He held up his hand. It shook like a coach bouncing down a bumpy road.

"You're about as much good as bloomers in a whorehouse, John Boot," she said. "Go on back to bed, then." She watched him, curious to see how he moved in and out of impossible places.

He stood, then cleared his throat. "I don't think I can go with you watching me. I always feel more... all together... when you're paying close attention to me."

Pearl turned away. "I thought only ladies were supposed to be modest." She listened closely, but heard nothing except the distant coughs and moans of the other prisoners. She turned, and John Boot was gone, passed through her cell walls like a ghost.

Hell, she thought, *now I'm up, I won't be able to fall back asleep.* She took a deep breath, then loosed a stream of curses at the top of her lungs. The prisoners down the hall shouted back, angrily, and soon cacophony filled the granite depths of the prison.

After listening to that for a while, Pearl slept like a babe.

Pearl gave up on John Boot after about a month, but she didn't figure out a better idea for two years. The boredom nearly crushed her, sometimes, but the time passed. She got to see John Boot a lot, at least—he came to her almost every night, and seemed weaker every time.

"The warden was in here the other day," she said one night. John Boot sat against the wall, tired after his latest halfhearted search for an escape route. "Telling me what a model prisoner you are, how you never spit on the guards at bed check or raise a fuss in the middle of the night. They said you're practically rehabilitated, and that you'd want me to behave myself." She punched her thin mattress. "They still think I'm a helpless innocent, led astray by *your* wicked ways, even though I've done my damnedest to show them otherwise. Stupid bastards."

John Boot nodded. He'd heard all this before.

Pearl, sitting on the edge of her bunk, leaned toward him. "I'm tired of being here, John Boot. Two years, and there's only so much hell I can raise from inside a stone box. We have to leave this place."

"I don't see how—"

"Listen a minute. All my life I've hated being a woman—well, not hated *being* one, but hated the way people treated me, and expected me to act. It's about time I used that against the bastards, don't you think?"

John Boot looked interested now. He hadn't heard this before. "What do you mean?"

She crossed her legs. "I mean it's time for you to leave, John Boot. Go ghost on me, fade away, get as tired as you want. I think if you hadn't been coming to see me every night, you'd have turned to smoke a long time ago."

His face betrayed equal parts confusion and hope. "But why? How will my leaving help?"

She told him what she had in mind.

"That might work," he said. "But if it doesn't..."

"Then I'll figure out something else. Don't waste time, all right? I'm not up for a sentimental goodbye."

He put his hand on her knee. "One last?"

She considered. Why not? "Just be sure to pull out. I don't want to start my free life with a swelled-up belly."

After, he lay against her in the narrow bunk. "I'm a little nervous now," he said. "I'll miss you."

She stretched her arms over her head, comfortable. "I wouldn't think it. You've seemed pretty eager to get away."

"Well... in a way. Don't you ever want to go to sleep, and never have to wake up again?"

"No," she said truthfully. "I'll sleep plenty when I'm dead."

He was quiet for a moment, and then said, "I don't think I have a choice. About loving you."

Pearl touched his hair, letting her usual defenses slip a little. "I'll miss you, too, John Boot. You're the only man I could ever stand for more than a night at a time. But it's time I let you go."

"Don't look," he said, getting out of bed.

She closed her eyes.

"Goodbye, Pearl," he said, his voice faint. He went away.

It took two days for anyone to notice that John Boot was gone—he'd been so unassuming that they overlooked his empty cell at the first bed check. When the warden and his wife came to tell Pearl that John Boot had escaped, she made a big show of breaking down and crying, saying, "He told me to stay strong, that we'd walk out of here together, that as long as I didn't give in to you he wouldn't leave me!" Weeping with her face in her hands, she could glimpse the warden and his wife through her fingers. They exchanged sympathetic looks—they believed it, the stupid bastards, they still believed that John Boot was the cause of Pearl's bad behavior.

Pearl's behavior changed completely after that. In the following weeks she began wearing a dress, and having polite conversation with the warden's wife, and even started writing poetry, the sappiest, most flowery stuff she could, all about babies and sunlight and flowers. The warden's wife loved it, her tough exterior softening. "Pearl," she said once, "I feel like you and I are much the same, underneath it all." It was all Pearl could do to keep from laughing—talk like this, from the woman who'd once gunned down a yard full of convicts! That was no stranger than a stagecoach robber writing poems, maybe—Black Bart aside, of course—but with Pearl it was an *act*.

She missed John Boot a little, but if his leaving could help get her get out of prison, it was worth it. The warden told Pearl that, with John Boot's influence lifted, she was blossoming into a fine young woman. Two months after John Boot "escaped," the warden and his wife came to visit Pearl again, both of them smiling like cowboys in a whorehouse. "The governor's coming to inspect the prison soon, Pearl," the warden said. "I've talked to him about your case, discussed the possibility of giving you a pardon and an early release... and he wants to meet with you."

"That would be just fine," Pearl said demurely, thinking, *Hot damn! About time!*

The governor came into her cell, middle-aged and serious. He wore a nice gray suit and boots with swirling patterns in the leather. The warden and his wife introduced him to Pearl, then stood off to the side, beaming at their new favorite prisoner. The governor looked at them, raised an eyebrow, and said, "Could I have a little time alone with Miss Hart, to discuss her situation?" The warden and his wife practically fell over themselves getting out the door. The governor stood up and closed the cell door. "A little privacy," he said.

"Sir, I'm so glad you decided to meet with me," Pearl began. She'd been practicing this speech for days. It had loads of respect, repentance, and a fair bit about Jesus. If it didn't get her a pardon, nothing would.

"Yes, well," he said, interrupting her. He took a pocket watch from his vest, looked at it, and frowned. Then he looked Pearl up and down, and grunted. "How bad do you want a pardon, girl?"

Pearl kept smiling, though she didn't like that look in his eyes. "Very much, Governor, I've learned my lesson, I —"

"Listen, little girl, that's enough talking. I don't care how sorry you are for what you've done. You're in the worst goddamn place in the whole desert, of course you're sorry, even a rattlesnake would repent his sinful ways if he got locked up here. Now I don't have a whole lot of *time*. There's one way for you to get a pardon, and it doesn't have anything to do with talking, if you see what I mean."

Pearl stared at him, her eyes narrowed.

He looked at his watch again. "Look, you can just bend over your bunk there, you don't even need to take off your dress, I'll just lift it up."

"You go to hell, you bastard," Pearl said, crossing her arms. If he tried to touch her, she'd put a hurt on him like he'd never felt before. She almost hoped he did touch her. The governor was just like all the others, like her husband, like all the men before she'd met John Boot. Boot seemed like just about the only good man in the whole world, and she'd pretty much had to make him up out of her own mind, hadn't she?

The governor went white in the face, then red. "You're going to rot here, Miss Hart. You could've given me five minutes of your time, done what you've probably done with hundreds of filthy men, and been free. But instead—"

"I may've done it with filthy men," Pearl said, "but I've never done it yet with a nasty old pig like you."

The governor rapped on the door, and a guard came to let him out. He left without a word. The warden and his wife bustled in soon after and asked how it went. Pearl thought about telling them, but what was the use?

"It went just fine," she said.

That night, for the first time in years, Pearl cried.

Pearl dreamed of lying in her old bedroom in Canada, giving birth. The baby slid out painlessly, crying, and she picked it up, unsure how to hold it, wrinkling her nose in distaste. The baby looked like a miniature version of the governor, with piercing eyes and grim lines around his mouth. The baby's tongue slid out, over its lips, and Pearl hurled the thing away in disgust. It hit the knotty pine wall and bounced. When it landed, its face had changed, and John Boot's eyes regarded her sadly.

Pearl sat up in the dark of her cell, shivering, but not because the dream disturbed her. She shivered with excitement, because she saw a possibility, a chance at a way out.

She lay back down and thought fondly of John Boot, her wonderful John Boot, her lover, her companion, calling to him in her mind.

Nothing happened, except for time passing, and Pearl's frustration rising. Finally she fell asleep again, fists clenched tight enough to leave nail marks in her palms.

"Pearl," John Boot said.

She opened her eyes, sitting up. It was still dark, but Pearl felt like dawn was near. John Boot was on the floor—no, *in* the floor, half in a hole, just like the first time she'd met him. "Am I dreaming?" she asked.

"No, I'm really here. You felt... very angry, Pearl. It pulled me back."

Maybe that's where I went wrong, she thought. *I tried to think sweet thoughts and call him that way, and he didn't feel a thing, but when I got mad, like I was the* first *time, here he comes.* "Pulled you back from where?"

"Someplace where I was sleeping, sort of."

Pearl knelt on the hard granite floor and extended her hand. He took it warily, as if expecting her to try and break his fingers. "I'm not mad at you, John Boot," she said. She wondered about the hole. It would no doubt close up when she wasn't paying attention, as modest in its way as John Boot was himself.

"Then what's wrong?" he asked, letting her help him out of the hole. "Did your plan work, are you getting a pardon?" He sat cross-legged on the floor, naked again, except for his fine boots.

She hesitated. She planned to use John Boot, no two ways about it. Pearl seldom shrank from saying hurtful things, but she hadn't ever hurt John Boot on purpose, and he'd done a lot for her. A little lie to spare his feelings wouldn't do any harm now.

"That's right, I'm getting pardoned," she said. "The governor was very impressed with me. I'm just angry that I have to wait for the order to go through, that I'm stuck here for a few days more... and that I'm going to be alone out there, without you."

He lowered his head. "You want me to come back?"

"I wouldn't ask for that." She put her hand on his bare knee. "But... I want something special to remember you by."

"What?"

"Sleep with me, John Boot. And don't pull out this time. I want to have your baby. We'll do it as many times as we have to, tonight, tomorrow, as long as it takes."

"You mean it, Pearl?" he said, taking her hand. "Really?"

"Yes." She got on the bed. "I want your baby in the worst way."

He came to her.

A little later, lying tight against him in the narrow bed, she said, "Let's go again. We've got enough time before bed check."

"We can if you want," he said sleepily. "But we don't have to."

"Why?"

"Because it took."

She pushed herself up on her elbow and looked at him. "What do you mean?"

"The baby. It took. You're kindled." He looked into her eyes. "I can feel it. I felt it the other time, too, when you... lost it. I wish..." He shrugged. "But it's all right now."

"Oh, John Boot. You've made me so happy."

"I should go."

"Wait until dawn? I want to see your face in the morning light one more time."

He held her. When the sun came, he kissed her cheek. "I have to go."

She nodded, then looked away, to give him his privacy.

"No," he said, touching her cheek. "You can look, this time."

She watched. He dissolved like the remnant of a dream, first his warmth fading, then his skin turning to smoke, until finally he disappeared all the way, leaving Pearl with nothing in her arms but emptiness, and a tiny spark of life in her belly.

Pearl waited two months, still behaving herself. Each time she saw the warden she made a point of anxiously asking if he'd heard from the governor. They hadn't, and the warden's wife clucked her tongue and said everything would work out. Pearl had no doubt about that.

After two months, Pearl asked to see a nurse. The woman examined her, and Pearl told her she'd missed two months in a row. The nurse blushed, but didn't ask probing questions. She went to report her findings to the warden.

Pearl's pregnancy created a difficult situation. As far as anyone knew, only one man had been alone with Pearl during her years of incarceration, and that man was the governor. He would say he hadn't slept with Pearl, of course, but she would say otherwise, and publicity like that wouldn't do anybody any good. She knew the governor would take the obvious way out, and avoid the scandal.

She didn't have to wait long.

"In light of your delicate circumstances," the warden said two days later, not meeting her eyes, "the governor has decided to grant you a pardon."

"It's about damn time," Pearl said.

On the day of her release a guard gave her a ride to the nearest train station. Pearl looked at the desert where she'd had her adventures, at the harsh ground that had birthed John Boot. She laced her hands over her belly, content.

There were a lot of reporters at the train station. They'd gotten wind of her plans. Pearl had decided that life as an outlaw was all well and good, but it demanded too much sleeping rough and missing meals. She had a baby to think about, now. Originally she'd planned to get rid of the baby at the earliest opportunity, but she was having second thoughts.

Pearl had a job all lined up as a traveling lecturer. A lady outlaw with risqué stories could really pack a room, and it wouldn't be nearly so strenuous as sharpshooting in a Wild West show. She wasn't much good with a gun anyway.

She waved to the reporters as she boarded the train. They only knew she'd been pardoned, not why. They shouted questions, but she didn't pay much attention. Her mind was on other things.

One question got through to her. "Pearl!" the reporter shouted. "Are you going to meet up with John Boot?"

They still thought she needed a man, after all this time. Would that ever change? "You're a stupid bastard," she replied mildly, and followed the porter to her compartment.

LIFE IN STONE

After ascending seventy-two flights of iron stairs, creeping past tentacled sentinels lurking in pools filled with black water, and silently dispatching wizened old warriors armed with glaives and morningstars that proved a close match for his pistols and poisoned glass knives, Mr. Zealand at last stumbled into the uppermost room of Archibald Grace's invisible tower. All Zealand's earlier murders were mere journeyman work compared to this final assassination, the murder of a man who'd lived for untold centuries, who'd come to America and enslaved Buffalo spirits, who'd built this tower of ice and iron on the far side of the Rockies as a sanctuary and stronghold for his own precious life.

Zealand rested for a moment, catching his breath. He got winded so much more easily now than he had as a young man, and he didn't sleep well anymore, which made him jangly all day, most days. He leaned against a filigreed pillar of white ivory, a tusk or bone cut from some prehistoric—possibly even ahistorical—leviathan. Archibald Grace had doubtless slain whatever monster this ivory came from. He was a killer of such stature that even Zealand found himself humbled. Grace had murdered monsters, while Zealand had seldom killed anything but men. He ran his hand along the spiraled carving on the pillar, one of a dozen in the round tower room, and then he walked to the arched, open window. He looked down from the tower's lunatic height onto the small town of Cincaguas, just another little place in the valley, whose inhabitants were unaware of the magical edifice rising on the outskirts of town, an invisible spire so high that Zealand could look down on a slowly gliding California condor.

Having regained his breath, Zealand turned to face the center of the room. He unzipped his black canvas shoulder pack and reached inside to touch the haft of a stone-headed axe, an ancient implement fitted onto an unbreakable carbon-steel handle. Zealand approached the center of the room, passing the pillars, and saw what he'd been led to expect—a square box, two feet to a side, resting on an ivory pedestal. The box was a simple thing, made of aged wood worn so smooth that the grain was nearly invisible. Zealand drew one of his remaining knives, this one made of ceramic, and used the blade to pry open and lift the lid.

The box was empty. Zealand stared at the space inside for a long time, going so far as to probe the inner edges with his knife, looking for a false bottom, but there was no such concealment. The stone simply wasn't there. Despite all the effort he'd spent making his way to the top of this edifice, there would be no reward. He'd learned long ago that mere effort didn't guarantee success, but this was an especially bitter reminder of that fact.

Zealand sank to the floor, sitting cross-legged, resting his head in his hands. He was too old for this by at least a dozen years. In his younger, hungrier days, such a setback would only have infuriated and energized him, given him an adrenal surge and a slow-burning determination to soldier on, but he'd long since grown out of such dedication to his work for its own sake. For many years he'd crafted an image of himself as an implacable nightstalker, relentless avatar of death, and he'd seen his work as a sort of nightmarish inversion of a holy mission.

But he'd just turned forty-five, he suffered chronic lower back pain, he found it increasingly embarrassing to sleep with prostitutes less than half his age, and he'd spent the past dozen birthdays and New Year's Eves alone in his home amid the redwoods above Santa Cruz, California. He'd lost all illusions about his career. He was neither avenging angel nor cinematic assassin; he was simply a man who'd spent a lot of years killing people for money. This job was more of the same, despite certain baroque complications and supernatural curlicues.

Though there was the promise of something more than money as payment if he succeeded in taking Archibald Grace's life.

Zealand got to his feet. No use mourning the moment of failure. Better to push himself, weary or not, onward to the possibility of success. He reloaded his pistols and redistributed his knives. Now he had to make his way back down to the foot of the tower. Maybe the guards wouldn't harry him so, if he was only trying to leave. He could hope for that much.

The next day Zealand met his client, the thus-far-immortal Archibald Grace himself. They shared their usual booth at their usual Italian restaurant, Grace drinking cheap house wine, Zealand sticking to water.

"Damn," Grace said. "I thought for sure I'd left it there." Grace looked like a young man, with a neat black beard and eyes the clear blue of synthetic sapphires.

"You were sure you'd left it in Mammoth Caves, too," Zealand said with practiced patience. "Sure you'd left it in the Great Sequoia Forest, certain it was in your old summer palace at the bottom of Lake Champlain, and positive it was hidden behind Niagara Falls. I am beginning to suspect you need a tutorial in the proper meaning of the words 'sure,' 'certain,' and 'positive.'"

"I am sorry," Grace said, looking into his wine. "You can have ownership of the tower, of course, as usual."

"Oh, good," Zealand said. "It will go nicely with the mud-slimed cave full of ghosts behind Niagara, and the sinkhole decorated with obscene pictographs in Mammoth Caves. Though I admit the palace in Champlain is nice. If it weren't also the den of an aquatic monster, I might even go back there. I'd like the tower better if it weren't full of homicidal beasts and your wizened homunculi."

"There's a phrase, to stop them from attacking you," Grace said, making a familiar grasping motion with his left hand. "But I've forgotten it. I've forgotten so many things." He still stared into his wine, as if he might find his missing memories at the bottom of the glass.

Zealand, who was not a man given to casual gestures of physical affection, reached across to touch Grace's hand. "Don't worry," he said. "I'll find your life, and I will crush it. You will die."

"I'm sure it's in North America," Grace said. "I moved everything with me when I came here. I came with the...." He made the grasping motion again.

"The Vikings," Zealand said, sitting back. "On the longboats. You've told me."

"I brought my life, my soul, hidden in a stone. Or, perhaps, an egg." Grace cupped his hands around a half-remembered roundness. "All the wizards and witches and giants and monsters knew the trick, to put your life somewhere safe, so your body couldn't be killed. So long as your life is safe, you live. We used to hide our souls in tree trunks, until the witch hunters began putting whole forests to the torch. As the trees burned, the souls burned, and sorcerers screamed across the continent." He clucked his tongue. "Then, for a time, it was fashionable to hide your life in the head of a toad, but toads are stupid, and often get eaten, or die. I was always smart. I hid my life well."

"I know," Zealand said.

"But I've forgotten where I put it." Grace looked up from his wine, into

Zealand's face, and for a moment it was clear he'd forgotten who Zealand was. "I've forgotten so many things. It's hard to know which things are worth remembering, when you don't have a soul."

"I know," Zealand said again.

"I used to be a giant." Grace looked wistful. "Before I was a man. I broke the spines of mammoths in my hands. But I've forgotten how to be a giant, and I don't want to be a man. I only want to die."

"I know," Zealand said, for the third time. Three times was usually enough to make Grace stop going over the usual elusive reminiscences again. "Where should I look next, do you think?"

"Look for what?" Grace said, blinking his beautiful eyes.

"Come, then," Zealand said. "I'll take you home."

Some weeks later, after another pair of fruitless searches for Grace's life, Zealand crunched through the snow-covered sand on the shore of Lake Tahoe. The water was still and blue, and though there was no wind, the cold was bitter and penetrating, making the inside of Zealand's nose burn with every breath. A woman stood on the edge of the water, a long black scarf hanging motionless down her back, her thick down coat the red of arterial spurt.

"Are you Hannah?" Zealand asked.

She turned, the lower half of her face covered by the scarf. "Mr. Zed?" she said, her accent British and precise. Her eyes were the color of the water, almost the color of Archibald Grace's own, which made sense, as Hannah claimed to be Grace's daughter. When she'd first contacted him, Zealand had been suspicious, partly because Grace's apparent sexual preference made the presence of offspring rather unlikely, but upon further consideration it was understandable that someone as old as Grace would have tried various partners and sexual permutations, probably many times over. Hannah had known things about Grace that Grace barely remembered about himself, and Zealand was reasonably certain her claim was true.

"You told me you know the whereabouts of your father's life," Zealand said. He was still fascinated by her eyes, so like Grace's.

"I do. I'll take you there, but you have to do something for me first."

"I'm not prepared to wait," Zealand said. His tone was polite, but the menace was implicit.

She laughed, harsh and hyena-like, quite unlike her urbane voice. "Father has lived for epochs. Another day or two won't matter."

"Nevertheless, I want you to tell me now."

She pulled the scarf down. Below the eyes, her face was inhuman, with two holes covered by membranous flaps where her nose should have been. Her mouth was lipless, filled by a score of two-inch-long interlocking incisors. She resembled nothing so much as a deep-sea fish, one of those horrors fishermen occasionally pulled up in their nets, and Zealand recalled Grace's claim to have spent years living beneath the sea. When Hannah spoke again, her mouth did not open, and Zealand realized that her human voice was a magical contrivance, not something born of her own vocal cords at all. "My father is almost a god, and my mother was the mistress of black oceanic caves. I will decide where we go, and when."

Zealand drew a pistol and fired a shot, blowing off Hannah's right knee. She screamed, this time opening her mouth, and it was an inhuman, gurgling sound. She fell to the sand, throwing her head back into the snow, her monstrous teeth spreading apart, her long tongue lolling out as she shrieked. She had a bioluminescent bulb on the end of her tongue, glowing a sick yellow.

Zealand put his gun away, wondering if he'd made his point sufficiently. Hannah had stopped screaming, so perhaps not. Feeling himself cloaked in a kind of prevailing numbness, what he had long thought of as his "working state," Zealand put one heavy boot down on Hannah's right thigh, just above her destroyed knee, then bent over to grasp her ankle in both hands. He wrenched her leg upward, grunting and twisting, pulling on her ankle while pressing down on the thigh with his foot, until her lower leg came free with a sickening pop. Hannah lashed and flailed at him, but the pain made her imprecise. Zealand noted with interest that she didn't bleed, though the wound seeped clear water. He hurled her lower leg into the lake, then stepped away from her thrashing limbs. "I hope you're part starfish, or that leg might be gone forever. You'll tell me where to find your father's life now."

Tears ran from Hannah's eyes. Her screams had subsided to whimpers, and the whimpering didn't stop when she spoke in her magical human voice—both sounds emerged simultaneously. "I only wanted to see my father again. I wanted you to take me to him. I've hated him for too long, hated him for his essential nature, and I wanted him to know that I forgave him, if he would forgive me." Despite her obvious agony, her voice remained clear and barely modulated.

"Your father has something like Alzheimer's, but more profound. He doesn't even remember your existence." Zealand had asked Grace if he knew anyone named Hannah, and Grace had given him that blank, desperate look and grasped at the air, but that was all. He'd been quiet and morose for hours after Zealand asked him, though, and Zealand suspected that Hannah's name had set up unpleasant resonances deep inside Grace, below his conscious mind. "But since he doesn't remember you, it means he doesn't hold a grudge for whatever drove the two of you apart, if that's any comfort."

"His mind is gone?"

"Not entirely, but it is degrading more every day. I think it comes from having lived so long without his soul."

"You intend to restore his soul to him?"

Zealand shook his head.

Hannah stared up at him, her monstrous jaw clenched. "Then you will kill him, destroy his life?"

"It's what he wants. It's why he hired me." Zealand gestured with a gloved hand. "You've exhausted my patience once already. Are you trying to do so again? Direct me to your father's life."

"I have to show you."

Zealand sighed. He trudged up the shore to his car and returned with his tool bag. He withdrew a pair of bolt cutters and snapped off Hannah's teeth, one at a time. Then he flipped her over onto her stomach and bound her hands behind her with thick plastic loops that tightened with a tug. He picked her up over his shoulder and carried her, his knees creaking under the combined weight of Hannah and his tool bag; at least she didn't thrash. He was breathing hard by the time they reached his car, an SUV rented under a false name. He put her in the passenger seat, and, after a moment's thought, pulled the scarf back up over the lower half of her face. Looking at her broken teeth and glowing tongue made him feel uncomfortable, and a little guilty, the latter an emotion that had plagued him more and more in recent years. His "working state" was already fading, and the emotions that replaced it were not welcome.

After he got into the driver's seat, Zealand said, "Guide me."

Zealand crouched on the edge of a creek in a wilderness area in the mountains above the lake. Hannah lay on her side in the snow nearby. Zealand was exhausted. He'd carried her nearly two miles from the trailhead, most of that well off the path, falling twice when the treacherous snow and ice gave way beneath his footsteps. His knees ached, and his feet were numb inside his boots, but he'd made it. Hannah had led him to a pretty place of tall pines, cracked gray rock faces, and a rushing mountain stream.

"It's filled with rocks," Zealand said, staring down at the bottom of the wide, swiftly flowing stream.

"It's white, speckled with red, egg-shaped, almost as big as your fist," Hannah said.

Zealand saw the stone, half-buried among water-smoothed rocks. He pulled off his glove, pushed up his sleeve, and plunged his hand into the water. It was deeper than it seemed, and he had to submerge his arm past the elbow before he could reach the stone. He grasped it and pulled it out of the water. Zealand's whole arm was numbed by cold, and he thought briefly how nice it would be to feel that way all over, inside and out, just cold and aching nothingness, the way he felt on a job, but forever. He couldn't even feel the texture of the stone in his hand, just the weight, which was greater than he would have expected.

He held Archibald Grace's life in his hand.

Dropping the stone into his coat pocket, he walked to where Hannah lay in the snow. "Thank you," he said. "Would you like me to kill you now? I can be quick."

"No!" Hannah shouted, her eyes wide.

"Your wounds are grievous," Zealand said.

"I'll heal."

Zealand looked down at her for a moment, then nodded. He thought she probably would. She was Grace's daughter. He squatted on his heels in the snow. "Tell me, before I decide what to do with you, how did you find Grace's life?"

"It was in his tower, at Cincaguas. I used to play there, as a child—there's a room that opens onto the ocean, onto the caves where I was born, so I could travel freely between them. I went to the tower last year, and Father hadn't changed the pass phrase, so the guards let me through. I thought I could make my father talk to me if I had his life, that I could use the stone as leverage. But I couldn't even *find* him. Then I heard you were working for Father, that you'd been seen around his old haunts, searching for his life. I didn't know he'd hired you to kill him, so I contacted you."

"I suppose you regret that now."

"I only regret not being able to talk to my father. I'd gladly give up a leg for that chance."

"Life is disappointment," Zealand said, and he'd never meant any three words so completely. He pondered the possibility of mercy. "I can throw you into the stream," he said, "or I can leave you for the coyotes."

"Stream," she said, without hesitation.

"And if I let you live today, will you come for me later, and try to kill me?"

"Never."

"Liar," Zealand said, almost appreciatively. He picked her up by her one good leg and the straps that bound her wrists, swung her a few times, and tossed her into the stream. He stood in the snow long enough to watch her wriggle away, eel-like, and disappear over the falls, flowing back down toward the lake.

Zealand kissed Grace just behind his left ear, and Grace moaned and moved his body back against him.

"I found your life yesterday," Zealand said. "Not forty miles from here."

Grace went stiff in Zealand's arms. They lay together in a wide, soft bed, mountain morning light filling the window and the room. "And now you want to use it to control me," Grace said, his voice heavy with disappointment, but not surprise.

Zealand put his hand on Grace's slim, bare thigh. "No," he said. "I just wanted to spend one more night with you, before smashing your soul apart."

Grace relaxed. "Good. That's good. I've lived for eons. Another day doesn't matter much."

Zealand shifted uncomfortably at this echo of Hannah's words. He shouldn't have treated her with such brutality. He was tired of doing things he regretted, tired of feeling ashamed, tired of bad dreams. How nice it would be to become immortal, and let his regrets drain away, or freeze over.

Apropos of nothing obvious, Grace said, "It's easier to be a sorcerer when you don't have a soul. It's easier to do the awful things you have to do, when you know the true sensation and emotion will be forgotten in the aftermath."

Not for the first time, Zealand wondered if Grace could overhear his thoughts. "How does it feel?" he asked. "Putting your soul aside?" It was an important question, and one he hadn't asked before.

"It's been so long since I had my soul, I don't recall the difference." Grace rolled away and sat on the edge of the bed. Zealand looked at the muscles in his unblemished back. "Fear is the first to go, which is liberating. Then other feelings fade. Your memories go, but it's the bad memories first, so it seems a boon. Finally the conscious will to live erodes, and you become like a moss or a lichen, living for the sake of mere existence. But you retain your mind, and so there is some dissatisfaction, some sense of..." He grasped at the air. "Eventually, you long for death."

"Do you wish to die, even when you're with me?" Zealand said.

Grace shrugged. "Perhaps moss enjoys the sensation of falling rain, or the warmth of sunlight. But that's not meaning. It's just pleasure." Without turning around, he said, "Do you still want your payment for killing me? Do you still want me to show you how to be immortal?"

Zealand didn't answer. It had seemed obvious, before. An immortal life, free from self-doubt, self-loathing, and fear—of course he wanted that. He touched Grace's back. Despite their time embracing, Grace's skin was cool, almost cold.

Zealand didn't answer Grace's question, and after a while, Grace forgot he'd asked, and went into the kitchen to get a piece of fruit.

After they made love a final time, after Grace taught Zealand the trick of putting his soul aside, they went out onto the deck that jutted over the cold blue vastness of Lake Tahoe. Here on the northern shore houses were fewer and farther apart than on the more tourist-friendly south shore, and they had a clear view of snowy mountains and evergreens. The brisk air made standing on the deck a bracing experience, and Zealand narrowed his eyes against the lake wind. He placed the spotted stone that held Grace's life on the redwood deck railing. Grace didn't seem interested in it; he just gazed, wide-eyed, at the mountains, as if seeing them for the first time. "Go ahead," he said. "I'm ready."

Zealand raised the old stone axe with its unbreakable handle. He thought about touching Grace, or kissing him, but the time for that had passed, and hesitation would only make this harder. He brought down the axe, and shattered Grace's life.

The spotted rock burst apart, and light the color of Grace's eyes shone forth, blazing so brightly that even when Zealand squeezed his eyes shut, he saw blue. After a moment the light faded, and Zealand opened his eyes.

Grace sagged against the railing, his whole body trembling, and when he spoke, his words were choked by sobs. "I have a daughter," he said, and then began pounding his head against the deck railing, slamming his forehead down so hard that the wood audibly cracked. Grace looked up at Zealand, his forehead gashed, blood running into his eyes, and screamed, "Finish it! Kill the body!"

Zealand lifted the axe again and brought it down between Grace's eyes. The man's forehead caved in, and the axe stuck there, embedded in Grace's skull, trapped fast in bone as old as the mountains. Grace fell back on the deck, dead.

Zealand went inside for the tarps and the chains he'd need to sink Grace to the lake bottom. His hands trembled as he wrapped Grace in the heavy plastic. The dead man had shaped nations, seduced monsters, and lived to the outer extremes of experience, but he'd died like anyone, like so many others at Zealand's hands—messily, and speaking only of regrets.

Zealand sat by Grace's corpse, holding the dead man's hand for a while, and contemplated the nature of immortality.

Zealand sat in the upper room of the tower at Cincaguas, holding an oblong piece of shaped marble in his hand. The stone was prepared according to Grace's instructions, as a receptacle for Zealand's life, and he could never make another—this was one-time magic, once and forever magic. Zealand heard the distant scrape and clang of weapons on the lower floors. He'd claimed possession of the tower with the pass phrase he'd learned from Hannah, and then he'd changed the phrase to one only he knew. But the guards were old, and Hannah knew her way around, so he was not surprised to see her limp in through the arched doorway. She apparently did have some starfish in her ancestry, because her leg had grown back, though it was knotty as coral, and a bit shorter than the other leg. She wore the slashed remains of a dark blue wetsuit, and she bled water from the wounds the guards had inflicted. Her teeth had grown back, too, though they curved off at strange angles, and some of them cut her face when she closed her mouth.

"You killed my father," she said, her voice emerging from the air before her, a calm statement of fact.

"He wanted me to," Zealand said. He didn't stand up.

"I don't care. Because of you, I never had a chance to talk to him, and make things right between us."

Zealand rolled the marble egg between his palms. "He mentioned you in his last words. He said he had a daughter, and I've never heard such anguish."

"He remembered me?"

"He remembered everything, and I think he wanted to die even more, once he did."

"I came here to kill you," Hannah said, but she didn't come any closer.

"I thought you might." He held up the stone, so she could see it. "I've been up here for weeks, trying to decide if I should put my life in this rock. I've never been an indecisive person, but I've been balanced on the edge over this." He glanced up at her, then away, and said, "I'm sorry for the way I hurt you." He set the egg on the stone floor.

Hannah sat down beside him. She smelled strongly of salt water. "My father never told me he was sorry for anything."

"He wasn't capable of being sorry, not while his soul was put aside."

"I'm sure that made his life easier."

"Mmm," Zealand said. "Are you still going to kill me?"

"Perhaps. Did you love my father?"

"As well as I was able. But I may as well have loved a cloud, or the stars, for all the feeling that was returned."

"I know how that feels." She picked up the marble egg. "I don't think I'll kill you. Not just now."

"I almost want you to. It would take the decision out of my hands. I wish I knew where to go from here."

She laughed, that harsh hyena sound, and Zealand realized that her laughter, unlike her voice, came from her own throat. "No one knows that." She put the marble egg back in Zealand's hand. "Not even my father knew where to go next. He just knew he was going to keep going on forever. Until you helped him find forever's end."

Zealand nodded. He stood and walked to the tower window, and looked down at the earth, far below. Hannah came and stood beside him.

"It's a long way down," Zealand said.

"Looked at another way," Hannah said, "we've come a long way *up*."

Zealand squeezed the stone in his hand. It was cold, and hard, and didn't yield at all under the pressure of his hand. He thought about irrevocable decisions.

Zealand dropped the marble egg out the window, and Hannah stood beside him as they watched it fall.

CUP AND TABLE

Sigmund stepped over the New Doctor, dropping a subway token onto her devastated body. He stepped around the spreading shadow of his best friend, Carlsbad, who had died as he'd lived: inconclusively, and without fanfare. He stepped over the brutalized remains of Ray, up the steps, and kept his eyes focused on the shrine inside. This room in the temple at the top of the mountain at the top of the world was large and cold, and peer as he might back through the layers of time—visible to Sigmund as layers of gauze, translucent as sautéed onions, decade after decade peeling away under his gaze—he could not see a time when this room had not existed on this spot, bare but potent, as if only recently vacated by the God who'd created and abandoned the world.

Sigmund approached the shrine, and there it was. The cup. The prize and goal and purpose of a hundred generations of the Table. The other members of the Table were dead, the whole *world* was dead, except for Sigmund.

He did not reach for the cup. Instead, he walked to the arched window and looked out. Peering back in time he saw mountains and clouds and the passing of goats. But in the present he saw only fire, twisting and writhing, consuming rock as easily as trees, with a few mountain peaks rising as yet untouched from the flames. Sigmund had not loved the world much—he'd enjoyed the music of Bach, violent movies, and vast quantities of cocaine—and by and large he could have taken or left civilization. Still, knowing the world was consumed in fire made him profoundly sad.

Sigmund returned to the shrine and seized the cup—heavy, stone, more blunt object than drinking vessel—and prepared to sip.

But then, at the last moment, Sigmund didn't drink. He did something else instead.

But first:

Or, arguably, later:

Sigmund slumped in the back seat, Carlsbad lurking on the floorboards in his semi-liquid noctiluscent form, Carlotta tapping her razored silver fingernails on the steering wheel, and Ray—the newest member of the Table—fiddling with the radio. He popped live scorpions from a plastic bag into his mouth. Tiny spines were rising out of Ray's skin, mostly on the nape of his neck and the back of his hands, their tips pearled with droplets of venom.

"It was a beautiful service," Sigmund said. "They sent the Old Doctor off with dignity."

Carlsbad's tarry body rippled. Ray turned around, frowning, face hard and plain as a sledgehammer, and said, "What the fuck are you talking about, junkie? We haven't even gotten to the funeral home yet."

Sigmund sank down in his seat. This was, in a way, even more embarrassing than blacking out.

"Blood and honey," Carlotta said, voice all wither and bile. "How much of that shit did you snort this morning, that you can't even remember what day it is?"

Sigmund didn't speak. They all knew he could see into the past, but none of them knew the full extent of his recent gyrations through time. Lately he'd been jerking from future to past and back again without compass or guide. Only the Old Doctor had known about that, and now that he was dead, it was better kept a secret.

They reached the funeral home, and Sigmund had to go through the ceremony all over again. Grief—unlike sex, music, and cheating at cards—was not a skill that could be honed by practice.

The Old Doctor welcomed Sigmund, twenty years old and tormented by visions, into the library at the Table's headquarters. Shelves rose everywhere like battlements, the floors were old slate, and the lights were ancient crystal-dripping chandeliers, but the Old Doctor sat in a folding chair at a card table heaped with books.

"I expected, well, something *more*," Sigmund said, thumping the rickety table with his hairy knuckles. "A big slab of mahogany or something, a table with authority."

"We had a fine table once," the Old Doctor said, eternally middle-aged and absently professorial. "But it was chopped up for firewood during a siege in the 1600s." He tapped the side of his nose. "There's a lesson in that. No asset, human or material, is important compared to the continued existence of the organization itself."

"But surely *you're* irreplaceable," Sigmund said, awkward attempt at job security through flattery. The room shivered and blurred at the edges of his vision, but it had not changed much in recent decades, a few books moving here and there, piles of dust shifting across the floor.

The Old Doctor shook his head. "I am the living history of the Table, but if I died, a new doctor would be sent from the archives to take over operations, and though his approach might differ from mine, his role would be the same—to protect the cup."

"The cup," Sigmund said, sensing the cusp of mysteries. "You mean the Holy Grail."

The Old Doctor ran his fingers along the spine of a dusty leatherbound book. "No. The Table predates the time of Christ. We guard a much older cup."

"The cup, is it here, in the vaults?"

"Well." The Old Doctor frowned at the book in his hands. "We don't actually know where the cup is anymore. The archives have... deteriorated over the centuries, and there are gaps in my knowledge. It would be accurate to say the agents of the Table now *seek* the cup, so that we may protect it properly again. That's why you're here, Sigmund. For your ability to see into the past. Though we'll have to train you to narrow your focus to the here-and-now, to peel back the gauze of time at will." He looked up from the book and met Sigmund's eyes. "As it stands, you're almost useless to me, but I've made useful tools out of things far more broken than *you* are."

Some vestigial part of Sigmund's ego bristled at being called broken, but not enough to stir him to his own defense. "But I can only look back thirty or forty years. How can that help you?"

"I have... a theory," the Old Doctor said. "When you were found on the streets, you were raving about gruesome murders, yes?"

Sigmund nodded. "I don't know about *raving*, but yes."

"The murders you saw took place over a hundred years ago. On that occasion, you saw back many more years than usual. Do you know why?"

Sigmund shook his head. He thought he *did* know, but shame kept him from saying.

"I suspect your unusual acuity was the result of all that speed you snorted," the Old Doctor said. "The stimulants enabled you to see deeper into the past. I have, of course, vast quantities of very fine methamphetamines at my disposal, which you can use to aid me in my researches."

Sigmund said, "Vast quantities?" His hands trembled, and he clasped them to make them stop.

"Enough to let you see *centuries* into the past," the Old Doctor said. "Though we'll work up to that, of course."

"When I agreed to join the Table, I was hoping to do field work."

The Old Doctor sniffed. "That business isn't what's important, Sigmund. Assassination, regime change, paltry corporate wars—that's just the hackwork our agents do to pay the bills. It's not worthy of your gifts."

"Still, it's what I want. I'll help with your research if you let me work in the field." Sigmund had spent a childhood in cramped apartments and hospital wards, beset by visions of the still-thrashing past. In those dark rooms he'd read comic books and dreamed of escaping the prison of circumstance—of being a superhero. But heroes like that weren't real. Anyone who put on a costume and went out on the streets to fight crime would be murdered long before morning. At some point in his teens Sigmund had graduated to spy thrillers and Cold War history, passing easily from fiction to nonfiction and back again, reading about double- and triple-agents with an interest that bordered on the fanatical. Becoming a spy—that idea had the ring of the plausible, in a way that becoming a superhero never could. Now, this close to that secret agent dream, he wouldn't let himself be shunted into a pure research position. This was his chance.

The Old Doctor sighed. "Very well."

"What's it like?" Carlotta said, the night after their first mission as a duo. She'd enthralled a senator while Sigmund peered into the past to find out where the microfilm was hidden. Now, after, they were sitting at the counter in an all-night diner where even *they* didn't stand out from the crowd of weirdoes and freaks.

Sigmund sipped decaf coffee and looked around at the translucent figures of past customers, the crowd of nights gone by, every booth and stool occupied by ghosts. "It's like layers of gauze," he said. "Usually I just see the past distantly, shimmering, but if I concentrate I can sort of... shift my focus." He thumped his coffee cup and made the liquid inside ripple. "The Old Doctor taught me to keep my eyes on the here-and-now, unless I *need* to look back, and then I just sort of..." He gestured vaguely with his hands, trying to create a physical analogue for a psychic act, to mime the metaphysical. "I guess I sort of twitch the gauze aside, and pass through a curtain, and the present gets blurrier while the past comes into focus."

"That's a shitty description," Carlotta said, sawing away at the rare steak and eggs on her plate.

The steak, briefly, shifted in Sigmund's vision and became a living, moving part of a cow. Sigmund's eyes watered, and he looked away. He mostly ate vegetables for that very reason. "I've never seen the world any other way, so I don't know how to explain it better. I can't imagine what it's like for you, seeing just the present. It must seem very *fragile*."

"We had a guy once who could see into the future, just a little bit, a couple of minutes at most. Didn't stop him from getting killed, but he wet himself right before the axe hit him. He was a lot less boring than you are." Carlotta belched.

"Why haven't I met you before?" Sigmund shrank back against the cushions in the booth.

"I'm heavy ordnance," Carlsbad said, his voice low, a rumble felt in Sigmund's belly and bones as much as heard by his ears. "I've been with the Table since the beginning. They don't reveal secrets like me to research assistants." Carlsbad was tar-black, skin strangely reflective, face eyeless and mouthless, blank as a minimalist snowman's, human only in general outline. "But the Old Doctor says you've exceeded all expectations, so we'll be working together from time to time."

Sigmund looked into Carlsbad's past, as far as he could—which was quite far, given the cocktail of uppers singing in his blood—and Carlsbad never changed; black, placid, eternal. "What—" *What are you*, he'd nearly asked. "What do you do for the Table?"

"Whatever the Old Doctor tells me to," Carlsbad said.

Sigmund nodded. "Carlotta told me you're a fallen god of the underworld."

"That bitch lies," Carlsbad said, without disapproval. "I'm no god. I'm just, what's that line—'the evil that lurks in the hearts of men.' The Old Doctor says that as long as one evil person remains on Earth, I'll be alive."

"Well," Sigmund said. "I guess you'll be around for a while, then."

The first time Carlsbad saved his life, Sigmund lay panting in a snowbank, blood running from a ragged gash in his arm. "You could have let me die just then," Sigmund said. Then, after a moment's hesitation: "You could have benefited from my death."

Carlsbad shrugged, shockingly dark against the snow. "Yeah, I guess."

"I thought you were *evil*," Sigmund said, lightheaded from blood loss and exertion, more in the *now* than he'd ever felt before, the scent of pines and the bite of cold air immediate reminders of his miraculously ongoing life. "I mean, you're *made* of evil."

"You're made mostly of carbon atoms," Carlsbad said. "But you don't spend all your time thinking about forming long-chain molecules, do you? There's more to both of us than our raw materials."

"Thank you for saving me, Carlsbad."

"Anytime, Sigmund." His tone was laid-back but pleased, the voice of someone who'd seen it all but could still sometimes be pleasantly surprised. "You're the first Table agent in four hundred years who's treated me like something other than a weapon or a monster. I know I scare you shitless, but you *talk* to me."

Exhaustion and exhilaration waxed and waned in Sigmund. "I like you because you don't change. When I look at most people I can see them as babies, teenagers, every step of their lives superimposed, and if I look back far enough they disappear—but not you. You're the same as far back as I can see." Sigmund's eyelids were heavy. He felt light. He thought he might float away.

"Hold on," Carlsbad said. "Help is on the way. Your death might not diminish me, but I'd still like to keep you around."

Sigmund blacked out, but not before hearing the whirr of approaching helicopters coming to take him away.

"I'm the New Doctor," the New Doctor said. Willowy, brunette, young, she stood behind a podium in the briefing room, looking at the assembled Table agents—Sigmund, Carlotta, Carlsbad, and the recently promoted Ray. They were the alpha squad, the apex of the organization, and the New Doctor had not impressed them yet. "We're going to have some changes around here. We need to get back to basics. We need to find the *cup*. These other jobs might fill our bank accounts, but they don't further our cause."

Ray popped a wasp into his mouth, chewed, swallowed, and said, "Fuck that mystic bullshit." His voice was accompanied by a deep, angry buzz, a sort of wasp-whisper in harmony with the normal workings of his voicebox. Ray got nasty and impatient when he ate wasps. "I joined up to make money and get a regular workout, not chase after some imaginary Grail." Sigmund knew Ray was lying—that he had a very specific interest in the cup—but Sigmund also understood why Ray was keeping that interest a secret. "You just stay in the library and read your books like the Old Doctor did, okay?"

The New Doctor shoved the podium over, and it fell toward Ray, who dove out of the way. While he was moving, the New Doctor came around and kicked him viciously in the ribs, her small boots wickedly pointed and probably steel-toed. Ray rolled away, panting and clutching his side.

Sigmund peered into the New Doctor's past. She looked young, but she'd looked young for *decades*.

"I'm not like the Old Doctor," she said. "He missed his old life in the archives, and was content with his books, piecing together the past. But I'm glad to be out of the archives, and under my leadership, we're going to make history, not study it."

"I'll *kill* you," Ray said. Stingers were growing out of his fingertips, and his voice was all buzz now.

"Spare me," the New Doctor said, and kicked him in the face.

By spying on their pasts and listening in on their private moments, Sigmund learned why the other agents wanted to find the cup, and see God:

Carlotta whispered to one of her lovers, the shade of a great courtesan conjured from an anteroom of Hell: "I want to castrate God, so he'll never create another world."

Ray told Carlotta, while they disposed of the body of a young archivist who'd discovered their secret past and present plans: "I want to eat God's heart and belch out words of creation."

Carlsbad, alone, staring at the night sky (a lighted void, while his own darkness was utter), had imaginary conversations with God that always came down, fundamentally, to one question: "Why did you make me?"

The New Doctor, just before she poisoned the Old Doctor (making it look like a natural death), answered his bewildered plea for mercy by saying: "No. As long as you're alive, we'll *never* find the cup, and I'll *never* see God, and I'll *never* know the answers to the ten great questions I've composed during my time in the archives."

Sigmund saw it all, every petty plan and purpose that drove his fellows, but he had no better purpose himself. The agents of the Table might succeed in finding the cup, not because they were worthy, but simply because they'd been trying for years upon years, and sometimes persistence led to success.

Sigmund knew their deepest reasons, and kept all their secrets, because past and present and cause and effect were scrambled for him. The Old Doctor's regime of meth, cocaine, and more exotic uppers had ravaged Sigmund's nasal cavities and set him adrift in time. At first, he'd only been able to *see* back in time, but sometimes taking the Old Doctor's experimental stimulants *truly* sent him back in time. Sometimes it was just his mind that traveled, sent back a few days to relive past events again in his own body, but other times, rarely, he physically traveled back, just a day or two at most, just for a little while, before being wrenched back to a present filled with headaches and nosebleeds.

On one of those rare occasions when he traveled physically back in time, Sigmund saw the Old Doctor's murder, and was snapped back to the future moments before the New Doctor could kill him, too.

Ray ate a Sherpa's brain two days out of base camp, and after that, he was able to guide them up the crags and paths toward the temple perfectly, though he was harder to converse with, his speech peppered with mountain idioms. He developed a taste for barley tea flavored with rancid yak butter, and sometimes sang lonely songs that merged with the sound of the wind.

"We're going to Hell," the New Doctor said.

"Probably," Sigmund said, edging away.

She sighed. "No, really—we're going into the underworld. Or, well, sort of a visiting room for the underworld."

"I've heard rumors about that." Hell's anteroom was where Carlotta found her ghostly lovers. "One of the Table's last remaining mystic secrets. I'm surprised they didn't lose that, too, when they lost the key to the moon and the scryer's glass and all those other wonders in the first war with the Templars."

"Much has been lost." The New Doctor pushed a shelf, which swung easily away from the wall on secret hinges, revealing an iron grate. "But that means much can be regained." She pressed a red button. "Stop fidgeting, Sigmund. I'm not going to kill you. But I do want to know, how did you get into the Old Doctor's office and see me kill him, when I *know* you were on assignment with Carlsbad in Belize at the time? And how did you disappear afterward? Bodily bilocation? Ectoplasmic projection? What?"

"Time travel," Sigmund said. "I don't just see into the past. Sometimes I travel into the past physically."

"Huh. I didn't see anything about that in the Old Doctor's notes."

"Oh, no. He kept the most important notes in his head. So why aren't you going to kill me?"

Something hummed and clattered beneath the floor.

"Because I can use you. Why haven't you turned me in?"

Sigmund hesitated. He'd liked the Old Doctor, who was the closest thing he'd ever had to a father. He hated to disrespect the old man's memory, though he knew the Old Doctor had seen him as a research tool, a sort of ambulatory microfiche machine, and nothing more. "Because I'm ready for things to change. I thought I wanted to be an operative, but I'm tired of the endless pointless round-and-round, not to mention being shot and stabbed and thrown from moving trains. Under your leadership, I think the Table might actually *achieve* something."

"We will." The grinding and humming underground intensified, and she raised her voice. "We'll find the cup, and see God, and get answers. We'll find out why he created the world, only to immediately abandon his creation, letting chaos fill his wake. But first, to Hell. Here." She tossed something glittering toward him, a few old subway tokens. "To pay the attendant."

The grinding stopped, the grate sliding open to reveal a tarnished brass elevator car operated by a man in a cloak the color of dust and spiderwebs. He held out his palm, and Sigmund and the New Doctor each dropped a token into his hand.

"Why are we going... down there?" Sigmund asked.

"To see the Old Doctor, and get some of that information he kept only in his head. I know where to find the cup—or where to find the map that leads to it, anyway—but I need to know what will happen once I have the cup in hand."

"Why take me?"

"Because only insane people, like Carlotta, risk going to Hell's anteroom alone. And if I took anyone else, they'd find out I was the one who killed the Old Doctor, and they might be less understanding about it than you are." She stepped into the elevator car, and Sigmund followed. He glanced into the attendant's past, almost reflexively, and the things he saw were so horrible that he threw himself back into the far corner of the tiny car; if the elevator hadn't already started moving, he would have pried open the doors and fled. The attendant turned his head to look at him, and Sigmund squeezed his eyes shut so that he didn't have to risk seeing the attendant frown, or worse, smile.

"Interesting," the New Doctor said.

After they returned from Hell, Sigmund and the New Doctor fucked furiously beneath the card table in the Old Doctor's library, because sex is an antidote to death, or at least, an adequate placebo.

* * *

"That's it, then," the New Doctor said. "We're going to the Himalayas."

"Fucking great," Ray said. "I always wanted to eat a Yeti."

"I think you're hairy enough already," Carlotta said.

Sigmund and the New Doctor sat beneath a ledge of rock, frigid wind howling across the face of the mountain. Carlsbad was out looking for Ray and Carlotta, who had stolen all the food and oxygen and gone looking for the temple of the cup alone. They wanted to kill God, not ask him questions, so their betrayal was troublesome but not surprising. Sigmund probably should have told someone about their planned betrayal, but he felt more and more like an actor outside time—a position which, he now realized, was likely to get him killed. He needed to take a more active role.

"Ray and Carlotta don't know the prophecy," Sigmund said. "Only the Old Doctor knew, and he only told *us*. They have no idea what they're going to cause, if they reach the temple first."

"If they reach the temple first, we'll die along with the rest of the world." The New Doctor was weak from oxygen deficiency. "If Carlsbad doesn't find them, we're doomed." She looked older, having left the safety of the library and the archives, and the past two years had been hard. They'd traveled to the edges and underside of the Earth, gathering fragments of the map to the temple of the cup, chasing down the obscure references the New Doctor had uncovered in the archives. First they'd gone deep into the African desert, into crumbling palaces carved from sentient rock; then they'd trekked through the Antarctic, looking for the secret entrance to the Earth's war-torn core, and finding it; they'd projected themselves, astrally and otherwise, into the mind of a sleeping demigod from the jungles of another world; and two months ago they'd descended to crush-depth in the Pacific Ocean to find the last fragment of the map in a coral temple guarded by spined, bioluminescent beings of infinite sadness. Ray had eaten one of those guardians, and ever since he'd been sweating purple ink and taking long, contemplative baths in salt water.

The New Doctor had ransacked the Table's coffers to pay for this last trip to the Himalayas, selling off long-hoarded art objects and dismissing even the poorly paid hereditary janitorial staff to cover the expenses. And now they were on the edge of total failure, unless Sigmund did something.

Sigmund opened his pack and removed his last vial of the Old Doctor's most potent exotic upper. "Wish me bon voyage," he said, and snorted it all.

Time unspooled, and Sigmund found himself beneath the same ledge, but earlier, the ice unmarked by human passage, the weather more mild.

Moving manically, driven by drugs and the need to stay warm, he piled up rocks above the trail and waited, pacing in an endless circle, until he heard Carlotta and Ray approaching, grunting under the weight of stolen supplies.

He pushed rocks down on them, and the witch and the phage were knocked down. Sigmund made his way to them, hoping they would be crushed—that the rocks would have done his work for him. Carlotta was mostly buried, but her long fingernails scraped furrows in the ice, and Sigmund gritted his teeth, cleared away enough rocks to expose her head, and finished her off with the ice axe. She did not speak, but Sigmund almost thought he saw respect in her expression before he obliterated it. Ray was only half-buried, but unmoving, his neck twisted unnaturally. Sigmund sank the point of the axe into Ray's thigh to make sure he was truly dead, and the phage did not react. Sigmund left the axe in Ray's leg. He turned his back on the dead and crouched, waiting for time to sweep him up again in its flow.

Carlsbad found Ray and Carlotta dead, and brought back the supplies. By then Sigmund was back from the past, and while the New Doctor ate and rested, he took Carlsbad aside to tell him the truth: "There's a good chance we might destroy the world."

"Hmm," Carlsbad said.

"There's a prophecy, in the deep archives of the Table, that God will only return when the world is destroyed by fire. But it's an article of faith—the *basis* of our faith—that when the contents of the cup are swallowed by an acolyte of the Table, God will return. So by approaching the cup—by *intending* to drink from it—we might collapse the probability wave in such a way that the end of the world begins, fire and all, in the moments before we even touch the cup."

"And you and the New Doctor are okay with that?"

"The New Doctor thinks she can convince God to spare the world from destruction, retroactively, if necessary."

"Huh," Carlsbad said.

"She can be very persuasive," Sigmund said.

"I'm sure," Carlsbad replied.

* * *

The fire began to fall just as they reached the temple, a structure so old it seemed part of the mountain itself. The sky went red, and great gobbets of flame cascaded down, the meteor shower to end all others. Snow flashed instantly to steam on all the surrounding mountains, though the temple peak was untouched, for now.

"That's it, then," Carlsbad said. "Only the evil in you two is keeping me alive."

"No turning back now," the New Doctor said, and started up the ancient steps to the temple.

Ray, bloodied and battered, left arm hanging broken, stepped from the shadows beside the temple. He held Sigmund's ice axe in his good hand, and he swung it at the New Doctor's head with phenomenal force, caving in her skull. She fell, and he fell upon her, bringing the axe down again and again, laying her body open. He looked up, face bruised and swollen, fur sprouting from his jaw, veins pulsing in his forehead, poison and ink and pus and hallucinogens oozing from his pores. "You can't kill me, junkie. I've eaten wolverines. I've eaten giants. I've eaten *angels*." As he said this last, he began to glow with a strange, blue-shifted light.

"Saving your life again," Carlsbad said, almost tenderly, and then he did what the Table always counted on him to do. He swelled, he stormed, he smashed, he tore Ray to pieces, and then tore up the pieces.

After that he began to melt. "Ah, shit, Sigmund," he said. "You just aren't *evil* enough." Before Sigmund could say thank you, or goodbye, all that remained of Carlsbad was a dark pool, like a slick of old axle grease on the snow.

There was nothing for Sigmund to do but go on.

"The cup holds the blood of God," the Old Doctor said. "Drink it, and God will return, and as you are made briefly divine by swallowing the substance of his body, he will treat you as an equal, and answer questions, and grant requests. For that moment, God will do whatever you ask." The Old Doctor placed his hand on Sigmund's own. "The Table exists to make sure the cup's power is not used for evil or trivial purposes. The question asked, the wish desired, has to be worth the cost, which is the world."

"What would you ask?" Sigmund said.

"I would ask why God created the world and walked away, leaving only a cupful of blood and a world of wonders behind. But that is only curiosity, and not a worthy question."

"So anyway," Sigmund said, sniffing and wiping at his nose. "When can I start doing field work?" He wished he could see the future instead of the past. He thought this was going to be a lot of fun.

The cup in Sigmund's hands held blood, liquid at the center, but dried and crusted on the cup's rim. Sigmund scraped the residue of dried blood up with his long pinky fingernail. He took a breath. Let it out. And snorted God's blood.

Time *snapped.*

Sigmund looked around the temple. It was white, bright, clean, and no longer on a mountaintop. The windows looked out on a placid sea. He was not alone.

God looked nothing like Sigmund had imagined, but at the same time, it was impossible to mistake him for anyone else. It was clear that God was on his way out, but he paused, and looked at Sigmund expectantly.

Sigmund had gone from the end of the world to the beginning. He was so high from snorting God's blood that he could see individual atoms in the air, vibrating. He knew he could be jerked back to the top of the ruined world at any moment.

Sigmund tried to think. He'd expected the New Doctor to ask the questions, to make the requests, so he didn't know what to say. God was clearly growing impatient, ready to leave his creation forever behind. If Sigmund spoke quickly, he could have anything he wanted. Anything at all.

"Hey," Sigmund said. "Don't go."

IN A GLASS CASKET

Billy Cates found the glass casket behind the burned-out Safeway, tucked in between the rusty dumpster and a stack of splintery wooden pallets. Billy leaned his bike against the soot-blackened brick wall and approached the casket. It was simply made, just an oblong box six feet in length, with beveled corners that reminded Billy of his dad's cut-crystal brandy decanter. Dad hadn't taken the decanter with him when he left (he hadn't taken much of anything), but Mom had smashed it in the fireplace.

The casket rested atop a board laid across two sawhorses. Billy stood at a respectful distance, looking. A girl lay inside, clothed in a red dress, white hands crossed on her stomach. Billy couldn't see the girl's face because of the sunlight glaring on the glass, so he stepped closer, sneakers scuffing on the asphalt. He wanted to see her face; he wanted to run away.

Curiosity won. Billy leaned close to the glass, his head throwing a shadow on the casket and cutting the glare so that he could see the girl's face. Her eyes were closed, which seemed only natural. Her dark red hair matched her dress, the color of cherry Kool-Aid stains on a white tablecloth. She looked about sixteen. There were girls at school prettier than her, in the higher grades—the girl in the casket didn't have much of a chin, and her hands were chubby. Her skin was beautiful, though, white and unblemished.

Billy wondered if she was dead, if this was the work of a serial killer, like in the movies—the Glass Casket Killer, something like that. If she was dead, Billy had to call 911 and tell the police. They wouldn't believe him, probably, but if they sent someone, they'd see it was true, a dead girl in a glass box. Or maybe she was a magic princess, like in that Disney movie, and she just needed a kiss from a prince to wake her. Billy wrinkled his nose. He wasn't a prince, and he didn't want to kiss her, and she was trapped in a glass box anyway.

His breath fogged the glass, obscuring the girl's face. Billy wiped the mist away, then looked at his hand in horror. Fingerprints—he'd just left fingerprints all over the glass! The police would be furious with him for sure.

Billy lowered his hand and looked back down at the girl's face.

Her cheeks were wet, and as he watched, tears ran from her closed eyes, down her face, into her hair.

Billy backed up a step. She wasn't dead after all, just trapped. Billy could think of one thing better than discovering a dead body, and that was rescuing somebody. The Glass Casket Killer liked to put women in glass boxes until they died, maybe that was it, but Billy could save her.

He looked around, then headed for a pile of broken-up cinderblocks. He picked up a heavy fragment of concrete in both hands and carried it back to the casket. He thought for a moment about tropical fish tanks, and about the Boy in the Bubble he'd seen in that video at school—maybe letting air in would kill this girl, maybe the casket was sealed to protect her. Billy dropped the concrete. He didn't want to mess anything up. The fingerprints were bad enough. What sort of trouble could he get in for destroying evidence, or for killing the girl by accident?

Billy had to go home for dinner soon. Mom didn't like it when he wasn't home when she got off work, and she wouldn't like him hanging around behind the burned-out store. Ever since Dad left last year she'd been like that, yelling at him half the time, hugging him close the other half. He took a last look at the crying girl and went reluctantly to his bicycle. Maybe Mom would know what to do.

Billy pedaled home, his bike wobbling in slow arcs back and forth across the cracked sidewalks and back streets, thinking about the glass casket, the way the beveled corners caught the afternoon light, the way the girl's tears fell into her hair. His helmet hung by its chin strap from the handlebars, forgotten as usual. Billy made it home and dragged his bike through the gate into the scraggly front yard. He chained his bike to a post on the porch, and remembered to put his helmet on so his Mom would think he'd been wearing it all along. He went through the front door, calling, "Hey, Mom!"

His mom was there, sitting stiffly in the straight-backed armchair, and a strange man sat on the couch. The man nodded to Billy. He wore a dark suit and had eyes as blue as Dad's poker chips. With his slicked-down black hair and his little mustache, he looked like a magician, someone who'd wear a tuxedo on stage and do card tricks, and for the grand finale he'd cut a lady wearing a sequined dress in half, or stick swords through her.

"Billy, this is Mr. Mancuso," his mom said. Her voice was wavery, and she looked at him funny, her eyes not quite focusing. "He used to know your father."

Billy looked at the man with new interest. "You knew my dad? Do you know where he is now?"

"I might be able to find him for you," Mr. Mancuso said. His voice purred, smooth, like a radio announcer on the classical station Billy's dad had liked. "I'm looking for someone, too, and I'm always willing to exchange help for help." Billy's mother didn't look at Mr. Mancuso as he spoke. She just stared at the blank television screen. That television had never been turned off in the evening, not in Billy's experience. When Mom was home, the television was on. Even when Mom had company, the most she'd do was turn the volume down low.

"Children see lots of things," Mr. Mancuso said, leaning forward, his blue eyes wide, his smile friendly but a little smirky, too. "They go places adults don't, see things adults wouldn't notice. Your mother... hasn't been much help." Mr. Mancuso frowned a little, like Billy's mom had disappointed him. "Neither has anyone else I've talked to today. But perhaps I've been talking to the wrong people. I wonder, have *you* seen the one I'm looking for?"

He's the Glass Casket Killer, Billy thought, *only somehow he's lost his casket*. Or maybe he really was a magician, and the girl in red was his lovely assistant, but the last disappearing trick went wrong somehow and he lost track of her. Those blue eyes—they were magician's eyes, for sure. Billy should help Mr. Mancuso. He should tell him anything he needed to know.

Billy opened his mouth to say, "She's behind the Safeway, sitting up on a couple of sawhorses," but then he remembered the tears. The girl in red was crying, even while sleeping, even while seeming to be dead. Was she crying because she was lost, because she wanted the magic trick to be over? Looking at Mr. Mancuso, Billy didn't think so. She was crying for some other, more through-and-through reason. Crying for something to do with Mr. Mancuso, maybe.

"I didn't see anybody," Billy said. "I had detention at school and then I rode my bike home straight after. I'm going to make a peanut butter and jelly sandwich, Mom." Billy hurried into the kitchen before Mr. Mancuso's blue eyes made him change his mind. Mom would never let him have a snack so close to dinner time, but she didn't object, and Mr. Mancuso didn't do anything more than grunt.

Billy went around the counter to the kitchen, wishing it was in a whole different room, not just sort of partitioned off from the living room. A pan of spaghetti sauce bubbled on the stove, burning and spattering, and the pot of water with the noodles in it had boiled down to almost nothing. It wasn't like Mom to leave the stove unattended, even with company here. Billy trembled all over, afraid from his skin to his bones—this was worse than having to go to the bathroom in the middle of the night after watching a scary movie, because then he only *imagined* monsters. Mr. Mancuso was *here.*

Billy turned off the burners and went to the cabinet to get the peanut butter, trying to act natural, like he had nothing to be afraid of. His heart thudded like he'd just pedaled his bike up a steep hill, and he listened as closely as he could for the creak of the couch, for any sound to indicate what Mr. Mancuso was doing.

When Billy turned back around to get the bread, Mr. Mancuso was gone. Billy hadn't heard the door open. His mom stood up, frowned at the TV, and flipped it on with the remote. She looked at Billy, opened her mouth, then closed it, shaking her head. "Put that peanut butter away," she said, walking toward him. "I'm fixing dinner."

Billy screwed the lid back on the jar, relieved in some way he couldn't define. Everything was okay, though his mom frowned at the stove and refilled the pot with water.

She didn't say anything about Mr. Mancuso at dinner. Billy didn't either, though he wondered if the man could really find his dad, really bring him back. Maybe he could. But if Dad had left once, wouldn't he just leave again? Probably so. Billy didn't mention the girl in the casket, either. His mom was in a bad mood, smoking cigarettes one after another, not talking much. He'd learned not to bother her when she was in moods like this. She'd just yell, or worse, start crying.

Billy watched TV with his mom for a while, then did his homework, not thinking about it much, probably getting half the math problems wrong. He waited for his mom to say goodnight and go to bed, then waited a while longer for the light to go off under her door, and then a little longer still for her to get good and asleep. Billy had never sneaked out of the house before, and he didn't want to get caught. He covered some pillows with a blanket so if his mom came to check on him it would look like he was still in bed. The pillow trick didn't look as convincing for real as it did in the movies, but maybe it was good enough in dim light. Billy put a flashlight in his bookbag, then crept to the garage. He opened his dad's little red toolbox and looked into it for a while, wondering what he'd need, finally deciding to take the whole thing.

Billy put the toolbox in his bookbag, wincing at the clank it made as tools bumped around inside, then he slipped out of the house, carefully locking the door behind him. He unchained his bike and rolled it into the street, glad that the playing cards he'd had clothes-pinned to the spokes had fallen off last week. The distinctive "click-click-click" would have probably awakened his Mom. He pedaled away through the empty streets toward the Safeway.

The area behind the grocery store, including the glass casket, was pretty well lit by a bluish light on a pole, but the shadows up against the building were scary. What if there was a homeless guy there, or a drug dealer? Or Mr. Mancuso? Billy just had to hope it was safe. He parked his bike beside a pile of pallets and went to the casket.

The girl inside was screaming, her mouth open wide, her head thrashing back and forth, but Billy couldn't hear anything. She pounded on the top of the casket with her pudgy fists, and lifted her knees convulsively, but the coffin didn't budge a bit, didn't rock or shift on its flimsy plywood pedestal. Billy stared at her, momentarily stunned, then he pounded on the side of the casket with his own fists, and frantically checked it for seams or hinges. The girl kept screaming—she didn't seem to notice him at all. Maybe the coffin was made of one-way glass, so Billy could see inside, but she couldn't see out. Billy tried to shove the coffin over, thinking that if it fell off the sawhorses the coffin would break open, and spill the girl out.

The coffin wouldn't budge. Trying to shove the casket over was like trying to push his house down. The girl inside subsided, her punches against the coffin lid slowing down, finally stopping. She crossed her hands over her chest. Her whole body shook, the way his mom's did when she was crying hard but silently. Then the girl's eyes closed, and she lay still.

Billy didn't know what to make of this, but he had to let her out—she wasn't a tropical fish, that much was clear, she wanted out. He opened his bag, took out the red toolbox, opened it, and removed a claw hammer. He held it a little uncertainly. If he smashed the side of the casket, the whole top part might fall on top of the girl. But if he broke the top, bits of glass would shower down on her. Well, he couldn't do anything else—he had to break it somewhere. He lifted the hammer over the center of the casket lid, and brought it down as hard as he could.

The hammer bounced.

Billy stepped back, frowning. It had seemed so easy when he'd imagined it. Why didn't it work? He went back to the toolbox, rummaging through it. A protractor. A socket wrench. Needlenose pliers. A chalk line reel—his dad used to joke that it was used for drawing the lines on elf baseball fields, but Billy didn't know what it was really for. A paint-stained calculator. His fingers closed on a Phillips screwdriver—what his dad called a "starhead" screwdriver—and he smiled. His dad had taught him how to chop wood, and shown him how wedges worked. Sometimes you couldn't get a log to split just by driving the ax in. So you set a wedge, and hit the wedge with a hammer, and that split the log. A glass casket wasn't the same as a log, and a screwdriver was no wedge, but it might be close enough.

Billy set the point of the screwdriver on the beveled edge of the casket, reasoning that the glass would be thinner at that point, and easier to break. He held the screwdriver in place, lifted the hammer, and hit the end of the screwdriver handle.

The glass splintered, fine lines spreading out from the point of impact. Billy hooted with pleasure. The girl stirred a little, her white hands moving, fluttering like moths. Billy moved the screwdriver farther down the seam and repeated the process. He hummed to himself as he worked his way around the edge of the coffin, tapping his screwdriver, smiling every time at the cracking sound. He'd done one whole side and gotten halfway up the other when he looked back at the girl.

Her eyes were open, staring at him. "Can you see me?" he asked.

She nodded, once.

He held up the hammer and screwdriver. "Am I doing the right thing?"

She nodded more vigorously.

Billy went back to work. She'd thank him, and maybe there'd be a reward, and best of all she'd have a story to tell him, how she wound up in the box, what it meant, who'd trapped her and why.

Billy hit the screwdriver for the last time, on the beveled edge above her head. Then he stepped back, unsure what to do next. If he tried to shove the top of the casket away, the edge would cut his hands to pieces. Maybe he could get a stick, or find some gloves, or—

The top of the casket rose up, away from the sides. At first Billy thought it was levitation, a magic trick, but then he saw the girl lifting it with her hands and her knees. She shoved the lid aside, and it fell to the ground, shattering with a sound so loud and startling that Billy dropped his hammer and screwdriver.

The girl sat up. She took a deep breath, then coughed, covering her mouth. Billy thought about the Boy in the Bubble again, and was afraid he'd done a very bad thing.

Then she laughed, and said, "I haven't smelled fresh air in a long time." She croaked more than she talked, but Billy could understand her. He went to the coffin, then wrinkled his nose. The girl *reeked*.

She frowned at him. "Try getting shut inside a box for... well... for a long time, anyway, and see how good you smell, kid."

Billy nodded, seeing the sense in that, and held out a hand to help her. She ignored his hand, stood up in the casket, then jumped out, landing on the asphalt in a crouch. She stood up, tugged down her dress, and grinned. "I got away from the old bastard again," she said. "Ha!" She looked down at Billy. "Thanks, kid. Where am I, anyway?"

Billy just blinked at her. She didn't sound like a Glass Casket Killer victim, or a magic princess, or anything. She sounded like the girls in the older grades at his school, that was all, a little snotty, like he was just a dumb kid. "How did you—"

She held up her hand in a gesture demanding silence, then lifted her nose and looked around. "Shit. He's nearby." She dug her heel into the asphalt—right on a shard of glass!—and dragged her bare foot along the ground, wincing. She left a little streak of blood on the pavement, like red crayon on black construction paper.

"What are you doing?" he said, staring at the blood.

"Making a protective circle," she said, gritting her teeth. "But it's too damned *slow*. Do you have a knife, or something?"

"Does it have to be blood?" he said, backing away. She had such beautiful white skin, and he couldn't stand to watch her tear it this way.

She paused. "No, if this was sand I could just drag a line through the dirt. The circle has to be unbroken, though, and I can't think of any way to do that here except for blood."

Billy didn't ask why she needed a circle. He knew why, though he couldn't say *how* he knew. Maybe he'd seen it in a movie, or maybe the knowledge simply lived in him. They needed a circle to keep the bad things out.

"Wait!" he said when she started dragging her foot again. He rummaged through the toolbox and came up with the chalk line reel. "Will chalk work?"

"Perfect," she said, snatching it from his hand. She knelt, and Billy could see the bottoms of her feet. The one she'd dragged was bloody, but the soles of both feet were covered in thin white scars, like they'd been scratched repeatedly and deeply by knives. She moved the chalk line reel slowly, drawing a ragged circle around herself, Billy, and the remains of the casket.

"What happened to your feet?" he asked when she'd finished drawing the circle.

She glanced at him, frowning. "Do you know the story of the little mermaid?"

"I saw the movie," Billy said.

"I don't know about any movie. I'm talking about the one where the mermaid is given legs so that she can walk around on land, but every step is agony, as if knives are being driven into her feet. That story."

"I don't know that story," Billy said. He looked at her feet again, fascinated. "You were a mermaid?"

She laughed. "No, kid. But my dad liked the idea, and thought making my feet hurt like that every time I left the house would be a good way to keep me from running off." She shook her head, her dark red hair swinging and obscuring part of her face. "Didn't work, though. I could ignore the pain for a while, and eventually I always found somebody to carry me."

"Your *dad* did that?" Billy couldn't imagine such a thing.

"Yeah. When that didn't work, he tried the box. He said it would keep me young and beautiful, and I guess it did, but he didn't tell me he never planned to let me out. But I'm my father's daughter, and I know tricks, too. It took a long time, but I finally managed to get away, glass box and all—"

"Caroline!" someone shouted.

Billy jumped, and the girl put a finger to her lips. "Shh," she whispered. "The circle keeps him from seeing us, but he can still hear us."

They sat very still. The voice called again. "Caroline! I know you're here."

Mr. Mancuso appeared, walking into the pool of blue-tinted brightness cast by the sodium-vapor lights. He headed straight for Billy's bike, propped against the pallets, outside the protective circle. "Oh, little boy," he called. "I know you're here. You found her, didn't you? My pretty little girl in the glass box."

Mr. Mancuso was Caroline's dad. Billy thought of her scarred feet and tried to breathe quietly.

"I knew if I followed you I'd find her," Mr. Mancuso said. "Little boys get everywhere, they see everything. Where've you gone? Come out and give her up, my boy. I'm used to young men doing foolish things for my Caroline, but you're a little younger than most." He laughed. "She's a bad girl, Billy, always running off, abandoning her old man. You can understand how much that hurts, can't you? Your father left *you*. Nothing hurts worse than being left behind. I'm offering a straight trade, boy. You give me Caroline, and I'll give you back your father. I know you're afraid he'd just run off again if he came back... but I can make it so he won't. I can make him *want* to stay."

Billy believed him, and part of him wanted to shout, to scuff away the chalk circle with his foot and let Mr. Mancuso in. Because he loved his dad, and he wanted him back. Mr. Mancuso was right. Nothing hurt like being abandoned.

Billy turned his head. Caroline stared at him, her eyes wide. She crouched perfectly still, watching to see what he would do. Billy thought about opening his mouth. He could scream before she stopped him, and then he'd get his dad back. His mother would be happy, and she wouldn't yell at him so much, and she would let him go and play with his friends.

But Billy remembered Caroline's tears, when she was inside the box. No matter how tough she seemed now, she'd been crying before. And her feet... if something like that, some spell, was the only way to make Billy's dad stay home, it was better to let him stay away.

Maybe some things did hurt worse than being abandoned.

Mr. Mancuso touched the bike's handlebars, then sniffed his fingers. He walked toward the coffin, frowning, squinting.

He stopped on the edge of the circle. "Now what's this?" he said. He waved his hands in front of him, frowning. "Something's amiss."

Caroline grabbed Billy's arm, her fingernails digging into his skin. She looked at her father, who was muttering, and moving his hands in strange patterns, and chuckling to himself.

Billy looked around. The far edge of the circle went right up to the wall of the Safeway. There was a hole in the bricks there, a small opening half-hidden by a broken pallet. Billy pointed toward the hole. Caroline frowned. Billy gestured more vigorously, a shooing-in motion. She shook her head.

Trust me, Billy mouthed. Caroline scowled, then nodded. She moved laboriously away on hands and knees, carefully avoiding the fragments of the casket lid. Billy got up and tiptoed to the casket. When Caroline reached the edge of circle, near the dark hole, Billy put his hands on the casket and shoved as hard as he could.

It didn't resist him this time. The glass box slid off the pallet and smashed on the asphalt, shattering just like Dad's brandy decanter had when Mom hurled it into the fireplace. Caroline scurried into the hole, the noise of her escape covered by the splintering of glass. Fragments of the coffin cascaded over the chalk line, breaking whatever charm had hidden Billy before.

Mr. Mancuso blinked at him, then stepped on the broken glass. "Where is she?"

Billy did his best to look like a scared kid. It wasn't hard. He whimpered and backed away. "I don't know. I broke open the coffin, and let her out, and then she drew this circle around me and told me that if I stepped outside it her dad would catch me, and put me in a glass box until I ran out of air and died."

"Why did you shove the coffin over?" His hands moved slowly, sinuously, as if independent of the rest of his body.

Billy shrank away. "You came so close, I was sure you'd find me. I was afraid you'd put me inside the box, so I broke it. I was afraid you'd put the lid back on and seal me up."

"That's just what I should do, too," he said. "Why didn't you do as I asked? Why didn't you take me to her? I would have given you your father back."

"I know," Billy said, and when he cried, the tears were real. He rubbed his nose with the back of his hand. "I know, I'm sorry, I'm sorry."

Mr. Mancuso kicked the fragments of the coffin. "I should punish you, little boy. I should tie you to your mother forever, make it so you vomit blood if you're ever out of her sight. Does that sound nice?" He grinned, and the snake-dance of his hands sped up. "You don't have the will my Caroline does, you'd never manage to break that bond. And when your mother dies—because all of you always die—you'll have to lay atop her grave just to stay alive. Yes. I'd make you a devoted son."

Billy closed his eyes and whimpered.

"Bastard," Caroline said. "Leave him alone."

Billy's eyes snapped open. Mr. Mancuso whirled around. Caroline was standing outside the circle. She must have crawled through the dark, charred inside of the grocery store and come out another hole in the wall. She held a large triangular shard of glass, from the coffin or just from the general wreckage around the store, Billy didn't know. She put the point of the glass against her throat. "Let the kid go, Dad, or I'm *really* going to leave you forever."

"You wouldn't," Mr. Mancuso said.

"You know I would."

Mr. Mancuso looked at Billy, then spat. "Fine. Come back to me, and I'll let the boy go."

"No negotiation, no compromise. Let him go now, or I'll cut my throat."

"If you kill yourself, I'll do anything to the boy I want." His hands were moving slowly again, hypnotically, but Caroline didn't look at them.

"You won't let me kill myself, though. Then you wouldn't have anything left."

Mr. Mancuso's hands stopped moving, and then he slumped. He suddenly looked very old. "Go on, then," he said, flapping a hand at Billy.

"I want your blood on it, Dad. That you won't harm him or anyone he loves."

Mr. Mancuso frowned. "Are you trying to trick me? You think he loves *you*, that you'll be protected?"

Billy looked at her, startled.

"He might love me a little, for coming back just now, but that's not what I mean. I mean his mother, and his father, wherever he is. You never try to hurt me, anyway, do you Daddy? You just try to keep me safe." She spat the last word, and pressed the glass closer to her throat, until a spot of blood welled.

"Fine!" Mancuso shouted. He held a long, shining blade in his hand, a slender silvery knife that had appeared as if by magic, but without sparkles or fanfare. Mr. Mancuso cut his palm and made a fist, dripping blood onto the asphalt. The blood hissed and smoked where it touched the ground, and Billy backed away, afraid it would spatter on his shoes. "I will not harm this boy or any he loves."

"Go on, Billy," Caroline said, lowering the shard of glass.

"But what will happen to you?" Billy said. "What about—"

"Don't worry about me," she said. "You let me out of the coffin. I'm better off now than I was before. I might get away clean this time."

"You're mine," Mr. Mancuso said. "You're my blood, and you will not leave me."

"Get on your bike and go, Billy," Caroline said. She sounded very tired, as tired as Billy's mom often did.

Billy took his bike and pedaled away, not looking back, crying as he rode, the wind blowing his tears away.

Once he got home, Billy crept into the house, only to find his mother lying on his bed with the lights on, clutching his pillow.

"Mom?" he said.

"Billy?" she said, sitting up, still holding the pillow. Her hair was mussed, her eyes red from crying. "I thought you ran away." She shivered, and stopped speaking, and sobbed, soundlessly, shaking.

Billy dropped his bag and got into bed with her. He held his mother in his arms and cried with her. "No, Mom, I won't run away, I'm sorry,

I'm so sorry."

"Never leave me, Billy," she said, her voice muffled against him. "Just stay with me, don't go, never ever go away."

Never? Billy thought. *Never ever?*

He held his mother close.

He said, "Shh.

TERRIBLE ONES

The Greek Chorus first appeared on Thursday night, as Zara lugged two paper bags full of groceries into the gravel public parking lot. The Chorus members wore tattered togas made from faintly flower-patterned, oft-washed bedsheets, and their faces were painted white with greasepaint.

Since she was in Berkeley, Zara assumed the Chorus members were performance artists of some kind, and didn't pay much attention when they drifted from out of the bushes and among the parked cars to stand in a loose semicircle a few feet behind her. As she unlocked her trunk and wedged the grocery bags between a box of mismatched shoes and a broken lamp she'd never gotten around to throwing out, the Chorus said—in a single voice, from many throats—"Crazed with rapture, she sings and trills, dark bird that loves the night." The line sounded familiar—Zara was an actress, and she'd done several classical plays—but she couldn't quite place it.

Zara straightened, slammed her trunk, and looked at the Chorus. The fading light and white make-up smeared their faces into blank anonymities. They might have been looking at her expectantly. "Fuck off," she said. "You're in my way."

One of the Chorus members cupped his ear theatrically. "What did you say? Never mind, I heard—as I hear your destiny. Weeping, cacophony, cries that assault the ear."

Zara got into her car, locked the doors, and threw it into the reverse. The Chorus scattered like pigeons making way for a bus. Once she'd backed past them, they reformed in front of her car, and their eyes shone in her headlights. She flipped up the high beams, and they shielded their faces from the brightness. Zara turned the wheel and drove away, leaving the Chorus to stand in the cloud of dust her wheels threw up from the gravel.

* * *

The Furies were old in those days. Alecto, Tisiphone, and Megaera lived together in the Tenderloin district of San Francisco, in an apartment building decorated with chipped carvings of lizards, between a strip club and a three-story liquor/erotic book store combination. Sometimes they became confused and lived for a while, cuckoo-style, in someone else's home. The rightful residents would go on drunken benders, or crack their skulls on curbs, or suffer hysterical blindness—whatever the specific cause, the effect was ignorance of the presence of the Furies in their midst. Eventually, inevitably, the ladies would look around and realize they'd been sleeping in strange beds, eating someone else's saltines and vanilla wafers, and they would leave, allowing the people they'd disrupted to recover their senses and resume their lives. Those intruded upon by the Furies in this way tended to throw open their windows and bundle their sheets down to the laundromat, for the ladies left a smell of dried blood and rancid olive oil behind when they departed.

Alecto was the most practical of the three. She did the shopping and kept the ants out of the kitchen. Megaera muttered darkly to herself, and walked the streets at night, hoping to be attacked—all she wanted was an excuse to do violence in self-defense. But in a place where murders were commonplace, no one ever threatened Megaera, who shuffled along in her housecoat until dawn. Tisiphone tended to stay closer to home. She went down the stairs fifteen or twenty times a day to check their brass-and-glass mailbox in the lobby, even on Sundays, though they never got anything other than take-out restaurant menus and pamphlets from upstart religions. Once, years before, when they were more self-aware, they received a jury-duty notice, addressed to the apartment's previous occupant. The ladies had a good laugh over that.

One day, while Alecto stood dropping dried scorpions and seahorses into a pot of boiling water on the stove, and Megaera sat staring out the window at the drug dealers and college students thronging the sidewalk, Tisiphone went down the creaking stairs to their mailbox. She opened the box with a tarnished key, and inside found a thick piece of parchment, folded in thirds, sealed with a dollop of red wax. The symbol embossed in the wax was a monstrous face, mouth gaping; an oracle's face.

Tisiphone broke the seal and opened the parchment. It was what she'd been waiting for, what they'd all been waiting for. A letter of commission.

Weeping a little, for reasons she could not have fully named, for happiness and anxiety and simply because the worn-down gears in her mind refused to mesh properly anymore, Tisiphone went back up the stairs, clutching the parchment, afraid it would disappear or transform into a Thai restaurant menu. She had to tell Alecto and Megaera. They had to prepare.

Zara got home, and kicked off her shoes, and hurriedly put her groceries away. She only had a few moments to eat before leaving for rehearsal. The red light on her answering machine blinked at a seizure-inducing rate. There were so many messages since this morning that even the machine appeared to have lost count. She pushed the button on her way to the kitchen, and Doug's voice emerged from the tinny speakers, calm and rational, a financial analyst's voice, saying, "I need you to beat me with a bamboo cane," and "I need you to plug my ass and lash me bloody." One message after another, a continuous litany—whenever the machine cut him off, he just called back and resumed his patient pleading. Zara rooted through her fridge for mold-free cheese, and cursed as she listened—this was the second day he'd called, and apparently he wasn't going to give up easily.

One of those assholes at the club must have given Doug her home number, probably for a substantial bribe. At least he wasn't calling her cell phone. She wondered, briefly, if he had her address, if she should worry. But if he showed up here, she could play along, get him naked and tied up, then shove him out in the hall, or call the cops, or try to reach his wife—surely someone like Doug, middle-management pillar of the financial district, would have a wife, someone who wouldn't approve of him going to clubs like Damien's Basement, or of his more expensive private play-partners, like that of her own summer-job persona, Mistress Zara.

Mistress Zara was just a role she played, no different than Ophelia, Medea, or Blanche DuBois—though she did enjoy whipping assholes like Doug, she had to admit, and it paid better than temping. She'd made enough money working at Damien's over the summer to concentrate on theater for the rest of the year. At the time, it seemed like the perfect job. She hadn't realized Doug would get so attached. He didn't understand that their relationship, such as it was, stopped when she put down the whip. She'd have to do something about him, eventually—get one of her big, tattooed friends to pay him a visit at work and tell him to fuck off, for instance—but she didn't have time to worry about it right now. Final dress rehearsal was tonight, and the show opened tomorrow.

Zara ate a cheese-and-wheat-bread sandwich while standing up at the counter, followed it with a gulp of lowfat milk, grabbed her bag, and slipped out of the apartment, with Doug still droning on her machine about how he *needed* her, she *owed* him, they had a *connection.*

In the empty apartment, a new voice spoke from the machine, another message hidden among Doug's. It was a woman's voice, smoky, throaty, like a torch-singer past her prime. "I know you won't hear this, Zara, but I've got to give you warning, and this counts, by the rules. There are three old ladies coming to see your play tomorrow night, and they're harsh critics. Maybe you should let your understudy play the lead. There. Advice dispensed. Nice and fair."

A click, and then it was Doug again, demanding all the torments he thought Zara owed him.

Zara ran to catch the BART train from the East Bay into San Francisco, thinking briefly that if Doug saw her dressed like this (in running shoes, a t-shirt, and loose cotton pants) instead of a leather corset, knee-high boots, and several silver piercings, it would help disabuse him of his illusions about their relationship. She went into the tiled, brightly lit station and headed for the escalator, only to encounter a blockade of scaffolding, sawhorses, and yellow tape—the escalator was closed. A crudely hand-lettered sign with an arrow directed her around the blockage. Cursing, sure she would miss her train, she followed the signs, walking along a passageway of covered scaffolding farther than seemed reasonable—was the train station really so *big?*—until finally reaching a stopped escalator that led, apparently, up to the platform for San Francisco-bound trains. She began to wish she'd driven, even though parking was nearly impossible in the part of the Mission district where the theater was.

After she ran up the escalator, she found the platform wholly deserted. She said, "Fuck," because there should be *some* people waiting, even on a Thursday night, unless she'd just missed the train. Which meant she'd have to sprint for the theater to make rehearsal on time. She hated making people wait on her, because she knew what it was like, sitting around waiting for the lead actress, thinking what a bitch prima donna she was—Zara didn't want to be seen that way, not even by the cast of a little experimental theater that could only seat about fifty people, tops. She crossed her arms and looked out at the darkened overpass and the Oakland hills beyond the platform. Odd—there should have been lights from the houses on the ridges, but the hills were just dark shapes in the moonlight. Were they doing rolling blackouts again? And why was there no traffic on the overpass? Was it closed for repairs, too?

Then a train pulled in, surprising her—there had been no announcement of an oncoming train on the PA system. Still, it was headed in the right direction, so when the doors slid open she got on.

There was only one other passenger, sitting in one of the sideways-facing seats with a newspaper held open in front of her face. Zara dropped down into the seat opposite, glancing at the woman's newspaper. It was written in Greek, which she couldn't read, and Zara shifted her gaze to the blackness beyond the windows as the train slid away from the station.

The woman across from her tossed her newspaper onto the carpeted floor. "Nothing but bad news," she said in a smoky, throaty voice, smiling. The woman was in her forties, probably, dressed in a tailored black business suit, her hair blonde and stylishly short.

"Oh," Zara said, not really in the mood for conversation.

"I'm Nikki," the woman said.

Because it was going to be a long ride under the bay and into the city, she said, "I'm Zara."

"Good to meet you." Nikki crossed her legs. "I'm a talent scout."

"Oh?" Zara said, feeling a stir of interest. "Like for a record company?" She had lots of friends in bands, some of whom would happily sell out in a heartbeat.

"For an agency, actually. We represent musicians, dancers... actors. We're always on the lookout for new clients."

Zara didn't say anything. She was ambivalent about the very concept of agents. She was more interested in the art than the marketing, which perhaps meant she *needed* an agent; on the other hand, perhaps it meant she didn't need one at all. Agents might want her to do things like audition for commercials. They might want her to get a tan.

"Are you a performer?" Nikki asked.

"Sometimes," Zara said.

"Actress?"

Zara nodded. Nikki looked at her expectantly. "I'm playing the lead in *Medea*," Zara said. "It's a contemporary version, set in the suburbs, very minimalist, but with some almost *Grand Guignol* touches at the climax."

"It sounds fascinating," Nikki said, and she sounded like she meant it. Zara wondered that Nikki could sound sincere no matter what she actually felt—maybe from one moment to the next she didn't even *know* what she was feeling. That had to be part of her profession, right? Sociopathology as an occupational hazard. Except for a talent scout-slash-agent, it wouldn't *be* a hazard, but an advantage. As her friend Dave the unemployed programmer liked to say, "It's not a bug, it's a feature."

"It's a good role," Zara said.

"I'll come see it," Nikki said decisively. "Has it opened yet?"

"Opens tomorrow."

"Where?"

Zara told her the address.

"I'll be there," she said.

"Okay," Zara said, shrugging.

Nikki frowned, as if she'd expected something more—most young, hungry actors probably dropped to kiss her boots at the merest whiff of interest, Zara supposed.

"Medea," Nikki said. "That's the one about the woman who murders her children, right?"

"That's the one," Zara said.

"I wouldn't miss it for anything," Nikki said, more decisively. The train stopped, and the doors hissed open. Zara didn't recognize the platform—it was underground, with marble walls, Doric columns, and stone benches. She didn't see a sign anywhere—was it the 12th Street station? If so, it had been extensively remodeled. It seems like she would've noticed that on another one of her trips. "See you," Nikki said, and left the train. The doors closed behind her, and the train pulled away into a dark tunnel.

Zara leaned her head back against the window, and closed her eyes. It took twenty minutes or so to get from Oakland to the Mission, and she'd left home in such a hurry that she hadn't brought anything with her to read except her script, which she had down cold at this point, and didn't want to look at anymore. She'd always been good at remembering lines. When she was really into a role, speaking her lines didn't even feel like recitation—it just felt like *talking*, saying what came naturally. That was her favorite feeling.

Someone coughed, and Zara opened her eyes and lifted her head. "Holy shit," she said.

The Greek Chorus was back—when had they gotten on the train? They must have come from another car, creeping quietly, sliding open the adjoining doors without a squeak. Or, more likely, Zara had fallen asleep, and just hadn't noticed them. They stood in the middle of the aisle, holding onto the grabrail above their heads, though there were any number of empty seats. They all stared at her, silently, swaying a little with the movement of the train.

Zara thought about getting up and going to another car, but what if they followed her? "This had better be a coincidence," she said. "We just happen to be going in the same direction, right? You aren't *following* me, are you?"

The Chorus did not answer, just looked at her. "So, what are you, mimes? You were plenty talkative before. Or are you just frat boys?"

Still no response.

Zara snapped open her purse (black vinyl, decorated with little silvery skulls) and rummaged until she found a mostly used-up tube of lip balm. She held it between her thumb and forefinger, took aim, and threw it at one of the Chorus member's faces.

The tube bounced off his nose, and he squawked like a bird and flinched away.

"Just fuck off," Zara said.

"We've heard things," the Chorus said, hesitantly, half of them mumbling, none of them quite in synch. "But only from strangers. Those who carry messages have no power."

"So you've got a message for me, then?" Zara said. "What is this, guerilla marketing? Viral advertising? How much do you get paid?"

"Torrents of blood will fall from the sky. Justice brings new pain; on a fresh whetstone, Fate sharpens her sword. Each charge is countered by another, and who can fairly judge between them? Yet whoever acts must be punished. Such is the law."

"The only law you should be concerned with is the one against pissing me off," Zara said. "If you don't get away from me, I'm going to kick your asses, concurrently or sequentially, whichever you prefer."

The Chorus member in front, the one she'd hit with her lip balm, said, "Go on. My heart trembles with fear."

"Is that supposed to be sarcasm?" she asked.

The Chorus leader bowed his head. "We are old. You are young. You must teach us."

Before Zara could reply—or throw something else—the train slowed down. Glancing out the window, Zara saw the familiar brightly tiled walls of the 16th Street Mission station, with people—*normal* people—milling around. "You assholes should be put to sleep," Zara said, and when the doors opened, she got off the train.

The Chorus didn't follow, but as she walked away, they called, "So you fall, abandoned, searching your heart for joy, but finding nothing—sucked dry, gnawed by monsters, a shell, a shadow, a—" Then the doors slid closed, and cut off their voices.

Halfway through the second act, Zara saw Doug poke his head through the door at the back of the theater, his expression unreadable at this distance. He came in and sat down in the back row as if he had every right in the world to be here, at a closed final dress rehearsal. So much for her hope that he hadn't penetrated the inner mysteries of her life—if he knew she was *here*, he knew as much about her as there was to know. She went on performing her scene with the actor playing Jason, deeply into the role of her suburbanite version of Medea. "Her" kids—actually the director's, a boy and a girl, seven and nine years old, remarkably well-behaved, practically raised in the theater—sat on the floor, the boy playing with dolls, the girl with a dump truck. The gender-stereotype-reversal was just one of the writer/director's countless tiny little flourishes.

She imagined, briefly, that Jason was Doug, and her bitter lines took on a new level of heat, but she forced herself to dismiss the comparison. Why give Doug so much power? He was just a client with an overactive fantasy life, who somehow failed to comprehend that "Mistress Zara" was nothing but invention. When the curtain came down on Act II, she'd tell one of the stage hands to get rid of him, and he'd be hustled away. Maybe she should think about calling the cops, or at least getting a restraining order.

But Zara didn't have the chance to do any of those things, because in the middle of a crucial monologue—the moment when Medea decides that the only solution to her problems is to murder and murder again—Doug rose from his place in the back row and came walking down the aisle. He was clearly fresh from work, dressed in a white shirt, dark tie, and slacks, his face handsome but a little doughy, poised somewhere between the end of baby-fat and the onset of middle-aged thickening—just another thirty-something member of the Gray Horde with a wider-than-average streak of kink. Zara didn't let her lines falter, even as Doug continued to approach the stage, even as the director stood up and said, "Hey, you can't be here," even as the children broke character completely and said, "Who's that guy?"

She continued her monologue as Doug climbed up on stage. He came up over the edge of the proscenium, just downstage of where she stood. His movements were clumsy and awkward, like a chubby kid hauling himself out of a swimming pool. "Mistress," he said, getting to his feet.

"How weak my heart must be," she said, still in character, "to be swayed by such pitiful pleas."

Doug frowned, then took out his wallet. He flipped it open, took out a sheaf of bills—fifties, mostly, it looked like—and threw them at Zara's feet. "There," he said. "Prepaid through the end of the month. Now get out of that stupid dress and put on something *good*. I had a hard day, and I need you to make my night even harder."

Zara stared down at the money on the floor of the stage, her lines forgotten. The rest of the theater was silent, even the children. "You mother*fucker*," Zara said, looking up at him. "You think I'm a *whore?*"

Doug grinned. "I guess so. I guess you'll have to punish me for that."

Zara rushed at him, put both her hands on his chest, and shoved him. He shouted, arms pinwheeling, and almost fell off the stage. He landed on his ass at the edge of the apron. "Get out of here," Zara said, through clenched teeth. "Never come near me again, you sick freak."

"*I'm* the sick freak?" Doug said, rising, wincing as he rubbed his ass. "At least I finish what I start." He nodded toward the stage floor. "You keep the money. I'll see you." Limping a little, he went down the steps and out of the theater.

There was silence for a moment after the door closed behind him. "Well," the director said finally. "Shall we take it up from the end of act two? Unless Zara has any other visitors...?"

The other actors laughed, a little tensely, and Zara squeezed her hands into fists. The story of *this* would spread all over—theater people loved to gossip. By next week everyone would think she was a prostitute, when the truth was she'd never even *touched* any of her clients, not skin on skin, let alone had sex with them. She'd just wielded the whip, or the crop, and prodded with latex-gloved hands, and talked the talk. It was just *acting*, but it would get all twisted around into something else in the stories. Now when the other actors looked at her, they wouldn't see Medea, they would see Zara, with the crazy john/boyfriend/whatever, with a wad of crumpled money at her feet. Doug had ruined the role for her, tainted the experience.

Well, fuck that. He was going to *pay*.

"Are you ready, Zara?" the director said.

"Yeah," she said. She kicked the money offstage. Let someone else have it.

Late that night, after the director wished them luck and Zara showered off the fake blood, she went in search of her revenge. Rodney, the doorman at Damien's Basement, refused at first, but Zara wouldn't let it go. "I know you gave that son of a bitch *my* phone number," she said. "So you can damn well give me his last name."

"He paid me," Rodney said sullenly.

"Yeah? I'll pay you by not telling Damien and getting your ass *fired*," she said.

"Shit," he said, but told her what she wanted to know.

Doug had mentioned the name of his company once or twice, in the awkward social moments before their sessions, and the same memory that made it so easy for Zara to retain her lines helped her remember where he worked. From that, it was short work on the internet to find an online directory for his company, complete with extension numbers for various employees. Humming a little—the thrill of vengeance, which probably wasn't much like what Medea felt, but it still made her feel connected to the character—Zara dialed the number for the company's vice-president. It was after midnight, so all she got was voicemail, but that's what she wanted.

After the recorded greeting, and the beep, Zara said, "Doug Mitchell calling," and pressed the "Play" button on her digital answering machine. Doug's voice came on, rambling about the indignities he craved—cock-shaped gags, butt plugs, floggings. He never mentioned her name, only said, "you": "I need you to," "I want you to," "You have to." Zara let the recording play for several minutes, over several messages. Then she paused the play-back, hung up, and dialed another number at Doug's company, this time the head of Human Relations, and repeated the process, introducing Doug and then letting his recording ramble. Then a woman's voice emerged from the answering machine, and Zara tried to stop the playback before the HR director's voicemail could record it. She accidentally hit the "Delete" button, erasing the woman's message. The voice had sounded vaguely familiar, but Zara couldn't place it, and she hadn't heard more than the first few words. Ah, well. If it was important, she would call back. Zara hung up on that voicemail, and called another extension. Now her machine held nothing but Doug's messages, and she poured his litany into dozens of voicemail boxes at his company, eventually dialing extensions at random, until she was too exhausted to keep going.

Doug was going to have an interesting day at work tomorrow. Zara had worked as a temp often enough to know how the Gray Horde oper-ated. They would play the messages for one another, put Doug's voice on speakerphone, argue over whether or not it was *really* him, and eventually decide it was, of course, it was. She'd been careful not to leave a message in Doug's own voicemail box. She wondered how long it would take him to figure out why everyone was laughing at him. This wouldn't exactly bal-ance things between her and Doug, but maybe it would give him the idea that she wasn't someone to be fucked with, and that she could hurt him in ways that had nothing to do with catering to his masochistic side.

Zara stripped and crawled into bed near dawn, happy and content, suffused with schadenfreude, definitely ready to play Medea the next night.

She dreamed of women with brass wings; of singing stones; of bloody tears; of scorpions the size of lobsters, arrayed on serving platters; of old women, weeping inconsolably over child-sized coffins.

Zara made it into the city that night without incident, encountering no grease-painted strangers, no weird detours in the BART station, no sociopathic talent scouts. No Doug. He hadn't called, either, but maybe he was just afraid to leave more incriminating evidence on her answering machine. She went backstage and got help with her make-up, hair, and costume. She was keenly attuned to any differences in the way her fellow actors treated her since last night, but for the most part, they concentrated on their own preparations. She supposed they were whispering about her in corners, wondering how much she charged, but that might have been simple paranoia. She closed her eyes and took deep breaths, inhaling the faintly sweet, powdery scent of her own stage make-up. Paranoia was fine. Paranoia could be used in portraying Medea.

Before curtain, the director came to give them a little pep talk. "You know what they say," he said, not even glancing at Zara. "A terrible dress rehearsal means a fabulous opening night. If that's true, we've got nothing to worry about now." Everyone laughed, and a little piece of Zara turned to cinders and ash inside. Getting her revenge on Doug hadn't solved everything— it didn't change what he'd done to *her*. But revenge had enabled her to sleep well last night, so there was something to be said for it.

"There's a full house out there," the director said. "Even people standing in the back. Some of them aren't even my relatives! So let's go, folks. Break a few legs."

The play began, and Zara waited in the wings for her cue. The actress playing her nanny talked to the children on stage, saying, "Go to your rooms, little ones. Your mother's had a terrible time lately, and it's best you stay out of her way. I can see everything welling up behind her eyes—every injustice, every sorrow—and I'm afraid of what she might do when it becomes too much for her."

Zara began speaking her lines as she walked on stage: "Oh, misery! The things I've suffered! And you, my sweet children, you little shits, every time I look at you, I see your father!"

The Furies arrived late, having gotten lost on their way to the address given in their letter of commission—they only found their way at all because a well-dressed, smoky-voiced woman they met on the street offered to show them the way. After they arrived, the Furies stood on the pavement outside the building for a moment, gazing without understanding up at the lighted marquee, the cars on the street, the people laughing on the sidewalks. Their lives had been a haze of bitterness, impatience, and plodding-along for years piled upon years, and even as they'd moved through the city these past decades, they hadn't really *seen* their surroundings, living mostly in their memories and minds. Now they were marginally more conscious, able to converse, able to take in the contours of the modern world as more than a cascade of lights and noise. They huddled together before the glass doors briefly, taking strength from one another. It had been a long time since they'd gone forth on an errand of justice.

A man in a wrinkled white shirt and a dark tie walked past them, muttering, then turned and walked back, pacing, his hands balled into fists. "Fucking bitch," he said, "I'll kill you, bitch, you can't do this to me." He didn't notice the Furies, and they looked at one another knowingly. The man was a poison-sac about to burst. Perhaps, now that they were active again, they would have cause to punish him soon, if his rage led him to transgress against those bound to him by marriage or blood.

"Inside, I suppose," Alecto said, and led the other two through the glass doors, into a vast room with red velvet walls, beneath a dusty crystal chandelier. The people standing behind glass counters and leaning on walls didn't notice the three of them at all, beyond slight headaches and sudden sweats.

Alecto looked around, frowning. "I've just thought. That woman, who showed us the way—how could she *see* us?"

"She didn't see us," Megaera snapped. "She saw three old ladies. What we need, the world provides. So it has always been. We needed direction, and she came."

"I'm just happy to be here," Tisiphone said. She paused, peering at the columns painted gold, the domed ceiling decorated with carved cherubs, all the faded opulence.

"Don't be *happy*," Megaera said. "We've been called, which can only mean blood, kin murdering kin, an affront to the gods, a cursed house. That shouldn't make you *happy*."

"I think we're old enough to be honest with ourselves," Alecto said soothingly. "We're *all* happy. I feel so... sharp tonight. Better than I have in ages."

"Hard work is good for the mind," Megaera said. "We've been idle too long."

"Where *is* that woman who showed us the way?" Tisiphone said. "I meant to thank her."

"We thanked her by not scooping out her eyes when she looked upon us," Megaera muttered.

"She seemed... familiar to me, as I think of it," Alecto said. She squinted around the lobby. "What *is* this place?"

"I thought someone said it was a theater," Tisiphone said, but she sounded unsure.

"Nonsense," Megaera said. "Theaters are *outside*." She gestured vaguely. "There are always... goats about. We used to go to the theater, and it was nothing like this."

"We used to be *in* the theater," Tisiphone said. "They used to have plays about *us*."

"Perhaps they will again, someday," Alecto said. "Come. We must find the murderess."

The ladies heard a collective gasp, beyond a set of double doors. They hurried forward, and threw the doors open.

A woman sat on a raised platform at the far end of the darkened room beyond, awash in a beam of white light. Gore clotted her hair, and blood streaked her arms. She cradled a pair of dead children, and stared up at the lights. She cried out: "Our children are dead! Surely that stings you!"

The ladies looked at one another and nodded. It was just what the letter of commission had told them to expect—a mother who murdered her children, in public, for revenge.

They linked arms. Their forms, the old-woman-shapes they'd worn for so long, rippled and fluttered, revealing blacker, more fundamental bodies beneath.

The Furies surged toward the stage.

During the penultimate scene, as Zara—as Medea—sat on stage with her dead children in her arms, everything went wrong. Zara was supposed to be under a single spotlight, but suddenly a dozen other stage lights came on, illuminating the blood-spattered wreckage of the suburban living-room set. She barely paused in her lines at first—the show must go on—but then the house lights came up, too, and she heard the keening from the back of the house, a high-pitched and strangely gleeful wail. The people in the audience should have turned around and looked back, craning their heads as Zara did to find the source of the noise, but they didn't move. In fact, they didn't move at *all*—they were perfectly still, even a man apparently just back from the bathroom, who hovered above his seat in the act of sitting down. Yet they weren't *frozen*—they trembled, and shifted slightly. It was like the moment in an improv exercise when the director calls "Freeze" and everyone stops and holds whatever position they happen to be in.

"What the *fuck?*" Zara said, and let go of the children. They slid down to the stage, still holding their curled-up-to-her positions. Something was coming down the aisle, toward the stage, something like a black sheet blowing in the wind.

Zara stood up, and the Chorus stepped onto the stage, half from stage left, half from stage right. They arrayed themselves behind her in a semi-circle and said, "Poor woman, swept up by tragedy! Who will give you succor? You have been led into a forest of horrors."

The black shadow swooped up on stage, toward Zara, howling and laughing. Zara glimpsed shapes in the roiling blackness—wings, stones, coffins, eyes, talons, scorpions, whips, spears, flails. She brought her hands up before her face. A flash of pain seared her—the taste of glass and blood in her mouth, ball bearings in her bones, something with serrated teeth gnawing deep in her gut. She gasped, and doubled over—

—and the pain passed, leaving only the bare hint of a memory behind. Zara lowered her hands to see three old women standing before her, dressed in stained housecoats. One of the women was regal, with the face of a queen; she looked stunned. Another was pinch-faced and hunched-over, and she glowered. The last had disheveled hair, and fluttering hands, and seemed on the verge of tears. "What... what *happened?*" this last one said.

"Cast change," said a smoky voice from the audience. It was Nikki, the talent scout, dressed in a black tailored suit, rising from her seat in the front row.

"You showed us the way here," said the regal old woman. "You gave us directions."

"Oh, I had a lot to do with bringing us all together."

"Somebody better start talking," Zara said, crossing her arms. "You have absolutely fucked up my show, and there'd better be a good reason."

"Show?" said the pinch-faced woman.

"Yes," Nikki said, climbing the steps to the stage. "It's a *play*, ladies. About Medea."

"I remember Medea," the regal woman said. She looked at Zara. "This is no Medea."

"Very true," Nikki said, looking down at the children. She nudged the boy in the ribs with the toe of her stylish low-heeled boot. "They are not dead, but only sleeping."

"But what—" the disheveled one began.

The regal woman interrupted her. "I think I understand. We're being... retired. You sent the letter of commission. We've been tricked." She squinted. "And I think I know you. Daughter of chaos. Mother of death and sleep. Nyx."

"Nyx? The goddess of night shouldn't be *blonde*," the pinch-faced one said.

"Why would you trick us?" the fluttering woman cried.

Nikki snorted. "There was a time when you couldn't have *been* tricked, ladies."

"Okay, I'm out of here," Zara said. "I clearly walked in on the movie halfway through. You can fight it out amongst yourselves. I'm going to get this blood off me, because it itches when it dries."

"Zara," Nikki said, and it was a tone of voice Zara recognized—she'd used it herself, on Doug, during their sessions. "Stay." It was a voice meant to be obeyed. Quite against her will, Zara found herself standing still. "These women are... the kindly ones, they were called sometimes. The solemn ones. The—"

"The *Furies*?" Zara said. "The Erinyes? The terrible ones?" At Nikki's look of surprise, Zara rolled her eyes. "I'm an actress, woman, remember? I've read the classics. Christ, I'm starring in motherfucking *Medea*, in case you hadn't noticed."

"Oedipus was the mother-fucking one," the disheveled old lady said, sounding pleased with herself. "Not Medea."

"Yes, well," Nikki said, glancing at the ladies, then turning her attention back to Zara. "The Furies are a force for vengeance. They punish those who kill their relatives. They saw you on stage, and thought you'd murdered your children, and tried to punish you. I imagine you felt the leading edge of that, hmm? But you *didn't* kill your children. By attempting to punish you unjustly, these kind ladies committed a serious transgression. By that mistake they proved themselves unfit to be the instruments of justice. In further fact—" and here she smiled, teeth as white as stars—"as the injured party, you now have the moral authority to punish them."

"We were deceived," the regal old woman said, voice shaking with barely suppressed rage. "We were told there would be murder tonight. We behaved rashly, yes, without the care we once would have shown, but we are not solely culpable."

Zara looked at the old women, then back at Nikki, and began to laugh.

"You don't believe me," Nikki said, still sounding smug.

"Shit, no, I believe you," she said. "Everybody in the audience looks like they got touched while playing freeze tag, and these white-faced freaks in the Chorus have been following me since yesterday, making with the portents. I'd be crazy *not* to believe you. I'm laughing because you expect me to take over from the Furies. Sorry. Not a role I'm interested in."

"You don't have a choice," Nikki said. "The ladies got too old, too boring, and... certain parties... decided there needed to be a cast change. You got the part, Zara. I'm the greatest talent scout there ever was. You should thank me."

"What certain parties?" Zara said. "The gods? Didn't that woman say you were, what, the goddess of night? What gives you the right to fuck with me? Nobody even *believes* in those gods anymore."

Now Nikki laughed. She sat down, cross-legged, in a puddle of fake blood, heedless of dirtying her clothes. "Oh, Zara, really. I've was born long before the gods, and I'm a child compared to the beings I work for. The gods are nothing. They were shat and belched and vomited up out of chaos, and that's where most of them have returned. The gods are just props—like these old ladies are, like you are, now. You're just part of the play. But who do you think *commissioned* the play? Who is the director of the play of the world, who is the producer of the universe? Those beings are the ones in charge, Zara. And the producers want you to take over as an avenging force in the world. These three women sprang from the blood of Uranus to avenge his murder. Uranus was killed by a family member, and the ladies took that as their guiding principle, and went on to punish other people for that same sin. And now *you're* vengeance personified. You can punish these women for *their* transgression."

Zara thought about the searing pain the Furies had inflicted on her so briefly. "So you're saying... I have power?"

"Yes," Nikki said. "Sometimes. When you have cause. The Furies only punished kin-killers. We're not yet sure what your specialty will be, but we're all very excited to find out." She glanced upward. "You know, some stories say I gave birth to the Furies—as I gave birth to pain, age, strife, and death—but it was never true. Until now. I feel something like a mother to you, now, Zara."

The house lights went down, and the stage lights, too, until there were only three spots—one on Nikki, one on the former Furies, one on Zara herself. Zara wasn't sure how, but she knew she was the one who'd made the lights change—her power was showing itself now, whether she liked it or not.

Nikki stood up and stepped away from her spotlight, into the dark. "*Now,*" she said. "Punish them, Zara, for what they did to you."

The former Furies stood, their backs straight, their heads held high, waiting.

"No," Zara said. "I won't do it." The spotlight found Nikki again.

Nikki sighed. There was no fake blood on her clothes, though she'd been sitting in a pool of it. "You don't have any choice—"

"There is always a choice," the regal Fury said. "We forgave Orestes. We were the benevolent ones, for a time."

"Yeah," Zara said. "I can be benevolent."

Nikki pinched the bridge of her nose between her thumb and forefinger, as if fighting a headache. "This isn't the way we meant things to go."

Zara slapped Nikki, hard, leaving a bloody smear across her cheek. The Chorus gasped and murmured. Nikki stared at her, eyes wide.

"This isn't a *play,*" Zara said, suddenly overcome by the pressures of the past few days—Doug, the Chorus, rehearsal, and now *this.* "You aren't my director. I'm not going to say the lines you wrote. You need to learn to tell the difference between what's real and what's not, or you're going to be in for a hard time." She turned to the Furies and snapped her fingers. The light on them went out. "Go on," she said. "Show's over. You're forgiven."

Nikki rubbed her bloody cheek. "What, you think you saved them? They'll just get old and die like normal people, now."

"That's better than me killing them because of something *you* tricked them into doing," Zara said.

Shaking her head, Nikki smiled. "Oh, Zara. We're going to have a great time watching you. You're going to cut a swath, aren't you?"

"I don't want the part," Zara said.

"Sure," Nikki said. "Whatever you say. I've got to be going. You might want to pick up the children and go on with your lines—time's going to come flooding back in here in a moment. You can finish your little play, take your bows, and then move on to more important things. I'll see you around—but you won't see me." Nikki stepped out of the spotlight again, and when Zara mentally shifted the light to follow her, it illuminated only the bloody stage. Nikki, and the ladies, were gone.

Zara sank back down to her knees and gathered the children toward her.

Getting back into the role of Medea for this last scene was going to be hell.

Zara begged off from the cast party, saying she didn't feel well, and after she'd cleaned up and changed into her street clothes, she left the theater by the side entrance. She had a lot of thinking to do. She didn't *feel* any different, didn't feel brimming with power. Maybe her life didn't have to change. Maybe she could just go on the way she'd always—

"Bitch," Doug said, stepping from behind a rusty trash container. "You called my office. You fucked with my life."

Zara moved toward him, fists clenched. "And what do you think you did to *my* life, you brainless prick?" she shouted.

Doug stumbled back, startled—clearly he'd run this scenario through in his head a few times, and it hadn't involved Zara being loud and aggressive. He rallied, though, and came toward her again. "I just wanted what you *owed* me. I paid you to perform a service, and you thought you could just stop, any time you wanted?"

"Yes, Doug, you moron. It was a *job*. I *quit*."

"But we had a real connection," he said, sounding hurt now. "I could tell by the way you acted with me that our sessions meant something to you, to both of us, by the way we synched up perfectly, anticipated one another's—"

"No," she said, not shouting now, just speaking quietly, and Doug fell silent. "No. I was acting. I'm an actress. It's not my fault if you can't tell the difference between a real connection and playing pretend."

"I'm sorry you feel that way," he said. "But you're lying to yourself. I'll make you understand." He reached into his pocket, and came out with a knife, a fancy one with a shining blade and a skeletal-frame steel hilt.

Zara narrowed her eyes. This was so... fucking... *melodramatic.*

A spotlight illuminated Doug, and he squeezed his eyes shut in the sudden brilliance. "What?" he said, bewildered, shading his face and looking up toward the source of the blinding white light—it was coming from the empty air.

Zara knew what to say. The words were there, in her head; the perfect words, the natural words, the ones that didn't feel like prepared lines at all. She wondered whether Nikki and her friends the producers had driven Doug crazy, set him on this path in order to bring about this confrontation, for their own entertainment.

Maybe so. But Doug was still an asshole, and he still had a lesson to learn. She wouldn't kill him, but there were other punishments. "You need to learn to recognize what's real, Doug," she said, her voice almost sad. "From now on, your life will be bathed in light and clarity. You'll never believe anything untrue again, and you'll never be able to tell untruths of your own, either. If you go to the movies, it will just be noise and flashing lights. If you go to the theater, it will just be people standing on a stage talking. Novels will be words on a page. You don't deserve to experience stories, Doug, because you can't handle the responsibility that stories involve." She waved her hand, and the spotlight went out.

Doug sat down in the alley. He whimpered. "I—I—" He fell silent, and dropped his knife, and covered his face with his hands, desperately trying to put the scales back on his eyes.

Zara walked out of the alley. Perhaps this was a role she could play after all. The Furies had lived to punish those who murdered their loved ones—that was the circumstance of their birth, after all. But Zara had gained her powers because some people couldn't tell the difference between what was real and what was only a story, and *those* were the kind of people she would punish. The world wasn't a stage, no matter what Shakespeare thought, no matter what Nikki and her producers believed. Zara wouldn't play the part they had in mind for her. She was going off book. She was going to *improvise.*

"Oh, Nikki," she said, and felt the night air tremble. "You fucked up, sister. It's my show, now."

As Zara walked out of the alley, a light, unseasonable rain began to fall. Once she was gone, the Greek Chorus emerged from behind garbage cans and piled boxes, to stand around Doug, who lay curled on the wet pavement.

"And so night fell," the Chorus said, "and the sky above the mountain of the gods was rent by a great light, and those above who penned the destiny of Earth and Heaven felt their hands tremble, and watched as blotted ink spread across the parchment in their hands, and wept to see their work undone." Then the Chorus stood, mouths half-open, as if unsure what to say next.

Their white make-up began to smear and run in the falling rain.

ROMANTICORE

Fucked half a hundred times by love, and still I look for more. I don't know why, but since I was fifteen I'm not happy—or don't even call it happy, I'm not *functional*, I'm not *awake*—if I'm not pursuing, or being pursued, or in the midst of an affair.

So this thing I'm going to tell you about, remember it's a love story, despite the lions and the murder and the jazz music; all that's important, but it doesn't detract from the essence of the thing. A love story. It's very important to me that I have one good love story, one where love conquers something, or saves someone, and I think this is it. Everything else, all the other times, might have been bullshit and wilting flowers, but this was real.

And while it's probably not the bloodiest love story you've ever heard, what with Shakespeare and all, I bet it ranks up there.

It all started two days after things finally disintegrated totally with Susie. (Even her name makes me curl my lip in disgust now; so infantile, so cutesy, such a conscious oxymoron sort of name for a woman with four silver rings in her face, slash-dyed black-and-henna hair, combat boots, eyeliner so heavy it almost makes a domino mask.) We broke up because she was cheating on me, which is pretty hilarious, really, since we had an open relationship. She could fuck anybody she wanted, date other people, I didn't care, I've never been the jealous type (unlike Martin, but we'll get to him, oh, boy, will we ever get to him). We only had two rules: have *safe* sex, and if you're fucking somebody else, tell me about it. That's all; precautions and disclosure.

So she starts sleeping with my best friend, and they don't tell me about it, because they think I'll be mad. Jesus. I would've been *happy* to hear she was screwing Nick. At least I *like* him, he's a definite cut above the usual buzz-cut muscle-shirt troglodytes she hooks up with, god knows why those guys want to sleep with her, when the closest she's ever come to a gym is standing outside of one smoking a cigarette while waiting for a bus. But Nick and Susie thought I'd fly into a rage, that they'd be stepping on some weird territorial taboo, so they snuck around behind my back until one day I came home early because the coffee shop where I usually work was being fumigated and I found them in my bed. And at first I was like, "Whoops, guys, I'll go grab a bagel and come back in a little bit," but they totally freaked out and then it was true confessions time, they'd been doing this for two months now, every chance they get, and they're so sorry and the secrecy is driving them crazy. Oh, and we're like totally in love, Susie says; and we're gonna make a go of it; and I'm moving in with Nick; and we're gonna be monogamous, because this open-relationship thing is just too stressful; and we're really sorry, Ray.

I don't know if they had safe sex or not, but it's not like I've never been in bed with Nick (I've been in like ten threesomes and one out-and-out orgy with the guy, we go way back) so it doesn't worry me too much.

After they said their piece I told them to fuck off, and they had enough respect for me to do so with a minimum of fuss, and fifteen minutes later I was sitting in my little apartment over the scary convenience store, smoking a cigarette and ashing into a beer can, wondering what happened. That morning I had a girlfriend, admittedly one who sulked a lot and borrowed money all the time, but still, a girlfriend, and I had a best friend to shoot pool and walk around downtown with and pick up chicks with, and now maybe I didn't have either one. So I put on some bitter emo-indie-punk music—Agent Ink, this band from down south somewhere, I think it was—and lay back on my futon staring at the ceiling with its totally appropriate nasty waterspots. Hello, squalor, my old friend.

I took a nap. Didn't get any work done, but none of my deadlines were exactly looming. I'm a writer, and I actually make a living that way (if you call this living, ha ha), with a lot of hustle. I do music reviews for one of the local papers, and anything else I can scrounge up, textbook articles, advertising copy, the occasional feature article. I fill in with proofreading and when things get really rough I work the door at a club a friend of mine owns, or run sound or lights somewhere. It's a pretty hand-to-mouth living, but I went to college on a scholarship and I've never even had a credit card, so I don't have the sort of debt most of my friends do. Don't own a car. I ghost along.

So that night I mostly moped and slept, tried to decide if I'd really miss Susie, knowing I'd really miss Nick, because he's the kind of guy who wouldn't be cool with hanging out with me after this. Slept badly, but slept. The next day I went to the coffee shop (which still smelled like bug spray) with my laptop and snagged a table in the one corner that the sun never hits all day long, and I drank cup after cup of black coffee and typed my fingers to the bone, like I do most every day. An article about the discovery of radium for a high school science book. Another about the battle of the Thames for a different book. Proofreading some boring-ass article about mixing boards for a music magazine. All of it good for keeping me from thinking about Susie and Nick, from wondering what they were doing that morning, probably having sex at Nick's place, which wouldn't bother me except I'll never be in bed with either of them again.

After work I went home, plugged in the laptop, and sent off the work I did to the interested parties. With luck checks would appear in my mailbox soon. Writing can be a bitch like that; the checks come whenever, usually about two days after you absolutely positively *must* have the money. When I think about how much my rent costs, I automatically tack on the extra $25 I get charged for paying late, since I can't remember the last time I managed to pay it on time. Then I puttered around online a little, looking for writing jobs, didn't find anything, looked at some porn, didn't get turned on, checked my e-mail, didn't have anything interesting. I decided to go out and get drunk because I've just been jilted by my girl for my best friend, and damn, that's a reason to get drunk, innit?

I went to Black Glass, which is dim and smoky and has Bikini Kill and Sparklehorse on the jukebox and live music lots of nights. I sat at one of the discus-sized tables and ordered a pint of Guinness, because I hadn't had dinner, and I'd heard you could live off Guinness if you didn't mind getting scurvy in the process. I figured I'd soften myself up with a few pints, then start ordering hi-test vodka to finish myself off. I could stagger home from Black Glass no matter how drunk I got; it was only three and a half blocks.

Halfway through my second pint, with Neutral Milk Hotel wailing on the jukebox, a bunch of college kids came in, dressed in full faux-punk regalia, clothes bought from expensive stores in the mall, meant to look like clothes scrounged out of the bin at the Salvation Army. They took the table next to mine and started babbling and braying and drowning out the music, bumping into my chair, generally being shits—and this was *before* they'd even started drinking. I gave them as baleful a stare as I could manage, glaring hard enough you'd think they'd turn to stone, but they didn't even notice me. So I slumped, defeated, and picked up my glass and relocated to the bar, where there were three empty stools. I sat on the middle one and felt pleasantly insulated from the cruel world. I drained my beer and looked at the smudged-up mirror behind the bar. (No, I'm not gonna take this staring-in-the-mirror-moment opportunity to describe my face. It's just a fucking ordinary guy's face.)

I looked in the mirror and saw *her*, down at the other end of the bar. Ash-blonde, probably in her late thirties but looking good, a face that was both pretty and *comfortable*, if you know what I mean; she wasn't caked up with make-up or hiding behind her hair or anything, just a nice pleasant face, looked like somebody you could talk to, and maybe more than talk to. She had her eyes closed, but not like she was sleeping; like she was listening. Her dress was loose and black, satiny-reflective. I must've been looking at her for two minutes at least before she opened her eyes, not blinking sleepily but *snap*, right open, and she looked right at me, my face in the mirror, my eyes.

Her eyes were as black and reflective as her dress, a solid dark gleam, without white or iris.

I jumped or something, I think. She glanced down, sort of secretly smiling at her drink, then looked back up at me, kind of coyly, but not in a bullshit way. I don't think I'd ever met a girl before who could look coy without also looking manipulative. Her eyes weren't black anymore, just normal eyes, though I couldn't tell what color in the dimness. That glimpse of blackness was just the bad light, I figured, or her face reflecting on a dirty part of the mirror, or just me being drunk. I didn't think about her black eyes again until much, much later.

We kept looking at each other in the mirror, her sort of smiling, me—I don't know what. Thinking she looked even better with her eyes open, probably. I wanted to go over and talk to her, sure, but more than that I wanted *her* to come talk to *me*. Then there'd be no chance that I was misinterpreting her look; I mean, maybe she wasn't looking at me at all. Hard to tell what's what, in a mirror.

Then she gave me a bigger smile, shrugged a little, put some money on the bar, and stood up, pulling her purse strap over her shoulder.

I looked down into my beer. Just a swallow left. I could stay here and get bombed out of my skull, to make a match for my bombed-out heart... or I could do something else.

I was just drunk enough to do something else. If I hadn't... but hell. That's an idiot's game, playing what-might've-been. You always lose that game. So I'll just tell you what *was*.

I followed her. She went out the door, and I came after

her and said, "Hey."

She stopped by the curb and looked at me. "Hey yourself," she said, and her voice was sibilant, smoky, a voice you could listen to for hours, a voice that would go down like good whiskey goes down, smooth and warm.

I held out my hand. "I'm Ray."

She shook my hand, briefly. "Lily."

And then we were looking at each other again, just like before, and I had no idea what to say, still, so I said, "Um, I wondered, I wanted to buy you a drink, but you left, so..." I shrugged. "What can I do instead?"

"Do you like jazz?"

"That depends. New Orleans, Traditional, Bop, Chicago style, Dixieland, ragtime, fusion...? I don't get into fusion much."

She cocked her head. I had the feeling I'd passed a test. "Pretty traditional. Five piece. Sax, drums, clarinet, trumpet, and upright bass. Called the Blue Rock Quintet. They're playing at a little place downtown, the Spiral Down club."

I waited for her to go on, but she didn't. "Is that an invitation?" I said.

"It's information. That's where I'm going, though."

I smiled. "Want to share a cab?"

Before two hours were gone, I knew I was in it again, that I wanted to know this woman. The Blue Rock Quintet was an all-female jazz group, a pretty rare thing, and they were good, really well-balanced, though the sax player was the best of them, a tall woman with short black hair, wearing a tux with tails. She was hot, and the music she played made her even hotter, but there was no one but Lily for me then, it was all about the way she lost herself in the music, the way she looked at me, the way she leaned in close to talk between songs.

Was Lily just a rebound? Shit, in my vocabulary, the only thing "rebound" means is the bounce off a backboard in basketball. I've been going from woman to woman my whole life, it's less a rebound and more like a skipped stone, or chain-smoking. Lily was there, and she was it, and she made me wonder why I'd spent so much time with Susie, that bundle of eye make-up and neuroses; when there was someone like Lily, so comfortable in her skin, making me so comfortable, too.

The Spiral Down was tiny, the tables right up against the stage, but the effect was cozy rather than claustrophobic. After listening to two sets, Lily leaned in close to my ear and said, "Let's go someplace we can talk."

I nodded, and followed her out. We walked down the block, chatting about the music, until we got to a mostly deserted café, nobody inside but a guy with a shaved head scribbling furiously in a black notebook, and a yuppie wearing headphones working at a laptop. We ordered drinks (she got coffee, just coffee, and I did likewise; a match made in heaven) and sat down in a corner, beneath a dangling mobile, crescents of steel, only shiny on the edges, hanging on wires.

"So," she said, looking at me appraisingly, half a smile hanging around her lips.

"So?" My left foot was tapping on the floor, seemingly of its own volition, and with an effort I stopped it. I felt jittery, really keyed up, and wondered if ordering coffee was such a good idea.

"Having fun?"

"Hell, yes. I didn't expect to have fun tonight."

She nodded. "Think you'll keep having fun if you keep seeing me?"

I tried to keep my big goofy grin under wraps, and only partly succeeded. "The current evidence seems to suggest that I will."

"Me, too. I'd like to go out with you again."

"I'm pretty sure I can free up my schedule."

She leaned forward, close to me, and for the first time I saw the little lines around her eyes, and the word that came to mind was *careworn*. I thought her face was beautiful, just touched by laugh lines, crying lines, life lines. "But there's something you should know. My relationship situation is a little unusual."

How many times had I started this conversation, mostly with girls who were maybe sophomores in college, explaining to them that I hadn't been in a monogamous relationship since I was seventeen, and had no intention of ever going back to the Land of Jealous Possession? I wondered if she was one of those hard-core polyamorous types, and if she'd start in about her co-primaries and her nested secondaries in an N-structure, and how we could at best have a tertiary relationship with bimonthly sex privileges. The jargon can get pretty extreme, though I don't have much use for it, myself, preferring to say, "Yeah, we're friends, and we sleep together sometimes," rather than "I'm her tertiary with secondary tendencies" or some shit like that.

But Lily didn't get into any of that. She said, "I have a boyfriend, named Martin, and we've been together for over ten years. He's a musician, though, and he spends about six months a year traveling, playing with different groups. I went with him a couple of times, and it was fun, roaming all over Europe—he gets a lot of gigs in Europe—but it's not the kind of life I'm built for. I'm too much of a homebody. So for the past eight years or so we've had a different arrangement. While he's here in town, for four months, six months, whatever, we're together, and it's great. And when he leaves, I see whoever I want, until he gets back." She shrugged. "It works pretty well. I don't get bothered about the women he sleeps with on the road, and he doesn't get bothered about the people I see when he's gone."

I mulled that over. "So he's on the road now?"

"Yep. In Greece, last I heard."

"When's he going to be back?"

"It's a little uncertain, but probably in October."

It was early May. Five months sounded like... forever. How many dates had I been on that turned into relationships that lasted longer than five months, anyway? Not many. And I knew about this Martin guy, so I could keep that in my head, not get too attached even if things did go well with Lily. "Sounds good to me," I said.

"And even if you and I really hit it off, that doesn't mean I won't see other—"

I held up my hand. "Say no more. It's cool." And I told her about Susie and Nick and the brief history of my love life, and we knew we understood each other.

That night was the beginning of something beautiful. In the short term, anyway. In the longer term, it was just a small part of something pretty monstrous.

The next five months were great. I could go on about it, tell you in detail about my summer of love with Lily. She was a freelance graphic designer, so her schedule was nearly as flexible as mine (though she got more work, and made more money, than I did). We did all-night film festivals, where we'd each pick out two movies and watch them on the DVD at her place. So she saw *The Brood* and *It Came from Outer Space* and *The Masque of the Red Death* for the first time, and I saw *The Lady Eve* and *Sullivan's Travels* and *Queen of the Nile*. We had picnics in the park, fried chicken and big roast beef sandwiches—I've never known a more joyfully carnivorous woman—and went roller-skating, which I hadn't done since junior high. We took a couple of weekend trips (her treat) to the country, which we spent in bed and on hiking trails in roughly equal proportion. And we went to dozens and dozens of shows, plays and concerts and poetry slams, and at every one she seemed to know a performer, or the guy working the door, or the woman working the lights, and half the time she got us in free, which is pretty much the epitome of cool in my book. She was so good for me, too. I mean, you know guys like me; I wear black, I smoke too much, I like obscure music, I talk shit, I'm the master of irony and sarcasm, I sleep all day and stay up all night, I'm cooler-than-thou; it's been my thing for years. But with Lily, I loosened up, laughed more, and the world didn't seem so painfully tedious and tawdry and stupid anymore. I was, to be as cliché as possible, stopping to smell the roses, and they smelled good.

And we had lots and lots of sex, occasionally great sex, but almost always really *good* sex. She was funny, and sweet, and she would sometimes have whole conversations with me in her sleep, her end of things matter-of-fact and surreal: "Have you seen my eyepatch?" she'd say, and laying awake I'd reply, "No, babe," and she'd say, "The statues are breaking in the rain," and I'd say, "That's what happens when you use cheap cement," and so forth. She never remembered those conversations the next morning, though she said she believed me; she'd always had the habit, she said, of narrating her dreams.

Neither of us dated anyone else, though we left the option open; we were together more nights than not, unless one of us had a deadline to finish. It was something. Something else. Something special.

I can't decide if all this is boring or not, if you care about the good times, or if you're just waiting for the monsters to start jumping out of the closet, if you're waiting for the train wreck you know is coming. I guess it doesn't matter. It's hard for me, writing about those good months, remembering. The thing is: she loved me. I wasn't just somebody to fuck while Martin was away, though maybe that's what she expected me to be at first. We had something more. It was the best relationship I'd ever been in, the most honest, the most unselfconscious, the most gentle, and it was good for her, too; she told me so often enough. So I thought that when Martin got back, there'd be *room* for me, that we could still see each other, that it wouldn't be the end, because I was *special*.

So in late September, when she said, "We should talk," I got this heavy feeling in my gut, like I'd just eaten a pound of ball bearings.

But before I tell you about that, I should maybe tell you about the lion dreams.

I've never really been into animals. I live in a city, and I don't see anything other than birds and squirrels, cats, dogs on leashes. I've been to the zoo a couple of times, but the monkeys interested me the most, probably because they're the closest thing to people. I hardly paid attention to the lions at all. But after I started seeing Lily regularly, I began dreaming about lions all the time, dreaming I *was* a lion, a big cat, slinking through the long grasses on the savanna, chasing down antelope, lazing in the sun, climbing over rocks. I loved the sun on my fur, the strength in my legs, the way dead animals smelled as good as hot brownies or espresso. I had that dream two, three times a week. I read about lions, even wrote an article about them, mostly about how badass they are, that I sold to a kid's magazine. Most of the dreams were set in the savanna, or in a rocky place, but there were other settings, to0. The one I remember most clearly was an island, with a weird building like a Greek temple on a hill. The beaches were white sand, and the water was blue as the lips of an asphyxiation victim. There were gray stone statues standing in the sand in front of the building, like it was the most white-trash front yard in the history of the world. Statues of people, birds, and all kinds of weird creatures from mythology. Roosters with lizard tails and multifaceted eyes. A pegasus with one wing broken off. A hydra, tipped over, with half its heads buried in the sand. A griffin, a centaur, a unicorn, and a cyclops—*that* one was as tall as a building itself. I padded through the statues, toward the building, but then I heard this *hissing*, like the air being let out of a hundred tires at once, coming from the dark behind the pillars. I looked around, and saw some lion statues, their faces frozen in snarls. I slunk back to the water, which churned, and seemed filled with monsters, and I was trapped, and desperate, and also *sad*. I woke from that dream with a sense of choking despair, and I clung to Lily like she was the only thing keeping me from sinking.

That was the last night I spent with Lily. The next morning she said, "We should talk," and here we are again.

We were in her white-and-yellow kitchen, having breakfast. I was having toast and coffee because my stomach doesn't appreciate much more early in the morning, but she had bacon and eggs and chicken-apple sausage and a big glass of milk. Lily ate neatly, without shoveling, but she could make mountains of food disappear.

"I thought we *were* talking?" I said, trying to keep it light.

She sighed. "I should've said something earlier, but things've been so good... I heard from Martin a few days ago. He's going to be back next week. Monday. I'm picking him up from the airport."

"Oh," I said. "Well, cool. I know you'll be glad to see him." Lily didn't talk about Martin much, though he naturally showed up in lots of her stories and anecdotes. The impression I got was that he was talented, moody, and capricious; the sort of guy who's a lot of fun to hang out with, but maybe a little exhausting, who decides to go to Vegas on a whim and convinces you to go with him, or who jumps in the car to go to the coast for a week and sleeps on the beach when he gets there. He played lots of instruments, but his best were trumpet and flute, and he'd played with just about every jazz and swing band on the planet at one time or another. He did well enough to tour like hell for several months and then take a few months off.

Lily nodded. "I've missed him, yeah. But what I really want to say is... I'm going to miss you. These past few months have been fabulous."

I put my coffee cup down; my hand was shaking. "Are you breaking up with me?"

She looked annoyed. Lily had precious little patience for bullshit, and I realized that's how I sounded to her. For a second her eyes looked black, just like they had in the mirror that first night in Black Glass. I'd seen that before, when she got angry, which wasn't often; just a flash of black, and then back to green. I'd convinced myself it was a little consistent hallucination on my part, that I sensed her mood and translated it into a creepy visual effect. "Ray, you knew all along there was a limit on the far side of this, that once Martin came back I was going to be with him again. I never lied to you."

"You haven't exactly brought it up lately," I said, bitter, not trying to hold back.

"I didn't think you needed to be reminded every half an hour, no. Was I mistaken?"

"So this is it, then? I'm out the door? You can't even see me on weekends, or—"

"No. I'm sorry. When Martin's here, he's for me, and I'm for him. He... it's an out-of-sight, out-of-mind thing for him. He doesn't care what I do when he's not around, but when he's back, he wants me all to himself." She shrugged. "That's the way it's always been."

"It doesn't have to be that way, if you don't want it to be."

She looked at me, totally cool, she might have been something carved from stone, and said, "No, it doesn't. If I don't want it to be."

And that was all. I knew how it was, then. She didn't want to be with me.

Though I hated myself for it, I said, "Don't you love me, Lily?"

She softened, and put her hand over mine. "Sweet Ray. Yes, I love you. But that's not what this is about. I love Martin, too, and I have for a long time. You've been my summertime, but Martin is my man for every season."

I nodded miserably. "When he goes away again..."

"Maybe," she said, but she wouldn't look me in the eyes. "It's hard to say. People change. I don't know how long he'll be here. He's even talked about retiring, these past couple of years, though I can't imagine him staying in one place for so long." She finally met my eyes. "I'll call you." I knew she meant it. I also knew she might not call for months. "I'm not asking you to wait for me. You know I'm not the one-and-only woman for you. We know that's just a bunch of dumb Hollywood crap."

"Yeah," I said hollowly, but for the first time I realized that the movies she liked most were those old romantic comedies, the ones where there really *is* just one person meant for you, one true love in a world of wrong choices. And I think that's a dangerous bullshit idea, I always have, and Lily said she did, too... but I wondered. I wondered if she didn't see Martin as her one-and-only, and everyone else as mere recreation.

"Take care," she said.

I mumbled something, pushed back from the table, got my stuff, and went to the door. She didn't follow. She didn't kiss me goodbye. I couldn't decide if that was cruelty or a kindness.

I got home and found an invitation to Nick and Susie's wedding. I pitched it in the trash. I'd been thinking about calling Nick, trying to convince him there were no hard feelings (and there really weren't; losing Susie was how I met Lily, and I wouldn't have traded that for anything), seeing if we could talk, but there was no way I could do that now. Too bitter. Why the hell should that idiot and that bitch be getting married, when I'd just been given the boot in favor of Martin?

So I'd suffer in silence, noble and alone, or maybe get drunk, finish the bender that Lily had interrupted all those months ago.

I didn't actually do that, though. I got into my work as much as possible instead, editing a long software manual that had been translated incompetently from the Japanese, writing an article about the early American oil barons, researching world death rituals for an anthropology professor at one of the universities. Filling my brain with more useless bullshit, and crowding out all the bad thoughts about Lily and Martin, Martin, motherfucking Martin. It was a struggle every day not to call her, and finally, in desperation, I got involved with a woman who lived in my building. Her name was Marie, and she was a waitress/actress, dumb as a thumbscrew and attracted to my old misanthropic-ironic pose, which I'd donned like a suit of armor when Lily gave me the boot. We went to clubs, drank too much, and screwed. Such was life; familiar, empty, simple.

And then one day I was sitting at the coffee shop, reading one of the local papers, getting pissed off because they'd put a typo in the *byline* of my latest music review, so now my name was "Roy," when I saw his name, that fucker's name, that bastard's name: Martin Chorus.

("His name's Martin *Chorus?*" I said, laughing. "He's a musician, and his last name is *Chorus?*"

("It was 'Khora' originally," she said, and spelled it for me. "A very old Persian name. But when Martin's ancestors came to America, the immigration officials spelled it 'Chorus,' so that's what it's been ever since. Just a funny coincidence, that he's a musician." That was one of our few conversations about Martin.)

Martin was playing at a little jazz bar on Saturday, which was that night, at 8 o'clock. I looked at my watch. Four hours. Shit. There was no question. I had to at least get a *look* at this guy. And if Lily was there... I'd just tell her it was a coincidence, or I was covering it for a review, or something. I called Marie on my cell phone and cancelled our date. She wasn't even that pissed. Marie was easy-going, and not bad in bed, but about as deep as a saucer. No comparison to Lily.

So I got dressed and went to the bar, a placed called The Stone Mirror, and took a table a bit back from the stage. It was a little before eight, and the place was filling up, but it was Saturday night, so that didn't mean Martin was any good; *every* place was full on Saturdays. I looked around for Lily, but she was nowhere to be seen, which didn't surprise me. She'd seen Martin play a million times, probably, and loving supportiveness only goes so far.

The band came on without introduction, setting up their instruments. A drummer, an upright-bass player, a guitarist, a keyboardist, a trombonist, and Martin, a trumpet case in one hand, a flute case in the other.

I'd never seen pictures of him—which was weird, when you think about it, it seems like Lily would've had a couple around—but the instrument cases gave him away.

I hated him at first sight. I wanted to eat his fucking eyes out of his head. I'd never had such a visceral reaction to someone before. It made sense; he'd stolen Lily from me, sort of, but still, my reaction felt extreme even from the inside. Martin had olive skin and curly black hair, and he wasn't all that good-looking, really; his face was too round, almost babyish, and the resting position for his expression was a kind of nasty smirk. He wore a dark suit with kitschy, wide lapels, and he introduced the band members, his voice was nothing special, kind of deep.

I watched him through the whole set, and he was good, the bastard. He played trumpet and flute both, wringing out music violently one minute, playing soft and gentle with a master's touch the next. I drank about four beers during that set, and once when the music stopped I heard myself *growling*, deep in my throat. I stopped once I realized I was doing it, and wondered if I'd been making that sound all along.

When the band took a break, I got up to leave, because I'd seen enough. He was a good musician, looked like kind of an arrogant bastard—he took his applause like it was his due, not gracious in the slightest—and what else could I expect to learn, just watching him?

On my way out the door, someone yelled, "Ray!" I should've left, but I stopped, and turned around, and there was Martin, approaching me, holding out his hand. I shook with him, feeling like my brain had been scooped out. He knew me. It hadn't occurred to me that Lily would have talked to him about me, or that he might've seen pictures, but of course there *were* pictures of Lily and me together, in the country, in the park, just hanging out.

Martin grinned at me, and he seemed to be friendly, but it was still a smirky smile, and I thought maybe he just had an unfortunate face, an asshole's face. "Good set," I said, which was the best I could come up with.

"Better than some, worse than others," he said. "Have a drink with me?" He should've been sweating after all that work he was doing on stage, but he was totally cool and fresh.

Having drinks with Martin was not an experience that fell within my comfort zone. "Thanks, anyway, no. I've had enough already tonight."

"Don't have a drink, then. On me."

I still wanted to kill him—and people say that all the time, but I *mean* it, part of me wanted to slam his face into a table until you couldn't tell where skin ended and wood began. But maybe it would be good to talk; hell, maybe he was going to tell me he was breaking up with Lily and I was welcome to take over, or that Lily dug me so much he'd decided to make an exception and let her see me while he was in town.

I know. Fat chance. But a guy's gotta dream.

"Sure, I guess I don't have anywhere to be." So we sat down at a tiny table, way too close together, our knees touching. I slid back and crossed my legs, crossed my arms over my chest.

"What made you decide to come here tonight?" he said.

I shrugged. "Heard there was a good band playing."

He looked amused. "You didn't know I'd be there?"

"Yeah, I knew it was you."

"You wanted to get a look at me."

I shrugged again, beginning to think this was a bad idea.

"You think I'm... competition. But you misunderstand the situation. There is no competition. Lily and I go way back. Farther back than you can imagine. We belong together. We're the same, I have a connection with her that you never can. We're closer than blood, Ray. She liked you, I know, though she didn't want to tell me much about you. I found the pictures tucked into one of her drawers, that's how I recognized you, but she didn't volunteer to show them to me. I wondered if I would see you around."

"Hey, Lily already dumped me, Martin. You don't have to do a follow-up, okay?" I wanted to make him eat a beer glass.

"No, no, that's not what this is about. What Lily and I have cannot be harmed or lessened, and for that reason, I *don't* see you as a threat. I am a... hungry person, Ray. I demand a lot of Lily's time. But..."

I uncrossed my arms. This sounded like it might be going my way after all.

"We occasionally invite people to bed with us," Martin said. "Women, men, whatever. I've romped with Lily and many of her other summertime romances. She didn't seem to think you'd be interested, but..." He raised an eyebrow and then, horribly, reached across the table, and brushed the back of my hand with his fingers.

"No thanks," I said, not even thinking about it, not even weighing the pleasure of being with Lily against the instinctive revulsion I felt for Martin—the revulsion won, with no calculation necessary. But I was already confused; Lily had told me that Martin was jealous, that he didn't play well with others, and now here he was, coming on to me! Was Lily lying, trying to get rid of me? Using Martin as an excuse for a breakup she wanted to happen anyway?

"Ah," Martin said. "Pity. Oh, well. I've got to play another set, Ray. Nice meeting you."

He went back to the stage, and I went out the door, miserable, thinking, *Sometimes it's better not to know.*

That night I slept alone, and dreamed of lions, but it was different, this time. Before I'd always delighted in my strength, my grace, the sheer wonder of my leonine form... but now I sensed that something was terribly wrong. Something was rotten on the savanna, and I don't mean the leftovers from my kills.

Walking, trying to find the source of my unease, I came to a place of tumbled rocks. An old lion lay stretched on a boulder, his mane pure white. He sat with his head on his forepaws, watching me, and I settled down before him, respectful, quiet. I was the head of my pride, the ruler of this territory, but I knew this old lion was something bigger— maybe even a god among lions, at the very least a wise old cat, to have reached such an age. If he was a god, I didn't feel any shock of the divine, or the overwhelming reverence that a human might have felt. I just felt respect.

There is a monster, the old lion said—or gave me to understand, it didn't use words. *An old monster. You must kill it.*

I lifted my head, full of strength and indignation, and made it clear that I would hunt this creature down and kill it.

The old lion shook his head. *Not here,* he said. *The monster is here, yes, but only as you are—in pieces, from long ago. You have to seek him out in the other world. It does not look like a monster there, any more than you look like a lion; but that is what it is, and what you are.*

"I don't understand," I said, and I wasn't a lion anymore—just me, naked and cold, crouching on freezing rocks.

Perhaps you will, the old lion said, and the sadness in him was as heavy as the world. *Or perhaps you will die.*

The old lion rose and padded slowly away, without looking back, and I woke up in bed, thinking: *Martin.*

No, I didn't decide Martin was a monster, and that I had to kill him. This isn't a story about me turning into a raving psycho—I don't think. At least, I'm convinced that the things I saw later on, the unbelievable things, were real, as real as hangovers and overdue rent. After the dream, I *did* think I was getting a bit obsessive about things. I mean, Lily had made it clear I was out of her life; whether the reasons she gave me were true or false didn't ultimately matter. If she'd lied to spare my feelings, hell, in a way, that was being *nice,* wasn't it? So I tried to forget about her, and Martin, and really get on with my life, not just pretend to do so.

And maybe that would've been it, I would've healed with time and all that, if I hadn't seen Lily, and if I hadn't known the guy she picked up.

Look, it's a big city, right? The odds of me running into Lily were pretty low, so I didn't worry about it. I avoided a couple of the bars that I knew Lily really liked, but otherwise, I went about my business. So it was a bad sharp shock when I was in a club called Ugly Everything, propping up the bar while Marie danced with whoever, swinging by every once in a while to urge me onto the dancefloor, but I just kissed her cheek and said I'd rather watch her dance, tonight. She was flirting pretty hard with a blonde girl in a short vinyl skirt, who kept throwing me these meaningful glances, and I thought there might be some intriguing three-way action in my future, which made me happy in a vague sort of way—and then I saw Lily.

Oh, she looked hot. She wore a tight black dress that stopped at mid-thigh, and she had her hair in pigtails, and she wore black boots. I'd never seen her dress like that; she wore dresses pretty often, but nothing so... well... *slutty*. I've got nothing against slutty, mind you; "slut" is hardly a pejorative term in my lexicon, it was just a surprising side of Lily, one I'd never seen before. I looked around for Martin, but didn't see him, and I had a funny feeling that I'd know it if he were here, sense it somehow, or smell him, like something rancid in the air. That didn't make sense, but I'd had enough to drink to accept the idea, almost enough to drink to go talk to Lily. Then I looked over at Marie and the blonde, dancing hard in the sweeping lights. I sucked back a little more of my drink, and decided I was better staying in my current situation. Hot sex was a poor substitute for true love, but it was miles better than loneliness and rejection and the ego-bruising I would surely take if I went and talked to Lily.

But why was she here, alone, without Martin? She looked like she was on the prowl, too, dancing with boy after boy (I couldn't help glancing at her, keeping track of her movements on the dancefloor). Had things fallen through with Martin, or had he left town already after just a few weeks, or was that stuff about them being exclusive just bullshit, as I half-suspected? I realized I was pissed-off at her, well and truly, and wondered how long I'd been feeling that way without realizing it, surprised I'd had to get a little drunk in order for those feelings to bubble up to the surface.

I didn't go over to her, and she never looked my way, but I saw her leave with Steven Lee. Steven and I had shot a lot of games of pool together, and gotten drunk together a couple of times; we weren't exactly friends, but we had lots of friends in common, and we got along well enough. So when I saw Lily leading him toward the door, holding his hand, while he grinned dopily at his good fortune, I almost shouted, almost told him to be careful, she was a viper, she had a stone cold heart... but I didn't say anything. I just watched them go, and even though I believed then that Lily *was* a tricksome viper, I was jealous of Steven, too. Because I still loved her. That shit doesn't go away. It's not like a poison you can suck out.

Then Marie bopped over to me, kissed me on the cheek, and told me she was going back to her place, she'd see me tomorrow. She left with the blonde, and I realized if there was going to be fun tonight, I wasn't invited. Sometimes things just don't go your way.

I made my way home, passing Marie's door as I walked to my apartment. Rage Against the Machine was playing from inside, loud; that was Marie's sex-music of choice lately. She liked something with a good driving beat to fuck along with. I don't remember when I felt more low. I realized that Marie probably felt the same way about me that I did about her; it was fun to be together, and the sex was nice, but there was no pretense at a deep connection. That depressed me further. I sat in my apartment and watched television, which I almost never do. I don't get cable, and the only thing on was a late movie, some interminably boring cop flick from the early eighties. I watched the whole thing, and then went to bed. I stared at the dark for a long time, and the loneliness settled over me like ashes. This was why I hated to be alone, basically; because in the night, I knew that if I died no one would mourn me, if I disappeared no one would really care; because if there was no one looking at me, shining their light on me, how could I even prove I existed at all?

I finally fell asleep, and I had the big dream, the monster-dream, the dream to end all dreams.

It began as the familiar lion dream, my muscles moving easily under tawny skin, the swaying grasses, the world broken into form and shadow. Everything was darker than usual; I didn't normally prowl at night, but there was an urgency now, a sense of hunting to be done, of some beast slouching through the night that had to stopped, had to be *killed*.

A horrible sound rolled across the savanna, shrill as a thousand car alarms, mingled with a low blatting noise. I hated the sound, and wanted to kill whatever made it, tear out whatever throat produced that sound. I ran toward the noise, knowing I'd never heard it before, also knowing it was the voice of my enemy.

I found the monster near the river, drinking, and it lifted its head from the water and gazed at me, smiling. I crouched, tensed to leap, but then just stood, frozen. I'd never seen a creature like this, in or out of waking life, and it smelled all wrong—like a man, and like a scorpion, and like a snake, and—worst of all—like a *lion*. No surprise; it was a mix-up beast, composed of all those things. It's body was that of a lion's, only larger than mine, with powerful haunches and a wide chest, and the fur was weirdly purplish, like clouds at dusk. Instead of a brushlike lion's tail, the thing had a segmented scorpion's tail, rising behind it in a deadly curve. A drop of yellow venom fell from the stinger as I watched, and where it struck the clay on the riverbank, it sizzled.

The thing's head was the worst. It had a human head, bald as an infant, chubby-cheeked, with green eyes that leaked brownish fluid from the corners. It opened its mouth, showing off a triple row of triangular teeth, like a shark's. It made that noise again—shrill piping, low blat.

It sounded like a flute and a trumpet, played at the same time.

Then, bang, I wasn't a lion anymore, I was a man, crouched stupidly on all fours by the river, looking across the water at this *thing*, this creature that was teaching me the meaning of the word "nightmare."

Then the monster changed, too, and became a naked man smeared with mud and blood. He walked toward me, arms outstretched, unsmiling—but I knew he still had a triple row of teeth inside his closed mouth, nothing but shredding incisors, a bite like knives. And once he reached me, he would wrap me up in his arms, and open wide, and fucking *eat* me. Because he was a man-eater. And, just my luck, I wasn't a lion anymore. I was a man. I was his favorite thing on the menu.

I woke before he reached me, and rolled out of bed, rushing to the bathroom. I splashed water on my face. Somewhere on the street a car alarm was whooping, and I stuck my head under the flow of water from the faucet so the water rushing by my ears would drown out the sound.

So the man, on the riverbank, in my dream?

Yeah. That's right. It was Martin.

The next day I was at the coffee shop, trying to work, every word a struggle, with my head full of bad echoes from the dream, that awful flute-and-trumpet cry, the monster with its tripled teeth. I'd just deleted another paragraph when my friend Jade-Lynne came in and sat across from me, huffing. "Have you seen that motherfucker Steven Lee?" she said, without preface.

I blinked at her. "Last night..."

"Everybody saw him last night. What I want to know is, where's he at *now*?" Her hair, an explosion of black braids woven with bright ribbons, waved as she shook her head angrily. "He was supposed to be at my house at 10 o'clock this morning to help me move. Now it's 2, and he's nowhere to be found. I beat on his apartment door for fifteen minutes, and called his cell phone, which is turned *off*, and paged him, and nothing."

"Ah," I said, just a meaningless syllable, while my brain swirled in its juices. Steven had left with Lily, doubtless to spend the night, so he was probably still there, right? Just lost track of time. But why wasn't he answering his phone or his pager? And Lily was an early riser, usually up with the daylight, so I couldn't believe they were still in bed, unless they were *seriously* hungover... "I don't know, Jade. I'll let you know if I see him."

"'Preciate it," she said, and wandered off.

I drummed my fingers on the table, sighed, and packed up my laptop. I went down the street a couple of blocks to a payphone. (I don't have a cell; sometimes I like to be unreachable.)

I plugged in dimes and nickels, slowly. This was crass; this was low-class; this was necessary. Steven was something like a friend, at least, and Jade-Lynne was definitely a friend, so I should do what I could to find Steven, right? Since I was probably the only person in the whole city who knew who he'd gone home with last night.

And, I admit, I wanted Lily to know I'd seen her leave with another guy. I wanted to put her on the spot. I wanted her to twist a little.

Love's not just sweetness; it's flowers wrapped in razorwire.

I dialed Lily's number.

It picked up on the second ring. "Yes?" Martin said.

I stood, frozen. I hadn't expected Martin to answer, but why not? Why wouldn't he be over there? Maybe they'd fucked Steven together.

"Hello, hello?" Martin said, more annoyed than amused. "Can I help you, Mr. Silence?"

I don't think I was even breathing. That voice. It was exactly the same as the voice in my dream. I might have been dreaming even then.

Then Martin shouted. I don't know if it was just something he did to fuck with prank phone callers, or if he knew it was me, and meant me to hear it.

He screamed, "Lions and tigers and bears, oh my! Lions and tigers and bears, oh my!"

I jerked the phone away from my ear and slammed it down.

Fuck this, I thought. Steven wasn't my problem, and Lily and Martin had zero bearing on my life. I went to my apartment, brewed a pot of coffee, and watched TV all afternoon and into the night.

Finally, about 10 o'clock, feeling stupefied, I roused myself. This was stupid, stupid. I shouldn't be wallowing. I called Marie, but she wasn't in, which meant she was probably out at a bar already, unless she was working. That almost put me down again, but I resisted the entropy that sucked at my bones, and put my shoes and jacket on. I wasn't happy with Marie anyway, and I wasn't going to find a better lover sitting around my apartment, so I had to go out. In the movies it's mostly women who are concerned about finding true love, while the men drift along, oblivious; that's just another bullet point on the list of bullshit Hollywood perpetrates, because men are out there looking for love, too, something true and deep and good that lasts. I'd spent too much time pissing and moaning over Lily, who didn't love me anymore, if she ever had. Now it was Saturday night; moving-along time.

I went to a bar, and then another bar, and then another, having a drink, sampling the crowd, moving on. Around 11:30 I bumped into Jade-Lynne, who was morosely drinking something made of vodka and Red Bull. "Did you ever find Steven?" I asked.

"No." She peered into her drink, then looked at me, her green eyes troubled. "I'm past pissed and approaching worried. Turns out a *lot* of people have been going missing lately. You know Charlie Johnson, plays bass for Dead Baby Joke?"

"Vaguely," I said.

"He's gone, too, he disappeared last week, poof. Some other guys, too, people I don't know. They go out clubbing one night, and they never come back." She gave me a wan smile. "So watch yourself, huh? I don't know what's happening, but I'd hate you to join the land of the missing."

"Shit." I leaned against the bar. "People are really disappearing?"

"That's the word. Half a dozen. Maybe more. I don't know if the cops are involved or what. I mean, missing persons, shit. What are they going to do? People go missing all the time."

I nodded. Maybe I should call Lily again; she might have been the last person to see Steven, and if he was just the latest in a long line of guys going missing... Or maybe Lily was involved. Of course that occurred to me, I won't pretend it didn't, but come on, I didn't really *believe* it. I wasn't living in some suspense flick, you know? The idea that Lily could have something to do with disappearances, it was just too *out there*.

Martin, on the other hand...

I dismissed it. *Not my problem.* That's been my mantra for a long time, and it's gotten me through some rough shit. "Take it easy, Jade-Lynne," I said, then paused. "You still need help moving?"

She raised her eyebrow. "Yeah. You offering?"

I nodded. We'd been close friends, once, and could be again, if I got my head out of my ass and my mind off of Lily. "I'll come over tomorrow morning."

"You're a good man, Ray," she said seriously, and I laughed, kind of embarrassed, and went out on the sidewalk to smoke a cigarette.

It was dark, and cold, and I was thinking of going home. Getting out of my apartment had cleared my head, and I felt better. The only problem with going home was that I might *sleep*, and that was no good, because I might dream about Martin as a monster again, or about Lily. There was no peace in being a lion in my sleep anymore.

I finished my cigarette and pitched the butt into the gutter, and then I saw the lion across the street.

I never thought for a second I was dreaming; I knew real life, and this was it, and there was a fucking lion across the street, but I didn't think it was an escapee from a zoo or anything, either, because it was the old lion from my dream, silver mane, dark eyes, the dignity of years. It stood across the street, in an alleyway, and it looked at me, then trotted down the alley.

"Damn," I said, and looked around, but there was no one else on the street at the moment, no one to say, "Shit, did you see that lion?" so I could say, "Yeah, we'd better call 911."

I crossed the street and stopped at the mouth of the alley. "Is there a lion in here?" I said, not shouting but not whispering either, peering into the dark.

"Nobody here but us chickens," said an old-man voice, and I almost jumped out of my fucking skin, because I did *not* expect to hear a human voice.

"Sorry," I said. "Didn't mean to bother you." So I *was* hallucinating. That was an interesting addition to my list of problems.

"Ray, do you work at being so dumb?"

I didn't move. "Ah. No. It's a native talent. Do I know you?"

"We've met." Something rustled, like a body moving on newspapers. "In dreams. 'In the jungle, the mighty jungle...'" His voice was sweet and high. "Do I have to draw you a picture? There is a monster, Ray. It's in your territory. My territory, too, but I'm old, and alone. You have people, a group, a *pride*."

I thought of Jade-Lynne, of Steven, of Susie and Nick, even of people I barely knew, like Charlie Johnson. They were the closest thing I had to family, a bunch of individuals swirling past each other, sleeping together and borrowing money and enacting petty betrayals, helping and hurting. Were they my tribe? Were they the pride I dreamed about?

"The monster is taking your people," the old man in the alley said. "You have to stop him."

"I don't get a magic sword or some stalwart companions to help me, do I?" I said, my mouth running on autopilot, as it so often does, while my mind played catch-up.

"This is real life, son. Even if parts of it *do* look like special effects."

"What am I supposed to do?"

"Look up the street," he said, and I did—

—and there was Lily, decked out in her sexy-red-dress best, getting into a cab, pulling some guy in with her, and the car drove away.

"Shit," I said, and wondered if that guy, whoever it was, was ever going to come home again.

"Follow that car," the old voice said, and chuckled. There was another rustling noise, and then nothing.

"Hey," I said. "Hey, I'm still in the dark about a lot of stuff, here," but there was no response, and I got the sense I was talking to empty space, anyway.

I found a payphone and called a cab, but it didn't come right away, so I stood on the street for twenty minutes, stomping my feet, thinking about my dreams, wondering if I was going crazy, wondering if it mattered, knowing I had to go to Lily's and find out what was going on.

The cab came. I gave the driver directions to Lily's neighborhood, and got out about a block from her house. There was light in her living room window, but the bedroom was dark, which might or might not have been a good sign. I walked toward her house, trying to think what I'd say, especially if Martin answered the door. "Hi, I changed my mind, and I would like to be in a wild three-way with you and Lily"? Or "Hi, an old lion in an alley told me you were a monster, could you get the fuck out of town"?

I didn't feel like much of a lion as I went up the walk, up her steps. I took a breath, and I knocked on Lily's door.

The inner door creaked open, and Lily stood behind the screen, wearing the white robe I'd seen her in so many times. Her hair was messed up, like she'd just had sex, and for all I knew, she had. Her eyes widened, then narrowed. "Ray, get out of here." But she didn't close the door, didn't move, so I didn't, either.

"Lily... look, we really need to talk."

She shook her head. "We had something good, Ray, but it's over now, I'm sorry. Please don't come here again."

"Fuck, Lily," I said, and banged my hand against the frame of the door; she didn't jump, just stared at me. "Look, I know something's going on. I saw you leave the club with Steven Lee last night, and nobody's seen him since, and I saw you with another guy tonight, and... shit, I've had these *dreams...* and Martin asked me if I wanted to have a *threesome* with you—"

Lily shook her head, sharply, and I wondered if she was drunk, or on something; she seemed distracted. "I know you met Martin, Ray, he told me. I thought you'd stay away after that, that it would be enough... you have to leave here."

"What do you care where I go? You dumped me like a sack of shit, Lily."

She stared at me. "I dumped you to *save* you, Ray," she said, her voice low. "I didn't let him... have you... even though he wanted you. I was always Lily with you, not the Judas goat."

I just looked at her, wondering what she was talking about, afraid I sort of knew. She started to close the door, and her robe fell open, and I saw the blood smeared on her chest, on her breasts. It wasn't her blood. I knew that.

I thought of her in bed with Martin, and another man, the man *between* the two of them, the man bleeding, and the blood smearing on Lily's breasts, and Martin's chest. I think I lost my mind a little, then. I couldn't make sense of what I knew of Lily, and of that image. They didn't fit together at all.

Somewhere in the house, a man screamed, and then the screaming stopped abruptly. Lily's eyes widened in alarm, and she turned away, the door not quite closed.

I didn't think. I just wrenched open the screen door and charged in.

"No, Ray!" Lily said, but I shouldered my way past her, into the living room. It was just like I remembered, but it was obvious Martin lived here, now; there were new books, instrument cases, a jacket hanging over a chair, boots by the door, little indelible traces of him.

I could *smell* Martin, like river water and desert sand, and I smelled blood; it was like being a lion in my dream, every sense cranked up.

I growled and went straight to the bedroom, expecting to see blood and horror, Martin crouched naked over a body, but the bedroom was empty, though there were more traces of Martin's presence, intermingled with Lily's. Where the hell was Martin, and the man who'd screamed?

"Ray," Lily said, clutching her robe closed again, doing her best to look serious and reasonable. "I don't know what you think you're doing, but you have to go." She hesitated. "Don't make me call the police."

I just stared at her. "I saw the *blood*. Go ahead and call the police, please! Where's Martin?"

"He's not here. What are you talking about, blood?" Her knuckles were white, clenching the robe closed all the way to her neck.

I went down the short hallway, but Martin wasn't in the bathroom or the little laundry room or the kitchen, and that was *it*, there was no more house.

Except there was a basement, the doorway tucked into one corner of the kitchen, and then stairs leading down. I'd never been down there. Lily said it was full of old filing cabinets and broken chairs and shit. Move along, nothing to see here.

Lily had trailed after me through the house, telling me to leave, but when I stared at the basement door in the kitchen she jerked open a drawer and took out a butcher knife. She held it, the point aimed toward my face, and stalked toward me. I backed up. This was some twisted shit.

"You have to leave. You have to stop making noise, or he'll know you're here... and then I can't be responsible. I don't want anything bad to happen to you, don't you understand that?"

I took a step forward. "Lily," I said, my voice breaking. "How could you get mixed up in this?" Whatever the hell "this" was. Martin was doing something nasty, and Lily was helping, but I didn't know what that had to do with lions or voices coming from alleyways; maybe nothing, maybe that was just the seasoning in this crazy soup.

"We all *need* things," she said. "Martin isn't like other people— he isn't like people at all, Ray. Anemics need iron, diabetics need insulin. Martin needs..." She shook her head.

"Sex? Death? Rabies shots?" I said, making an effort to speak quietly, because that seemed to chill her out, a little.

"Blood," she said. "And... everything else. Flesh. Clothes. Life. He consumes it all. I don't have to watch that part. I do help with the rest, sometimes, with the luring-in, the seducing." She sighed. "He doesn't do it often, Ray, you must understand, almost never, but... every few years... he binges. He has to, to stay alive, it's his nature. Martin is very old, Ray, he's an old *soul*. He says I have an old soul, too, that there are myths under my skin, that he can help me live forever. Who else can love me for so long, Ray? Who else could love me forever? Not you. You could love me as well as Martin, but not for so long." Her eyes were pleading. She wanted me to *understand*.

"Baby, Martin is fucking with your head. I don't know what he's told you, but what do you mean, you could live forever? I don't—"

"We *all* have myths inside us, strains of the old creatures, shreds of the old spirits. Our ancestors mated freely with spirits of the desert, with giants of the earth. It's only traces in the bloodline, in most people, but some of us... some of us have more, in some of us, the old blood runs strong." She touched her hair self-consciously. "Martin says I have an island woman far back in my ancestry, a strange ancient sort of woman who turned her lovers to stone, but loved them just the same... Martin says he can help me grow into those powers. Just being in Martin's presence brings it out in me, I get younger, healthier, his presence does that to *everyone* who has the old blood. Martin won't say what *you* have, but he told me about meeting you at the club, told me he saw something strong and dangerous in you. He wanted me to bring you home, bring you to *him*, so he could take what you have into himself... and I *denied him.*" She shook the knife at me like a maraca. "I have never denied him *anything*, but I would not let him have that, I wouldn't let him have you, you stupid shit, because I *love* you. But now you're here, and if you don't get out now—"

"What about Martin's ancestry? What myth does he have under *his* skin?" The things she said were crazy, but they took place in the context of a greater madness in which they made sense; because suddenly I *knew* what I had, far back in my spiritual ancestry. Some multiple-great grandparent of mine had mated with something on the savanna, some lion god, and the lingering effects were still with me. But what the hell had Martin's ancestors mated with?

Lily shook her head. "Martin isn't like us, he isn't a half-breed. He *is* the myth, the thing entire. He was born in the heat of a jungle before civilization was born, and he has lived in deserts and groves. He is *mardkhora*, man-slayer, manticore, with a tail of stinging spines, a triple row of teeth in a human head, his voice like trumpet and flute played together..." Her voice was dreamy, distant, and her words had the flavor of a recitation; they chilled me down to the guts and marrow. "He was always *partly* a man, and he can make himself seem to be completely a man. Except..." she glanced toward the door at her back.

I understood. "Except when he feeds. Right? Then he's all monster." I shook my head. "At least he's got an excuse; it's what he *is*. But you chose to help him." My voice thickened; I thought I might cry. "I can't believe I ever loved you."

"I think you can't love as deeply I do," she said, simply, without malice, and it made my heart clench. "And you must know, I love you as much as I do him. He will simply be with me longer, and I had to choose."

"I'm going to kill him."

"You'll die, if you try that." She lowered the knife. "I don't *want* you to die."

"He's part lion, isn't he, Lily?"

She frowned. "He... has a lion's body, sometimes."

"I think that's why I hate him so much," I said. "Because he's a, a *per-*

version of what I am."

"What you are? You're... a lion?"

I looked at the basement door. "I have to go."

"I didn't know you were brave," she said. "A lion." There was wonderment in her voice, and worry. She stared at me, her eyes wide, her expression fixed. Her hair fluttered, as if moved by a breeze.

I ground my teeth together, as suddenly my arms and legs became too heavy to move. I felt like I'd been turned to stone; there might have been concrete poured into my stomach, lead wrapped around my bones.

But my enemy was below, in his lair, and I could *smell* him, and he was killing my pride.

I grunted and took a step forward, breaking whatever spell Lily had put on me, whatever weight of myth she'd brought to bear. She'd tried to turn me to stone... and the worst part was, she wanted to do it for my own *good*, to save me. She gasped when I moved, and dropped her knife with a clatter, and fell to her knees. Something had snapped in her head, I think, or else I'd snapped it when I fought her, put too much strain on her psychic sinew and torn it. She crouched, swaying, shaking her head. She would be all right, or she wouldn't—I couldn't do anything about it.

I picked up the knife with my left hand, looking at the blade, thinking of what might be waiting for me, down below. Lily could turn people to stone, maybe, sort of, and Martin was an out-and-out monster; suddenly having the soul of a big cat didn't seem like such hot shit. But I'd do what I had to. I opened the door.

I expected the basement to be dark, but I guess Martin liked to see what he was doing, because there was track lighting down there, bright as the inside of a supermarket. The basement was one big room, and there were dark stains on the concrete floor, some of them several feet in diameter.

Martin was...

When I had my dream of Martin by the river, I could see him, I could *see* the monster. And having that experience—ephemeral though it was—gave me some context for understanding what I saw there in the basement, seeing what Martin *really* was. I don't think most people are capable of seeing and interpreting shit like that. If humans ever could see and understand such things, that ability has been pretty much bred out of us as a species.

Martin was a monster, a manticore, but he shifted—his fur was the purple of dusk, then a matted red, then faded orange, and then tawny, lion-colored. His tail rose, segmented like a scorpion's, long spikes sprouting from the tail and then disappearing. For a moment, I swear, his tail became a serpent, with a hissing head on the end, and it looked at me with yellow eyes, comprehending me totally. Martin, the monster, had his back end toward me, his head bowed over something that I could only see parts of—legs, a hand. His latest victim.

I growled, and I must have stopped thinking and let instinct take over totally, because I *jumped* down the six or seven stairs to the floor. I landed in a crouch, the knife in my hand. I want to say I was not myself then, that I was possessed, that some greater force was moving *through* me—but it's not true.

I was me, all the way down, more myself than I'd ever been before.

Martin didn't even notice me. He was too busy eating. I didn't want to see that, to understand how it could be possible, how something his size—a little bigger than a lion—could devour a whole person, clothes and all.

The tail was a scorpion's then, not the terribly self-aware snake, and so I approached almost without fear, my knife raised high, and plunged it into his back with a cry.

The tail smashed me aside, though I kept my grip on the knife, and I fell to the concrete, landing so hard on my shoulder that my right arm went totally numb. The monster turned his face toward me, eyes slitted in fury, blood pouring from the wound in his side. I could only lay there, staring. The monster's head like a baby's, smooth and round, fat-cheeked, but it was also clearly *Martin's* face. He opened his mouth, revealing the triple rows of teeth, and music came out, flute and trumpet.

I rolled over onto my stomach, protecting my softest spot, and lifted the knife with my left hand.

"You *hurt* me," he said, in that bass-treble blatting voice. "I didn't think you had so much lion in you."

I bared my teeth and struggled to my knees. His tail lifted, curling, and the spikes reappeared, sliding out like cat's claws. The spikes were a foot long, poison, instant death, I *knew* it.

"I'm part lion," the manticore said, all trumpet now, all blatting. "I *was* a lion, long ago, but my line... diverged. *Improved.* The pure lions still hate me for that. Even your bastard, half-imagined blood has some potency, enough to *sting* me, but that's all."

He wasn't going to die from the stab wound. That was quite clear. I'd hurt him, sure, but not enough. I wondered if the old lion from the alley would come crashing through a basement window, jump on Martin's back, tear him a new asshole.

I didn't think so. I didn't think it was a night for that kind of miracle.

"I'll never know what Lily saw in you," he said, and his tail twitched.

It was too much. Such a fucking prosaic old-boyfriend thing to say, and it was coming from this fucking inhuman thing, this shiny baby-headed monster with spikes on his tail.

I laughed. That was all I had left, right? He was going to kill me, but I laughed. And I still had the knife, after all. Maybe I could jump at him, stick it in his eye, get to his brain. What did I have to lose?

Martin scowled, and his tail uncurled, the spikes dripping venom. I looked him in the eyes. "I bet I'm better in bed than you are," I said.

His tail drew back, and I tensed to jump, to laugh in his face and stab before his spikes nailed me.

Then his tail stopped, and began to change. At first I thought it was just another transformation, that his tail would become a snake and bite me, or that the spikes would sprout barbs. But that wasn't it—the tail was turning gray, and then tiny cracks appeared in it, like stress fractures. The spikes fell away, shattering on the concrete floor. Martin looked back at his tail, his human face wearing an expression of total horror. The grayness crept up his tail, up his hindquarters, and his horrible too-human eyes widened as his legs turned to stone.

We both looked up the stairs. Lily was there, sitting on the steps. Her robe was open, and her front was all blood. She wept, her face shiny with tears, and her hair positively *writhed*, like a nest of angry snakes.

"Lily," Martin said, his voice all trilling flute, as the petrification crept up his body. She didn't look at him. She didn't look at me, either, though.

Martin snapped his jaws. The gray slowly crawled up his neck, and then his head. He froze that way, his jaws open. He looked like a gruesome piece of cement lawn art—more cartoonish than monstrous in this fixed state, more comprehensible to human eyes.

I dropped the knife and ran toward the stairs, but by the time my foot touched the bottom step I couldn't move any farther—it was like trying to walk through a solid stone wall. Lily looked past me, at Martin.

"You saved me," I said. "You *chose* me."

"You would both have died," she said tonelessly. "Martin would have killed you, but you would have stabbed him before you died, and there is enough lion in you for that wound to be fatal. I know; my ancestors were oracles, and I can see enough of the future to know what would happen. I wanted to save one of you. I couldn't turn *you* to stone, not entirely, you're too human... but Martin is more susceptible to these old things, these old powers. A weakness to go with his strength." She looked at me then, her eyes all pupil, all black, her hair twisting on her shoulders. "I hate both of you," she said. "I hate both of you for making me choose."

She went up the stairs. I couldn't follow—the air stayed thick for another half hour, and even then I had to fight my way up the stairs, one at a time.

I never saw Lily again.

The next day I helped Jade-Lynne move, and we talked about Steven, how we hoped he was okay, wherever he was. I didn't tell her Steven was in the belly of a statue of a manticore in a basement across town. She wouldn't have believed me. I carried boxes all day. Jade-Lynne flirted with me, even, and any other day it would have gone somewhere, but no way, not then.

This all happened a while ago, you know, months and months, but I still haven't figured out how I feel about it. I still dream about being a lion, but I haven't seen the old lion again. Maybe he died. I spend more time with my friends, but I haven't been on a date in ages, haven't had sex, either.

I went to Nick and Susie's wedding last weekend. They held hands at the altar, like they couldn't stop touching each other for even that long. I decided they were better off together, just the two of them, for now, for the moment, and that had to be enough, didn't it? I cried at the ceremony, and even I'm not sure why. Everything hurts, more or less, every day.

You know what I wish, mostly?

I wish Lily had turned my heart to stone. Just my heart. That would have been enough, I think. To have a still, stony heart; something heavy, but not so heavy I couldn't forget about the weight, light enough that I could forget, sometimes, why I was still carrying it around.

LIVING WITH THE HARPY

Living with the harpy presented certain difficulties. Her feathers clogged the shower drain, and the smell of unsavory meats cooked over chemical fires drifted from her room. She screamed profanity sometimes, as if afflicted with Tourette's, but with obvious glee. I occasionally found drowned mice in the coffeemaker.

Even so, I'd had worse roommates, during college when I shared a house with three boys who liked to try to catch me naked in the bathroom (though I wasn't as beautiful back then as I eventually became). The harpy seemed content with our living situation, too. It is in the nature of her kind to roost, if not to nest.

Besides, I loved the harpy. I always loved the *fact* of her, and sometimes, when she was in her pleasanter moods, I even loved the particularity of her.

I met Jocelyn at a dyke bar in the city. She had clearly never been in such a place before, smiling awkwardly, dressed in glittery club-clothes that didn't seem to fit quite right; I later learned that no clothes hung on her properly, that she always seemed ill-attired, that she only looked comfortable when she was naked.

I knew she would never approach me, or anyone else, not tonight. She was trying to get the lay of the land, not to get herself laid. I liked her right away, if only because she was so different from the other women in the bar—her hair was all crazy nut-colored curls, held in a clump on top with a clip, as if she'd given up hope of taming it, and despite her stylishly sequined black top and short skirt she carried a big purse, rainbow-striped, clearly homemade. I found the unself-consciousness of her fashion clash endearing, but it just drew sneers from the rest of the crowd.

I drifted through the bar, toward the pillar she leaned against. She was drinking a gin and tonic. Before the night was over, I planned to taste the gin on her lips.

We'd go to her place, if she was amenable, or else go no place at all. I couldn't take her home. Because of the harpy.

I'm a voice actor. In the television commercial about the new yeast-infection treatment, I'm the soothing female narrator. Every few months I adopt a sultry tone and read erotica for a books-on-tape company run by a pair of oddly feminist lesbians who enjoy dressing in Victorian garb, corsets and all. They say I get the breathless sighs just right. Sometimes I get movie work, and though several directors have offered me access to their beds as a route to screen time of my own, I have always declined. I don't like spotlight any more than the harpy does, I suppose. We're a lot alike.

My voice used to be nothing special, dull, a bland Midwestern accent, but since I've been living with the harpy, it has grown mellifluous, polyhymnal. I worked for a sex phone line at first, before I got into more respectable voice work—that was an experience that put me off dating men for a long time, though I've always been attracted to both genders. The harpy likes my voice. When I sing in the shower, she doesn't screech. She listens.

"So what's this mystery roommate's name?" Jocelyn asked.

"Harp," I said.

"Harp? Like the beer?"

"I suppose," I said, watching the movie. I had a part in the film, as the disembodied voice on the loudspeakers, warning of imminent core meltdown, just another threat for the hero to overcome.

Jocelyn giggled. "Harp? Like the type of seal?"

"Like the musical instrument," I said, strangely offended.

"Do you ever call her Harpo?" Jocelyn said.

"Shh," I said. "You'll miss my line." From the vast speakers, I counted down the moments to a fabricated destruction.

I've never seen the harpy's face. The nearest thing was one day when I came home early from a recording session and caught the harpy in the living room. She rushed into her room straightaway, of course, but I saw her stained white housedress and the mass of dirty, pigeon-gray feathers on her head.

Mostly I see her in the bathroom. Our shower has pebbled glass doors, so everything viewed through them is distorted, transformed into blobs of color, angles rendered round, lines turned curvaceous. Sometimes when I shower, the harpy comes in, and sits on the toilet, and talks to me in her raucous, cawing voice, her head a gray blur through the glass, her body white. We talk about inconsequential things, usually: repairs that need to be done around the apartment, items I need to pick up at the store. Sometimes she talks about the history of her kind (or perhaps the history of herself; it is never clear), about forests of twisted trees in caverns underground, women who weep blood, men without eyes, the futility of suicide. Sometimes she speaks Greek, or guttural Latin, or the lost tongues of mountain hordes. The harpy speaks wistfully of flying, and eating fresh raw livers, but says she is too old for such pursuits now. These are generally monologues, and if I try to respond, she simply ignores me and talks on.

The day the harpy first moved in, when I was afraid of her, she came into the bathroom and told me how she would pay her rent. "The coin of a better life," she called it. "Sucking the poison out," she said. I'd never been really beautiful, really lucky, really brave. I knew right away I couldn't reject the harpy's offer. She'd known the same thing before she even asked.

Ellen Bass, the poet, has compared two women making love to arm-fuls of lilacs wet with rain, among other things, and that may be true, sometimes, but sex with Jocelyn is more like being in the briar patch. She is fierce, scratching with her nails, nipping with her teeth. I've never had such a rough lover, but I enjoy it, the way she holds on to me so tightly, the way she drags her fingernails along my skin, and I reciprocate, leaving suck marks on her breasts, scratches on her shoulders.

One afternoon, lying in bed at her place (always her place), after, she touched the unbroken skin of my back. "I can't believe I didn't leave a mark on you," she said, a soft note of sadness in her voice.

"I'm thick-skinned," I said, though the truth is more complicated. Since I've been living with the harpy, I don't bruise, or scar, or burn. Nothing leaves a mark on me. It's part of the rent. The harpy says if I live with her long enough I'll become indestructible. Even suicide would cease to be an option, not that I've ever really considered it.

"Sometimes I wonder if I've left any mark on you at all," Jocelyn said, and began to cry.

She let me hold her, but she wouldn't talk about it, she wouldn't explain what she meant.

* * *

When I told the harpy I wanted to invite Jocelyn over for dinner, the only response was the sound of shattering glass from her room, some-thing heavy and fragile thrown against the wall.

"Is that okay?" I asked, leaning my forehead against her door. "If it's not okay, say so, and I'll tell her she can't come."

"Sing to me," the harpy said.

So I sang "Frank Mills," that song from *Hair*, because it's one of the few songs I know by heart, and the harpy likes it. I hesitated over the line about loving someone, but being embarrassed to walk down the street with them. My voice might have broken, if it were capable of breaking anymore. I don't think the harpy noticed.

When I finished singing, after a moment of silence, the harpy said, "Do whatever you like." Her voice was like something gnawing itself in pain.

"You're too perfect for me," Jocelyn said.

"Oh, stop it," I said. "You'll embarrass me."

"It wasn't a compliment," Jocelyn said. She sighed. "It was a statement of fact. You don't need me. I don't know what you need. Maybe nothing. Too perfect."

"That's a pretty strange thing to complain about," I said.

"If you think so, then you don't know me as well as I thought you did," she said.

I'd been so hesitant to invite Jocelyn over, but I could tell it was a crucial step, that Jocelyn's reservations about me—her sense that I keep secrets, her fear that I was using her somehow—were growing. I had to show willing. I had to let her in.

And the harpy was quiet. Jocelyn and I made dinner, drank wine, nuzzled on the couch. There were a few feathers here and there, but I told Jocelyn that my roommate Harp raised pigeons, that feathers got stuck to her clothes, and Jocelyn believed me. I should have felt guilty about lying to Jocelyn, but I didn't—I felt guilty for lying *about* the harpy, as if I were ashamed of her, when really I was just keeping her identity a secret.

After half an hour of long kisses, Jocelyn took my chin in her hand, met my eyes, and said, "Thank you for letting me come over. Can I stay the night?"

"Of course," I said. I wondered if the harpy was listening.

* * *

When I came home the day after the first night Jocelyn slept over, I found coffee grounds dumped all over my pillow, and telltale feathers everywhere, and the glass cracked in my favorite oval hand-mirror with the tortoise-shell back.

I went to the harpy's door (I was even thinking of her as "Harp" then, though she'd never needed a name in the days before I needed a lover), knocked gently, said, "We should talk."

There was only silence. Not even the rustle of her feathers. Not even weeping.

"So why have I never met this Harp?" Jocelyn said. "I know she raises pigeons, and she's shy, and I hear her thumping around back there, but why doesn't she ever come out of her room?"

I shrugged. "She doesn't like people."

"There's got to be more to it than that," she said. "A... a pathology."

"It's not a pathology. Harp's an albino." I improvised wildly. "She has a port-wine stain on her forehead and across one cheek. She doesn't like people to see her. Even I hardly ever see her." I wondered if the explanation was too outlandish, and waited for Jocelyn to laugh, but she didn't, so I assumed it was so absurd that Jocelyn assumed it must be true.

"Poor thing," Jocelyn said.

One day when I came home I discovered that we had a fireplace, which we never did before. The hearth was made of rough gray stone, the bricks stained with the ash of a thousand fires. There were feathers scattered all around, and I pictured the harpy kneeling there for a long time. I knelt, too, and in the fireplace I saw shards of glazed pottery, scraps of thick paper, and bundles of dried flowers, all partially burned. I put out my hand, and the stones still radiated heat. I supposed the harpy must have been working a spell. I wondered what kind. Probably something to make Jocelyn leave me, which more and more seemed like the saddest of all possible outcomes, and which more and more seemed like something that would happen whether the harpy worked her dirty magics or not.

I hadn't talked to the harpy in weeks, not since Jocelyn brought up the subject of moving in with me. That day I told the harpy what Jocelyn had suggested, and asked what would happen if she did come to live with me, with us. The harpy answered me in Greek. I couldn't understand her. It sounded like she was choking on something as she spoke. I hadn't tried to communicate with her since, had only seen the indirect evidence of her continued presence—the wads of bloodied tissue paper in the kitchen, the piles of white sand in the hall.

I knocked at her door, once, twice, thrice, and she said "Come in."

I stared at the grain of the wood. She had never asked me to come in before. I had never seen the inside of the harpy's room. Before she moved in, my apartment only had one bedroom, mine, but when the harpy came, she brought her own space with her.

"I just wanted to talk," I said. "I don't have to come in." My legs were shaking. I could barely stand. I couldn't imagine passing through that door, seeing the harpy's face, seeing her nest, her home within our home.

"I'll be here," the harpy said, and her voice seemed smoother than usual, though perhaps she was only being quiet. "When you're ready, come in, and we'll talk. But not before."

I went to my room. I called Jocelyn. I asked her to meet me for a drink.

The next time, I didn't knock. I just turned the knob, and pushed open the harpy's door.

Inside was a cave, I think, but it was so dark, I couldn't really see—there was just the underground smell, the distant plink of water, the rustle of wings in the shadows, the sense of cavernous space. I stood in the doorway. "Harp," I said, and winced, because that wasn't her name. She didn't have a name.

"Harpy," she said, somewhere far back in the shadows. "I am here. You've come to tell me. To tell me what you're giving up, and what you're giving it up for. Me, for her."

"It's not that simple," I said. "I just... I feel so isolated, like I can't let anyone in, can't let anyone get close. Before Jocelyn, I felt so alone, and now that I have her..."

"You have me." Her voice was harsh, but it was always harsh, and I'd never been good at understanding her moods, her emotions, based on the sound of her voice.

"Yes," I said simply, because there was no way to deny that, and no changing the fact that, even so, I always felt alone. "You know I love you," I said, the beginning of something, some soothing sentiment, but the harpy interrupted.

"You know I love you," she hissed, and I couldn't tell if she was mocking me, throwing my words back in my face, or making a confession of her feelings. "But you'd rather grow old and die with Jocelyn than live forever with me."

"It's not an easy choice," I said.

"The only easy choice is suicide," she said. "At least you aren't one of those. When I leave, you know... I'll take it all with me. The balance—my ugly for your beauty, your melody for my cacophony, it all goes away. You'll be what you were, before. Not so beautiful. You'll bleed. Your voice will crack. Dandruff. Loss of nerve. Crying fits. Bad cramps. Failure."

"I know," I said, thinking of Jocelyn, of her imperfections, and how they made me love her even more; thinking of the way Jocelyn had described my eyes, once, as being like the mirror-side of one-way glass, impossible to see into.

"She might not love you, then," the harpy said.

"You did. Didn't you? You told me yourself, you never really changed me. You just sucked the poison out, stripped the ugly things away, shielded me from harm."

The harpy sighed, and I heard a heavy rustle, like a woman at a fancy-dress ball gathering her voluminous skirts. "I'll be gone by morning. I wish I could say I wish you well."

"Harpy. Thank you. Thank you for understanding."

She laughed. "If I understood, I wouldn't live alone in a cave. You should leave, shut the door. This place won't be in your apartment for much longer."

I hesitated. "The things in the fireplace," I said. "The things you were burning. Were they some kind of a spell?"

"No," the harpy said. "They were gifts for you. A vase of flowers, a sheaf of letters. I was going to give them to you. For the fifth anniversary of my moving in. But I was angry with you, and I destroyed them."

My heart felt like a snail's shell, crunching under someone's foot. "I hope you find another place you like," I said.

"Go away," the harpy said.

That was the last time we spoke. The door to her room didn't disappear, but the next time I opened it, there was just a dusty, empty room on the other side.

The night after the harpy left, I was slicing carrots to make dinner for Jocelyn, and the knife slipped, cutting my finger. It hurt horribly. It was just a tiny cut, but the pain was unbelievable. A bead of blood welled up, and I put my finger in my mouth and sucked.

I realized I'd forgotten the taste of blood, the taste of pain, and I closed my eyes in horror at what I'd done to myself by sending the harpy away.

Then Jocelyn put her arms around my waist, and cooed soothingly in my ear, and I leaned back against her, and let myself bleed.

"You should invite Harp to the wedding," Jocelyn said a few months later.

"I never hear from her anymore," I said, and I think I was too quiet, and reserved, all the rest of that night. Jocelyn went to take a bath, probably just to get away from me. I thought about going to sit by the tub so I could talk to her while she soaked, but I didn't know what I wanted to say. In the end, I didn't say anything at all. But that night, snuggled under the feather comforter, I whispered an apology into her sleeping ear.

Jocelyn and I were married in the summer, in a park, the ceremony presided over by a pagan priestess friend of hers. Jocelyn and I both had flowers woven into our hair, and we both wore white. As we exchanged vows, the sky went dark, a shadow passing across the sun, and all the guests looked up. A cloud of feathers drifted down like a slow, gray snowfall. One feather fell onto Jocelyn's head, sticking up among the flowers and braids.

"I don't see any birds," she said, looking up, looking around. "That's so weird."

"It's a wedding gift," I said. "From Harp."

She looked at me, her nose crinkling, her eyebrow quirked as if she knew I was making a joke, but one she didn't understand.

I plucked the feather from her hair, and let it fall to the ground. I nodded to the priestess to start again. I had promises to make.

KOMODO

The trouble began when I met my new lover for the month. I bumped into him at the little Chinese grocery around the corner from my building. He was an attractive young man with some watered-down Asian ancestry in his features, buying ox blood and chicken feet. (I was buying lo mein and pork buns, but I have a high tolerance for people with stranger tastes than mine.) We got to the register at the same time and he gestured that I should go first, the sort of casual chivalry that I appreciate, as long as there's no hint of condescension. Then he offered to walk me to my car, this being a dangerous neighborhood for a woman out walking by herself. "It's *my* neighborhood," I said, "and I don't own a car, but you can walk me a couple of blocks if you want." We chatted as we went. His name was Kasan, and he was a personal trainer and lifeguard at a local gym. He wasn't a big guy, but he was wiry, and I could believe he was a swimmer. He seemed a bit awkward in conversation, as if he didn't speak to people much, and I wondered if he'd been scrawny and unpopular earlier in life, and gotten into physical stuff to help his self-esteem.

I told him one of my standard half-truths, that I'd made a lot of money day-trading a few years ago and that I was spending most of my time now reading and making art for my own amusement. My true ambitions are rather different, but I could hardly tell a stranger that my goal in life is to rack up a mostly positive karmic balance and eventually make a bid for immortality.

We stopped at the front steps of my building, a weathered old town-house that had been divided into flats. I glanced skyward, though I knew full well what the moon had to say. It was dark of the moon tonight, a good time for new beginnings, as any enterprise undertaken tonight would only grow in the following weeks as the moon waxed. I hadn't cultivated a new lover in many months—the last one had fulfilled all my wishes and, as he'd requested, was now living happily at the bottom of a local river, slowly decaying into the bottom-mud and learning the languages of fish and pollution. In another hundred years or so, if the river didn't dry up entirely, he might become a minor river god. Kasan had appeared just in time. I had certain things to accomplish over the course of the next month, and the energy that came with a new lover could serve well to fuel those endeavors.

"Want to come upstairs for a while, Kasan?" I asked. I'm beautiful. I'm desirable. I know how to sense when a potential partner is interested. I can say these things with no particular pride, because such powers require relatively small magics to achieve. People seldom say no to me. I never compel anyone to make love to me—such mental domination is possible, but it's also essentially rape, and cannot be condoned. I entice my lovers with beauty, and bring them back again and again by giving them the best sex they've ever had. There's no magic to that, just years of experience and sensitivity to the needs of my lovers. I am good at what I do. Sex is my vocation and my devotion.

Kasan wanted me, and agreed to come in. I led him upstairs, to the apartment on the top floor, where I've made my lair for these past half-dozen years. "It's a nice apartment," he said, and it is, wine-red couch, tapestries in muted blues, and lots of bookshelves crammed with everything from a complete run of Burton's translation of *The Arabian Nights* to paperbacks with their covers ripped off that I'd bought from street vendors.

"It is nice," I said. "You should see the bedroom. It's even nicer. But there's a dress code in there. You're not allowed to be dressed."

Kasan stripped so fast his clothes might have been on fire, and his body was lean, young, and excited.

I took his hand, feeling excited myself. Sex is my life and livelihood, but I haven't grown tired of it yet, and a new partner always thrilled me. I took him into my bedroom.

Some time into the second round of lovemaking, he stopped moving long enough to touch my shoulder and get me to turn my head and look back at him. "I'm embarrassed," he said. "I never asked your name."

"Delanie," I said. That's what it had been for the past few decades, anyway.

"Rhymes with felony," he said, grinning. He had a toothy, bright smile, but I didn't think anything of it at the time.

"We're not committing any of those, unless you're under eighteen and you didn't tell me."

"Nope. I'm legal. Just turned twenty last week."

"That explains the twice-in-an-hour thing we're doing here. So, birthday boy—ever had anal sex ?"

He seemed surprised, but he agreed readily enough. Most men do. For my part, I like anal well enough, if I'm in the right mood, but the main reason I wanted to do it was magical. There's a different flavor of power to sex when it's explicitly, incontrovertibly non-procreational, and all that potential power of creation can be turned to other uses. (Oral sex works just as well, but I have to take the seed into my body for maximum effect, and I've never liked the taste.) Plus, in this culture at least, there's a whiff of the transgressive about the act which further fuels its potency. We'd have a lot of anal sex in the next month, if things went my way—I needed the power. I had to renew my life force soon, and restore the wards on my building, and there were certain other rituals to be performed, steps on the long road to true immortality and the bottom rung of godhood.

"You can lose the condom," I said, handing him a bottle of lube. "I've got a recent clean AIDS test, if you want to see it."

"Aren't you worried about catching something from me?" he said.

"Should I be?"

"Well, no."

"Then I'm not worried," I said. He could have every disease known to humankind, and it wouldn't hurt me; that's one of the benefits of magical life-extension. I don't have to worry much about purely physical threats.

I lay face-down, and with only a little awkward fumbling and guidance from me, he slid in. When he orgasmed, not long after, he bit down on my shoulder, his teeth breaking the skin. He apologized for the bite afterward, embarrassed, looking away. "I've never done that before. I just lost control."

"I've had worse," I said, dabbing at my shoulder with a damp cloth. It wasn't a very deep bite. "I'm flattered I had such an effect on you. Give me your number, and in a couple of days we'll see if I can make you lose control again." He scribbled down his home phone, cell number, pager, fax, and e-mail address. He was so eager, I wanted him all over again. In four weeks or so I'd reveal my powers to him and offer to invoke a vision to find his path to greatest happiness, and help him toward it, as I did for all my lovers. It was a small reward in exchange for how much I drew from them during our month-long liaisons, and it kept me in favor with certain forces that were far above personal mortal concerns, but nevertheless retained an interest in human affairs.

"I, uh, have to get up early tomorrow," he said, gathering his clothes, not looking at me.

"No worries," I said. I wouldn't have let him stay the night anyway; I had work to do. Most of the men I picked up wanted to sleep over, though. His desire to leave was probably just due to the shyness I'd sensed earlier. I doubted he was very experienced with women. We kissed goodbye at the door, though it was a bit hurried and awkward, and I wondered if I was his first one-night stand. I found his nervousness rather endearing.

After his footsteps receded down the stairs, I went to my bedroom and opened the walk-in closet to my shrine, the stone altar, the crystals and figurines, the beads and candles, all the physical bric-a-brac that helps me focus and externalize the power that grows inside me each time I make love. I renewed the daily protections on my building—I had many old and formidable enemies—then went into the kitchen and poured myself a glass of shiraz. I stayed up for a while, reading a bit, and went to bed when the moon set at 3:30 a.m., still warmly pulsing from the power of the night's sex.

I spent the following morning rearranging all the fictives in the building, because it's dangerous to leave them in one position for too long. I owned the whole building, and every apartment but mine was filled with cheap furniture and those incredibly expensive, creepily realistic life-sized sex toys known as "Real Dolls." The dolls are made down in San Marcos for about $6,000 each, and they appear convincingly human at first glance. I didn't have any interest in the dolls as masturbation aids, but since they have articulated skeletons and realistic (if silicone) flesh, they're human enough to fool all sorts of nasty spirits who have a tendency to think all people look alike anyway. In the old days I made do with scarecrows and, later, mannequins to create my fictives, but their effectiveness was questionable at best. The dolls were the next best thing to hiring real people living in the other apartments, which was a bad idea for many reasons. Every day or two I moved the dolls around, posing them at various stations of life—at the sink, in the shower, sitting around in the living room. They all carry little tokens of my body, bits of my hair woven in with their own, mostly, or fingernail clippings tucked in their mouths, under their soft rubber tongues. There are creatures looking for me, tracking me by half-remembered scents, and having bits of myself secreted away in so many lifelike figures scrambles their ability to detect me, and where they *should* see me they see a blur of too many bodies, and move on in confusion. The fictives have other uses, too—anyone attempting to harm me magically is likely to affect one of the dolls instead.

In apartment 2-B, I found one of the dolls melted into a lumpy puddle of rubber, stuck to the carpet. The dolls are rated to survive temperatures in excess of 400 degrees Fahrenheit, so this wasn't a simple case of my leaving her by the sunny window for too long. Bits of her steel joints poked up gruesomely through the skin-toned silicone, and her eyes stared up from widely separated points in the mess. I shivered—someone had aimed a devastating attack at me some time in the past couple of days, and I hadn't gotten any warning of it at all. The protective spells that surround the building are supposed to erupt in divers alarums if anyone attacks me magically, but in this case, nothing had happened except the melting of my silicone proxy.

I needed to clean up the doll, but I wasn't sure where to begin—she'd fused solid to the carpet. I'd have to buy some industrial solvents or something. In the meantime, I needed to investigate, and find out who'd attacked me, and why.

Before I could start a ritual meant to uncover the psychic spoor of whatever malevolent entity had targeted me, someone buzzed at my front door. I wrapped myself in a bathrobe and went down the creaky stairs to the foyer, where I opened the pebbled-glass door.

A man in a short-sleeved white shirt and a tie stood on my steps, holding a clipboard bulging with papers. "You own this building?" he said, looking down at his clipboard.

"I do."

"I'm the building inspector. I just checked out the exterior, and just to let you know, there are going to be a lot of fines. You've got structural problems, the fire escapes are deathtraps, I can tell right off that the windows in the back are too small for emergency fire exits... well, it goes on. You'll get a copy of my report. I'll need to come in to the building and inspect a couple of the apartments, too."

"Why, exactly, are you doing an inspection?" I asked. He still wasn't looking at me. This would be much easier if he'd just look at me.

"Routine," he said, which was no answer at all, though it wasn't the first time a building inspector had come by—I'd used magical persuasion to sidestep such an inspection when I took over the building, and there was apparently an unresolved file about this property at City Hall. I'd have to deal with it eventually, but I had too many other things to worry about now. At least *this* problem was easily remedied. I was still filled with power from my time with Kasan the night before, and I could twist this man's will in a moment.

I touched the inspector's chin with the tip of my finger, and he looked up at me, surprised. Once he looked into my eyes I said, "I'm sure you'll find everything in order." It wasn't a question, or a request; it was a command, and I put the force of my powers of compulsion behind it. Something twinged inside my head, a sudden flash of migraine-intense pain, there and gone in an instant. I kept myself from wincing, though the pain worried me. "I'm sure those other things you noticed are fine, too. You should probably check again and reconsider your report."

He frowned and looked back down. "No ma'am, I don't think so. I'm fairly thorough. I'll come back to do the interior inspection later this week. My office will call you to set up a time." He walked away.

I stood in the open doorway for a moment, then shut the door and leaned my forehead against the glass.

My powers had failed me. That building inspector was no adept-in-disguise, I could tell, and I hadn't felt any sort of protective spell wreathing him. My power simply hadn't *worked*, and that hadn't happened to me in more decades than I could count. I'd long since moved past the awkward early years of hit-or-miss magic, into a realm of greater mastery. I might fail at more ambitious magic, if I tried to expand my skills or did my work sloppily, but a simple compulsion laid on an unsuspecting human? It should have worked. It should have been as easy as breathing.

I went upstairs again. Whoever had attacked me had done more than just melt one of my fictives. They'd somehow interfered with the flow of my power, and I could not allow that. I'd do my ritual, which should at least point me in the right direction, and I'd find out which old or new enemy had decided to come for me.

The ritual didn't work.

The candles burned, the crystals sparkled, the words filled my mind, but it didn't *work*; I was like a boat on becalmed seas. My sails were useless, without the wind of magic to fill them, and my magic was gone, as if I'd used it all up trying to compel that little building inspector. This was bad on more than one level. Without magic, I couldn't renew my life force, and in another week or so I would begin to age and die, the years catching up with me exponentially. On the first day after I failed to renew the spell I would age one year, on the second day two years, on the third day four years, and so on, the amount doubling each day. A week later my body would be over a hundred and fifty years old, and I'd be dead.

That was assuming I survived *this* week. Without my magic to maintain the protective spells on my building and keep the fictives activated, various old enemies would probably take the opportunity to strike. I had a day, perhaps, before those protective spells weakened. The whole reason I'd slept with Kasan the night before was to gain more power to work these magics, and now some assault had drained me.

Which meant it was time to call Kasan, and get him to come over again. A marathon session of fucking would fuel me enough to strengthen the protections on my building, at least, even if I had to cast the spell during the act itself, letting the power pass through me and directly into the workings of magic.

I called Kasan's home number, and a pizzeria answered. Annoyed, I called his cell phone. The number was not in service. His pager number went to a nursing home. I tried his e-mail address, and it bounced. His fax number didn't go to a fax at all, but to a local used car lot.

I pressed "Stop" on the fax machine to cut off the querulous voice of the car salesman coming over the speaker. Kasan had given me fake contact information.

I was surprised, and a little hurt, and a lot suspicious. I had apparently misjudged him—it now seemed likely that I *wasn't* his first one night stand, and that he had the fuck-and-slip-away technique down to a science. He'd certainly fooled me with his shy-and-awkward approach, and I was normally a good judge of such things.

Unless. Was Kasan something more sinister than an opportunistic lover? Was he an enemy sorcerer in disguise? Had he fucked some kind of poison into me, something to steal my abilities? How could I possibly find him, and find out? I wondered if I was being paranoid, grasping at remote possibilities because I couldn't figure out how to investigate more likely ones.

I sank down to the floor, wanting to curl up and whimper. I'd begun studying magic in order to protect myself, to control my destiny, to author my own fate, so that I would never be helpless or dependent on anyone else. And now that power had been taken away from me. I didn't know how to cope.

I forced myself back to my feet. Curling up in a ball did not qualify as coping, and if I didn't know what to do next, I'd just have to think about things until I *did*.

* * *

I walked around the asphalt multi-use path until I reached the wooded side of the lake, a little natural realm in the midst of downtown, the tops of buildings visible over the trees. The day was springtime-cool, blue and clear, and the lake reflected the sky like a mirror. It was too pretty a day to be thinking of last resorts, but here I was.

I went into the trees until the path was invisible behind me, and only the occasional flash of light reflecting on water showed in front of me. I knelt on the leaves beneath the oaks, before a large stone, rounded as if it were the top half of an egg buried in the soil.

"Barry," I said. "I need it now."

I waited. After a moment the leaves rustled, and the earth opened up before me, the rock rolling aside as if pushed by invisible hands. Dirt began to slide apart, neatly piling up in heaps on either side of the growing hole.

Down at the bottom, a lump of dull, round stone the size of a coconut rested. It rolled up out of the hole, coming to rest between my knees. The dirt poured back into the hole.

The wind rose, blowing my long hair, lifting it off my shoulders. Barry had always liked it when I wore my hair up, to show off my neck. He'd been a good lover, and a good friend. Ever since he'd been a little boy he'd had dreams in which he was bodiless and all-seeing, a spirit of the wind. After our month was over, many years ago, I helped him attain that wish, sacrificing his body and his mortality to become a local spirit of the lake and the oaks. His desire was not so different from mine, though the path I followed took far longer, and had far greater potential rewards. Barry would only exist for so long as his grove of trees did, while I sought true immortality. Still, he would live long past his normal human span, in happiness and contentment, and I'd helped him reach that point. As thanks, he'd been watching something for me. I picked up the lump of cold stone and brushed clinging bits of soil away, slipped it into a canvas grocery bag over my shoulder, and stood up. "Thanks, Barry," I said, and headed back home.

I set the stone orb on my altar, then picked up a perfectly mundane claw hammer. I cracked the orb with the hammer, and it split neatly in two, halves falling to reveal the sparkling crystals inside. It was a geode, beauty hidden in a drab exterior, but it was more than that, too—it was my life savings. I'd made this object many years before at great cost, draining myself of power over several successive months, pouring it off into this orb. I'd done no other magic for the half a year it took to make this orb, and using it now was almost painful, like being forced to spend your life savings on emergency medical expenses. This was magic, *my* magic, but not contained within my body, and so safe from whatever corruptive influence had tainted my powers. The orb was a one-use device, unfortunately, and its power would be expended on whatever spell I cast now.

I set up the investigative ritual again, this time putting the geode at the focal point of the objects I arranged around me.

When I lit the last candle and said the last word, the room thrummed with energy, and the crystals in the geode began to turn black, one by one, as the power stored within them dissipated.

I closed my eyes. The ritual worked. Knowledge fell upon me.

The vision is difficult to describe. There were voices, images, and implicit knowledge seemingly dropped into my mind, all in the service of answering my questions: Who had attacked me? How had they wrought this harm?

The main thing I saw in the vision was Komodo dragons. You've seen them on television, probably, if not at the zoo. Native to Indonesia, they're the largest lizards on the planet these days, weighing in at up to 300 pounds, twelve feet long, carnivorous, carrion-eaters, relentlessly predatory, snouts full of teeth so sharp and protruding that they actually slice open the flesh of their mouths every time they bite down. Most importantly, the mouths of Komodo dragons are acrawl with some of the world's nastiest bacteria—fifty different kinds, at least half a dozen of them septic. Any animal a Komodo dragon bites dies, even if it escapes immediate evisceration, because the resulting infection from the bite is so virulent. It's not venom, not like snake poison—it's just *germs*. Komodo dragons are the perfected form of natural biological warfare.

The bacteria are nasty, but the Komodo dragon's *own* immune system has no difficulty keeping the germs under control; otherwise, the dragons would die the first time their teeth broke the skin in their own mouths. A lot of doctors are interested in Komodo dragons for that very reason, hopeful of finding a human application for the dragons' supercharged immune systems.

Komodos eat people, sometimes, but then, they eat *anything* they can rip apart and swallow, and they aren't picky about avoiding hooves, skins, or entrails. They can *swim*, too, which a lot of people don't know, especially people who jump into the water to try to escape a hungry one. They're vicious, wicked, relentless, single-minded—perfect predators for their environment.

And, according to my vision, I'd recently had sex with one in human form.

It was possible that Kasan was some sort of Komodo dragon spirit, or a sorcerer who'd fully taken on the totemic powers of a Komodo dragon, or something even stranger. Ultimately, it didn't matter. The effect on me was the same. After the ritual, I went to the bathroom and looked at my shoulder in the mirror. The place where Kasan had bitten me was still red, but didn't look obviously infected. It probably wasn't infected, not physically, but Kasan's bite was the *magical* equivalent of a Komodo dragon's bite, and it had corrupted me psychically. No wonder my magics had failed. My body would likely have died, too, if not for the protective power of the fictive, which had melted in my place. I was lucky to be alive, but my spirit-body was still swarming with magical infection.

I went back to the living room and looked at the geode, all its crystals turned black, all that carefully hoarded power spent on the ritual. I was powerless again.

No. That was the wrong kind of thinking. I was *magically* powerless, but there were other forms of power.

I went to a cabinet and opened the bottom drawer. Inside, nestled in velvet, were my ritual knives. They were meant for occasional personal bloodletting, for cutting up sacred ingredients, and for other magical purposes, but they were also sharp, curved, and perfectly adequate for other uses. Using them on a person would taint the blades, make them profane and unfit for magic, but with luck, I wouldn't *have* to use them, just make the threat.

Still, the knives felt good and familiar in my hands. I slid two into sheaths on my ankles, beneath my long black skirt, and tucked others into my waist. If they became tainted with the blood of Kasan the Komodo-man, I'd have to consecrate new ones. With luck, I could convince him to fix what he'd done to me, and I wouldn't need to resort to violence.

The visions had given me knowledge of Kasan's whereabouts, an image of him in his home, a run-down little one-story house, and I could recite his street number as if I'd known it for years.

I went out, afraid but determined, and wondered if that was the way all dragon slayers felt as they set out on the hunt.

I knocked on Kasan's door, and when he opened it he was clearly surprised to see me. Even knowing what he was, I still thought he was cute.

"Oh," he said. "I didn't expect to... Shit. Melanie, right?"

I seethed. "*Delanie*," I corrected. "What did you do to me, Kasan?"

He leaned against the doorjamb, as if we were having a casual conversation. "Bit you," he said. "Didn't mean to, didn't *plan* to, but it happens pretty much whenever my self-control slips." He frowned. "I don't usually hear from the people I bite again, though."

"That's because they usually die, Kasan."

"Yeah, well." He scratched his head. "It's not like I go back to check or anything. I don't quite have the hang of being human yet, but I'm working on it, you know? I'll get over the biting thing eventually. I've only been doing this for a few months. I didn't mean for anybody to die."

"Why did you give me fake phone numbers?"

"Like I said, I'm learning how to be human. That's what men do when they have a one-night stand, right? Give the girl a fake phone number?" The expression on his face was almost painfully earnest, as if he were worried about being reproached.

I'd give him more than reproach if he didn't start saying something useful. "Sure, asshole, lesson well-learned. But I'm not a typical girl, and here I am, seeing you again. I need you to *fix* me. Give me the antidote, or suck the poison out, or do whatever's necessary to make me normal again." I paused. "Or else."

"I would if I could, really, but I've got no idea how to undo the effects of the bite. You should be impressed that I manage to pass for human, don't expect me to be some kind of doctor, too. I *bit* you. You're infected. Most people just die, I guess, like you said. I don't know what'll happen to you if you stay alive. Maybe you should get a blood transfusion or something. Or maybe it'll pass."

"Infection doesn't just pass, you idiot. And this is a *psychic* infection, it's magical, so I don't think a blood transfusion will help. I'll probably get the supernatural equivalent of gangrene, and all my magic will rot off." At least, that might happen if I was going to live longer than two weeks, which seemed unlikely.

"You're some kind of witch, right? So can't you... do something witchy?"

"Sure," I said. "Human sacrifice is starting to sound appealing. You're not strictly human, but you'll do." Kasan was useless, whether he was a lizard-god or something stranger. He didn't know how to fix me. Killing him wouldn't change that, but it wouldn't hurt anything, either, and if I was going to age unto death, I didn't want to be the only one who died. I slipped my hand into my waistband to pull out one of my knives.

"Look, I'm sorry about the bite, but I can't help you. Sex with strangers is risky. You know that."

I don't think Kasan even noticed I was going for the knife. He just shut the door in my face, apparently tired of talking to me. I stood there for a moment, holding my knife, then I rattled the knob, but it was locked. The windows were barred—this wasn't a great part of town—so breaking one of those wasn't an option. I pounded on the door with my free hand and shouted. If I'd had my powers, that door would have been *splinters*, and Kasan wouldn't have fared much better.

"I'm calling the police!" he shouted, and appeared briefly at his barred window, showing me the phone. Then he closed the curtains.

I kicked his door, then turned and stalked off. I couldn't decide if Kasan was malicious or genuinely clueless, if he was really trying to be human and just following the wrong role models—certainly there were plenty of men out there who treated women the way Kasan had treated me. I wondered if he could be shown the error of his ways.

I can't help it. Even at my most furious, I'm a romantic at heart. When I make love to someone, I want very much to like them afterward. Even, apparently, when they bite me and poison me and take all my powers away.

I walked the block from the bus stop to my apartment building, but stopped on the far side of the street from my front door. There was something wrong. I may have lost my power, but my senses were as good as ever, and my well-developed awareness noticed certain things out of place—curtains had moved in some of the fictives' apartments, the doormat on the steps was askew, and there was the faint suggestion of a shape on the far side of the pebbled glass in the front door.

Something was inside my building. Up on the third floor, in the apartment where I lived, a curtain twitched, and I caught a glimpse of something red and slick touching the cloth, leaving a blood-colored splotch on the fabric.

I faded back fast, half-hiding behind a line of newspaper boxes. My apartment building had been breached. The protective spells had faded, and now my enemies—the long-lived, nonhuman ones, creatures I'd bested or cheated or outwitted in battles long ago—had come looking for me, creeping through my rooms, profaning everything they touched. The red thing in my apartment was not the smartest or the most aggressive of my enemies—thus, he'd been stupid enough to show himself. But if he was inside, then there were certainly others, more dangerous ones.

I couldn't go home. It was getting dark, and I was tired, and dispirited, and I couldn't even go home.

I walked another few blocks and caught another bus, paying with the last of my change. I rode to the lake, and made my way to Barry's glade. I collapsed among the trees, curling up on a bed of leaves. Barry fussed around me, making the branches sway, trying in his wordless way to comfort me and offer whatever solace he could.

I thought about dying there, just laying in among the trees until my age caught up with me. I'd used up my only reserve of power, and now I had nothing left, nothing to fall back on, nowhere to turn.

I dozed in the dirt, my body exhausted, my mind overwhelmed, and Barry gently swept a covering of leaves over me, the best blanket he could muster. His efforts made me smile, wanly, and I said, "Thank you, lover."

And suddenly I was wide-awake. I sat up, scattering leaves all around me. I put my hand on the egg-shaped stone that had once marked the resting place of my reserve power. I'd always thought that was the only thing I'd managed to save up over the years, my only rainy-day protection. But that wasn't true. I'd saved up something else, too.

"Barry," I said. "I need you to deliver a message for me. Several messages, actually."

The next morning, I rode in a limousine to Kasan's house. I'd slept in a bed that night, and had a fine meal earlier in the morning. I was still poisoned, still dying, but I was no longer as bereft as I'd been.

When we arrived, the chauffeur opened the door for me. His face was a tenuous blur, his body almost transparent in places. Both the chauffeur and the car were mere ghosts, but they were solid enough to take me and the others to Kasan's house in style.

I walked to Kasan's door alone, but with a legion prepared to come forth if needed. I knocked. No one answered. I had the idea that Kasan slept in. So I knocked again, and this time the sound reverberated deep into the house, rattling the windows. I heard swearing inside the house, and a moment later the door opened, revealing Kasan, sleepy-eyed and still damnably cute. "Delanie," he said. "You couldn't wait until after noon to come and try to kill me again?"

"I've been thinking about Komodo dragons, Kasan," I said. "They have tremendous natural immune systems, as I'm sure you know. Doctors have been studying them for a while, trying to find out how those hyperactive immunities work, hoping to develop a way to use them to help humans."

"Great," Kasan said. "That explains why I never get colds." He started to shut the door. I stopped it with my hand. Kasan pushed harder, and though he should have been able to force me back with his superior physical strength, the door didn't move.

"It explains more than that," I said. "Since your bite has magical consequences, I think your immune system does too, and that you're immune to magic—to your own, at least, the same way Komodo dragons are immune to their own bacteria. That's a pretty useful ability. It's so useful, I want it for myself."

"What are you talking about?"

"Sympathetic magic. I want to borrow some of your power. Not *steal* it—just borrow it. To save my life, among other things."

"Uh huh," Kasan said. "And does this involve chopping me up, wearing my guts as a belt?"

"No. Just a ritual, some magic, some words, some concentration, some sex. We fuck, you bite me again, I bite you, I take in your blood, you take in mine."

"If I'm immune to magic, how are you going to cast a spell on me?"

"I can temporarily suppress your immunity," I said. "I have a potion." I patted a pouch at my waist.

Kasan frowned. "So why should I do this? What's in it for me?"

"This is your chance to be a good guy, Kasan. You've gotten the hang of being an asshole, but there are other options available to an astute student of human behavior."

"Hmm. If there's one thing I've learned, it's that people are liars. I think you're probably lying to me now. I bet you do want to wear my entrails for a belt. I saw those knives you brought last time. So you'd better take off, before I call the cops again."

"Okay," I said. "Plan B, I guess." I stepped off the porch.

And two score of my old lovers stepped forward. Well, some of them stepped—others floated, or shifted into this visible plane, or rose up from puddles of shadow, or precipitated out of the air into a cloud of shimmering gray particulates, or made their presences known with the jingle of little silver bells, the smell of cut lemons, a sensation of sudden dry warmth.

Kasan tried to slam his door again, and still failed, though this time there was no one visibly holding it open.

"I thought you'd lost your power," Kasan said, backing away, into his house.

"This isn't my power," I said. "These are just my friends. Old lovers, who remember me fondly. You might want to take notes, because this is something else humans sometimes do—we make friends, we inspire loyalty, and we do things for each other." I'd realized it the night before, lying in the dirt—that I'd saved up a lot of goodwill over the years, and I didn't necessarily have to deal with all my problems alone. I'd made love to these men and women, and helped them become their better selves. My old lovers weren't perfect people. Some of them were short-sighted, temperamental, self-centered, judgmental, and lazy, just like any cross-section of the population, but they all had good qualities, things in them that I could love, and there were things in me they loved in return. And this particular two score of my old lovers were even more exceptional, because these were the ones who had longed to rise above their limitations and flaws, who'd wished in their deepest hearts to be something *more* than engines of appetite and guilt—these were the ones who didn't care about having the most money or fucking the most people or getting revenge. They had wished for transcendence, and I'd done what I could to help them toward that goal.

They all still loved me, a little. And like anyone who feels fond toward an old lover, they hated to see me hurt by a *new* lover.

They swept into Kasan's house, and with their arms of light and shadow, their hands of wind and invisible weight, they held him down on the floor. I came into his dim, shabby house, and set up candles and cloths, items my lovers had brought me the night before and that I'd hurriedly consecrated. The ritual was prepared. Now all I had to do was pour the potion down Kasan's throat—my old lovers would make sure he swallowed it. Then I could tear open his clothes, climb on top of him, and...

I slumped on the carpet, put my head in my hands, and said, "Damn it."

My old lovers stirred and fluttered, unsure what to do. They released Kasan, who sat up, wary, and looked at me. "What's happening?"

"I can't do it. I can't take you against your will. I won't *rape* you. That's what it would be, even if it is to save my life. It goes against everything I am. I could murder you more easily than I could fuck you against your wishes. I thought I could, if I had to, if you wouldn't see reason, but..." I shook my head. I could have raped Kasan, and gone on living, but I wouldn't have been able to live with myself afterward, and it would have tainted all my powers forever. Maybe it would be better to just kill myself. That might be more pleasant than being killed by the monsters in my building, or hiding out, waiting to age and die.

Kasan looked around the room. "All these... things... they're really your old lovers?"

I nodded, wiping my tears away. "Old lovers, old friends. They wanted to help me."

"They used to be human, and you helped them become what they are now?"

I looked around, smiling despite myself, because it made me happy to see how well they were all doing. There was Michael, a little djinni of air and dust in the corner, who'd left the broad deserts he loved exploring to come help me. There was Serafina, a swirling shadow creature, who in her bodiless dark form sprawled across the galaxies, tasting the space between stars. Carlo, who lived in the space between universes, endlessly conversing with the vast, strange intelligences who held conflicting realities at bay. Martindale, who'd been a brewmaster in his mundane life, and who'd learned how to make magical potions—he was the one who'd concocted the magical-immunity suppressant I'd planned to force-feed to Kasan. They were here, and so many others, and this didn't even count my lovers who weren't here, the ones who had retained their human forms, who I'd helped pursue their dreams to create art, or to live in the deep woods off the produce of the land, or to grow grapes in the south of France. My lovers made it possible for me to live forever, and I helped them live their own dreams. "Yeah, of course I helped them. We had fun, and we cared for each other. It was good."

Kasan touched my leg. "Could it go the other way? Could you help someone who's not human *become* human? I've watched people, men in bars, men at the gym, and I've tried to do what they do. But this, these people... I don't understand this, what you do together, what you had together. I want to understand. I used to be a spirit of the islands, a dragon made of smoke and sea mist, but since the first time I saw a human, I've wanted to *understand*."

I stared at him. He was, fundamentally, a voracious, septic reptile. But something had made him try to be human. To make the leap from being an animal spirit, or a totemic force, or a demigod—a creature of appetite, living in the moment—to being a man. Some urge for betterment within him had enabled Kasan to attempt this only-partial transformation. He might have been lying to me—he'd done so before—but I believed he was telling the truth about wanting to be a better man.

In every relationship, there comes a moment when you can't go forward unless you're prepared to risk trusting the other person.

"Yes," I said. "I can help you. Start by drinking this." I took the glass bottle containing the potion from my pouch.

"And we'll make love again? I liked that." He was shy again, looking away, and this time I thought it was genuine.

"Yes," I said. "And I liked it, too."

He drank the potion. My old lovers watched him, and once he'd swallowed it all, they slipped, melted, vanished, and flew away from the house. If anything happened to me at Kasan's hands, they would come for him. Kasan must have known that, but it didn't seem to worry him at all, which told me I'd been right to trust him, this time.

"I really didn't mean to bite you the other night," Kasan said.

"I believe you."

We made love, there on his living room floor, and as the power filled me I let it pour back out again before it could become tainted, let the magic surround us, until finally I bit his shoulder, and he bit mine, and his power flowed into me, and some of mine, I think, flowed into him.

Afterward, we lay together, and I felt full of magic again, and knew that I could contend with the difficulties that lay ahead. Kasan was still just a bad mood away from being a man-eating reptile, but now I was immune to his bite, which meant I had nothing catastrophic to fear, and I could help him find out what kind of man he should be.

There might be things for me to learn from him, too. I wondered if I'd been missing the point all these years, striving for immortality and godhood at the expense of being human. Kasan was trying to go in the other direction, which certainly made me question some of my assumptions. And all these long years of limiting myself to a month at a time with any given lover... maybe that was a mistake. Maybe there would be advantages to a longer relationship.

"Kasan," I said, running a fingernail down his chest.

"Hmm?" he said sleepily. He might have been any of my lovers, then, sated, happy, and warm.

"Would you take me to the islands, where you're from, sometime?"

"Sure," he said. "We'll go in a few months, when it's summer there. It's beautiful then."

"I'd like that," I said.

BOTTOM FEEDING

Graydon sat in a lawn chair beneath a bedraggled weeping willow, by the pond where Shiteater lived. A canvas grocery bag rested in the mud on his left, bulging with his most prized possessions, carefully chosen that morning—a mason jar filled with smooth stones and sea glass that he'd gathered during childhood summers at the beach house; the copy of *Watership Down* his brother Alton had been reading before he died, tattered bookmark still in place; a twist of braided blonde hair Rebekah had given him to remember her by, the summer she went off to Ireland and met Lorrie; the program from the first play he'd ever directed in college. All the things he was finished with. All the things he had to trade.

Graydon sipped strong coffee from his thermos, and watched the sun begin its day's climb up from the east. Graydon had been here for an hour already, mostly in the dark. He was crying a little, off-and-on, almost absent-mindedly.

A loaded speargun lay across his lap, bought two days before at a sporting-goods superstore in Atlanta for more money than Graydon had expected. The clerk had asked where he was going fishing, and Graydon said, "A pond behind my house." The clerk had laughed, thinking it was a joke, and gone over the basics of handling the speargun with Graydon, who'd never used anything more complicated than a rod and reel before.

"All right, then," Graydon said, wiping tears from his cheeks. He lifted the speargun in one hand and the canvas bag of treasures in the other. He waded into the murky green water, up to his waist, and upended the bag upon the water. The braided hair floated, as did the book and program, their pages darkening with water, but the full mason jar sank, ripples spreading around it.

A light rain fell, making more ripples, and thunder rumbled. Those were good omens for this kind of fishing.

"There's your bait," Graydon said. "Come on, Shiteater." He held the speargun as the clerk had shown him, and waited for the thing he hunted to swim up from the depths.

The salmon of knowledge lived a long time ago, in the Well of Segais, where the waters ran deep and clear as rippling air. He swam there, thinking his deep thoughts, coming to the surface occasionally to eat the magical hazelnuts that fell into the water from the trees on the bank. Every nut contained revelations, but the salmon was not a mere living compendium of knowledge—he was a wise fish, too, and so chose to live quietly, waiting for the inevitable day when he would be caught and devoured. The salmon dimly remembered past (and perhaps future) lives, experiences inside and outside of time, from the whole history of the land: being blinded by a hawk on a cold winter night, hiding in a cave after a flood, running from a woman who might have been a goddess, or who might have been a witch.

The salmon did not look forward to being caught, and cooked, and eaten, but knowing what the consequences would be for the one who caught him, he had to laugh, insofar as fish (even very wise ones) are able to laugh.

Graydon started fishing the summer after he got kicked out of college. Lacking any other direction, still stunned by his brother's sudden death, Graydon had returned to his hometown of Pomegranate Grove, Georgia, and rented a two-bedroom house with a fireplace, on the edge of town. He had a spare room full of Alton's things, as he was the sole inheritor—their father was long dead, their mother in a nursing home, victim of early-onset senile dementia. Every day Graydon sorted through the piles of his dead brother's things, touching objects both familiar and foreign, and one day he found a rod, reel, and tackle box. He and Alton had gone fishing often when they were children, and suddenly that seemed like the proper monument, a way to honor Alton's memory and simultaneously pass the empty days, so Graydon made a lunch and took the rod and tackle out back, to the pond by the woods behind his house. It wasn't much of a pond, maybe thirty feet across at its widest, with a few reeds in the shallows and one big weeping willow close to the water. These ponds could be deep, though, and it wasn't trash-strewn or visibly polluted, so he thought there might be fish.

Graydon sat on the bank and put a flashy red-and-yellow lure on the hook. Probably all wrong for whatever kind of fish lived in this pond, if any, but he didn't care if he caught anything—he just wanted to sit, and think, and hold the pole, and watch the red-and-white bobber float. That's what fishing was about, he recalled. Actually catching anything was sort of an optional extra.

He cast the line out into the middle of the pond and settled down with his back against the willow tree, thinking about Alton, who'd taught him how to climb trees, and cheat at poker, and, when they were older, how to take a hit off a bong. Graydon hadn't used any of those skills in a long time. Alton had taught him to fish, too, though neither one of them had ever been any good at it. Graydon wondered if the two of them had ever fished in this particular pond, and couldn't remember—it was possible, as they'd tried little fishing holes all over Pomegranate Grove.

The bobber sank under the green surface of the pond, and the rod moved in Graydon's hands. He reeled the line in slowly, wondering what kind of fish had been fooled by the flashy lure, but whatever had snagged on the hook didn't move like a fish, or like anything alive. Something dark and round broke the surface, as big as a human head but smooth and shining. Graydon reeled it in the rest of the way and bent over the water to fish it out.

He'd caught a motorcycle helmet, a black one with a star-shaped crack on one side. The line was tangled around the chin strap, and Alton's flashy red-and-yellow lure was gone.

Graydon turned the helmet over and let the water run out of it, into the pond.

Alton had died in a motorcycle accident, had lost control and smashed into a guardrail on a bridge, then gone flying off the bike into the shallow swamp-water below. He'd landed face-down, probably knocked unconscious, and though his head struck a rock in the water, the blow didn't kill him—the helmet had protected his skull. Instead, Alton had died by drowning in two feet of water.

Graydon touched the star-shaped crack, then threw the helmet violently back into the pond. Remembrance was one thing, but pulling up something like that was too morbid by half. The helmet hit the water and floated, open end up, like a little plastic boat.

Something broke the surface of the water, mud-brown and slickly shining. It was a catfish, the biggest Graydon had ever seen. Its huge head stayed out of the water for a long moment, teacup-sized black eyes staring at Graydon. Long whiskers sprouted from around its mouth in nasty profusion. The catfish dove under the water again with a flip of its stubby fins, then reemerged beside the floating helmet, its gaping fish-mouth open wide enough to swallow a basketball.

The fish ate the helmet in one bite, and disappeared beneath the ripples.

Graydon whistled. He'd heard of catfish that big—they were the stuff of Southern rural legend. Huge catfish, decades old, and when they were finally caught and cut open, all sorts of things were found in their bellies. If this fish was big enough to eat a motorcycle helmet... well. Graydon wasn't going to catch a fish like that with Alton's old rod and reel. There was little chance of catching it at *all*. That fish was older than him by many years, probably, and had doubtless outwitted scores of better fisherman.

Still, that would be something, wouldn't it? Catching something so big, so old, so wily. Even if he didn't succeed, it would be fun trying.

And just like that, Graydon had a goal for the summer.

Here are some things that have been found inside the bellies of large catfish in the American South:

License plates, diamond rings, steel buckets, beer bottles, lugnuts, picture frames, doorknobs, alarm clocks, boots, credit cards, stolen hotel ashtrays, rubber duckies, cowbells, candles, dinner plates, floppy canvas fisherman's hats, spectacles, wallets with money still inside, one-armed Teddy bears, other fish, snapping turtles, spark plugs, toy pistols, hubcaps, wheelbarrow tires, coffee cups, thermoses, roofing shingles, human hands, telephones, and screwdrivers.

Here are some things that have never been found inside the bellies of large catfish in the American South:

Solace. Hope. Lost ideals. True love. Things that smell nice. Glory. Everything you ever dreamed of having, but never received. A reason to go on living.

On Friday, the week he started fishing, Graydon drove into Atlanta to have coffee with his oldest and most bewildering friend, Rebekah.

Graydon arrived at the Pelican Café first, and took a table by the windows, beneath an art student's painting of sinister mermaids fencing with human thighbones. He ordered a glass of chardonnay and sipped it, thinking of catfish, mostly, until Rebekah showed up, only fifteen minutes late, her honey-colored hair knotted in a profusion of small and not very tidy braids. She wore white shorts that showed off her legs and a pale-yellow blouse, open at the throat. Graydon had adjusted to the situation with Rebekah long enough ago that he no longer felt a pang at her loveliness, but he still noticed it. They'd grown up together in Pomegranate Grove and dated briefly, in high school, before Rebekah met Lorrie and realized she was a lesbian. After a few bumpy months following that revelation, the two of them had become friends again, though Graydon still had trouble warming up to Lorrie, with her sharp features and her New Age affectations, her astrology and proselytizing vegetarianism.

Rebekah apologized for being late—she might as well apologize for being Rebekah, Graydon thought—and spread her things out on the table. Textbooks, a notebook, highlighters, pens, a cup of coffee, a bottle of beer, all squeezing Graydon onto a tiny edge of the table, with barely room for his wineglass. Rebekah's things always expanded to fill the available space, and her personality did much the same.

"How's life?" Graydon asked.

Rebekah shrugged. "Schoolwise, I'm getting fluent in Old English, for what that's worth. Chaucer's never been funnier. The freshmen I'm teaching are functionally illiterate, and the professor I'm TA'ing for is more interested in my T&A than my ideas. Lorrie's gone from vegetarian to vegan, and if I see another bean sprout I'm going to scream. I've been sneaking out to eat cheeseburgers for months now, and I'm getting tired of living a dietary lie. Lorrie says my aura's getting all black and spiky, which I figure can't be good. But mostly I'm too busy to worry about how I'm doing." She smiled brightly. "You?"

"I've been fishing," he said, and told her about catching the helmet and seeing the catfish, though he hadn't seen the fish again in the three days since, despite spending hours at the pond each day.

"I've heard of that fish," Rebekah said. "Dad told me about it. We used to live about a mile from your place, you remember that? At least, I guess it must be the same fish. I'm surprised it's still alive. Dad said people have been trying to catch it since he was a kid. I think trying to catch that fish used to be a major pastime in the Grove, but I suppose that kind of thing's gone out of style."

"I blame video games," Graydon said.

Rebekah ignored him. "The fish even has a name. Guess what it is."

"Mr. Whiskers?"

"Sineater. Except when my dad told me about it, he *started* to say 'Shiteater,' I think, and then decided to protect my delicate ears from such profanity."

"Shiteater," Graydon repeated. "That's charming. When I catch him, you can come over, and we'll have a big catfish dinner."

"I'm coming over anyway," she said. "You're going to let me stay the night next weekend, and I won't take no for an answer. I've *got* to get away from Lorrie for a while. She won't even eat fish anymore, that used to be our big compromise, but now she says it's 'morally repugnant.' She only ever ate salmon anyway, she said everything else was too fishy-tasting. I mean, c'mon, it's *fish*. What *should* it taste like?"

"Catfish is pretty bland, I guess," Graydon said.

"It's not bad, fried with the right spices," Rebekah said. "So can I come over? You can cook for me, though I don't think you'll be feeding me Shiteater, as appetizing as that sounds. You'd need more than a rod and reel to pull him in anyway."

"I don't know," Graydon said, thinking of the mess in his house, all of Alton's things in the spare bedroom, also thinking of how hard it would be to sleep in the same house all night with Rebekah and not be able to touch her—he hadn't had sex since a bad one-night stand at school in New York. Rebekah knew that, and she must know that he still had feelings for her; he hadn't made it much of a secret. But it sounded like things were going badly with her and Lorrie, and Rebekah and Graydon *had* been lovers, before, in dim pre-college antiquity, so...

Rebekah snorted. "Come on. Like you're too busy? You've got too much other stuff to do?"

Graydon didn't answer, didn't let any expression touch his face at all.

"Oh, hey, I'm sorry, Gray," Rebekah said, reaching across the table to touch his hand. "I didn't mean anything by it, you're getting your head together, figuring out what you want to do, and that's fine."

Graydon nodded, but he didn't think Rebekah believed what she'd just said—for her, life *was* work, being active, moving forward. She wouldn't be treading water if she were in Graydon's position. Hell, she'd never have let herself get into Graydon's position in the first place, blowing off classes, avoiding advisors, finally being "invited to pursue graduate studies else-where," as he'd been. Rebekah didn't have much patience for self-pity.

"Sure," he said. "Next Friday?"

Salmon aren't much like catfish. Salmon are beautiful, insofar as fish can be beautiful, with silver scales and graceful bodies. Catfish are ugly, whiskered, mud-colored, slow. Salmon are wiser than other fish, wiser than many people, wiser than some bears. Catfish are not wise, but they are wily. Salmon, it is said, eat hazelnuts. Catfish eat shit and garbage and dead things. Salmon are patient as gods, only hurrying to spawn. Catfish are patient as death, only hurrying to feed. The flesh of salmon is delicious. The flesh of catfish is bland as rainwater. Salmon sometimes grant wishes, when that seems the wise course. Catfish can grant wishes, too, but different wishes, for different reasons.

Salmon know more than catfish, but catfish remember everything.

That weekend, Graydon studied how to catch giant catfish. It was surprisingly uncomplicated, at least in theory, according to the books and websites he consulted, but the definition of "giant" seemed to be thirty or forty pounds, which he thought was far smaller than Shiteater. He looked further, and discovered that the largest catfish ever caught in the U.S. had come from a pond in Tennessee, and weighed one hundred and eleven pounds. Graydon had no idea how big Shiteater was, but he suspected it was bigger than that. The record-breaking fish had been caught with deep-sea tackle, but one trip to a sporting goods store showed Graydon that he couldn't afford that kind of equipment, not with the dregs of his student loans running out.

Still, Graydon was hardly an expert on catfish, so perhaps he'd overestimated Shiteater's size. Starting Monday he tried the recommended approaches for catching giant catfish from the shore, setting multiple poles and lines on the bank, with hooks set at various depths. He tried different baits, from small fish to rotten chicken and beef, but none of it worked, and the bait came out again sodden but untouched, and there was no sign of the big fish at all, not even a ripple.

Graydon didn't catch *anything*, as if there were no other fish in the pond at all, which he supposed was possible. Shiteater could have eaten them all. By Wednesday Graydon had given up on catching the monster, already bored and frustrated by the effort. It had been hubris to think he could catch such a monster, just one more instance of his reach exceeding his grasp.

On Thursday he sat on the bank with his dead brother's fishing rod jammed into the mud, line in the water, staring at the sky. The fishing rod was almost a formality now, just a prop, set-dressing. It justified his sitting by the water, in the shade, listening to the willow's drooping branches sway in the breeze.

The rod fell into the water. The bobber was submerged—had Shiteater bitten the hook and pulled in the rod? Graydon splashed into the pond, up to his knees, going after the rod, which was already floating away.

He reached for the rod... and something passed before him, brushing against his legs. He looked down, and there was Shiteater, *far* bigger than one hundred and eleven pounds, as big around as a barrel. Shiteater took the fishing rod into its mouth, like a dog picking up a thrown stick, and dove with it, disappearing.

Graydon stared down into the water for a moment, then shouted and slapped at the water angrily. "You fucking fish! Bring that back!" Shiteater ignored food, it ignored everything, but it tried to eat his brother's *fishing rod?* What kind of beast was this?

Graydon slogged out of the water and sat, dripping, beneath the willow tree, thinking dark thoughts about fishing with dynamite, or about blasting Shiteater with a shotgun, but he didn't have dynamite, or any guns at all.

Something drifted on the surface of the water, eddying gradually toward the bank, until it floated just offshore in front of the willow. Graydon leaned forward to look at it.

It was a dreamcatcher, a wooden hoop threaded with string and hung with wet feathers. Alton had given one of those to Graydon years and years ago, after a trip he took to an Indian reservation in the Southwest. Graydon had lost it in one of his many moves, and he'd missed it, a little. Graydon reached into the water and lifted the floating dreamcatcher out.

It was the same. The same snapped threads, the same gray-and-white feathers, the same size, everything. It was the dreamcatcher he'd lost, the one Alton had given him, he'd almost swear to it.

Graydon looked at the pond for a while. He'd baited his hook, that first day, with one of Alton's lures. He lost the lure, but found a motorcycle helmet. Now he'd lost Alton's fishing rod, and found a dreamcatcher.

The thoughts that occurred to him were ridiculous.

But, on the other hand, they were testable.

Graydon went back to the house, and came back a bit later, carrying some of the things Alton had left behind.

There are myths about salmon, but catfish don't warrant much more than folklore. Some say that catfish bite well when it thunders, or that they're easy to catch when it rains; that catfish will bite a hook dipped in motor oil, or that you'll be lucky fishing for them if your pockets are turned inside out. If an owl hoots in the daylight, the catfish are easy to catch.

All of those beliefs are true. But some of them confuse cause and effect.

By nightfall, Graydon had thrown almost all of Alton's possessions into the pond, and received an equal number of things in return. Throwing in Alton's class ring brought back one of his brother's running shoes, his initials written in permanent marker on the inside of the tongue. Throwing in freshman algebra class notes brought back a sparkling geode

Alton had used as a bookend, though Graydon had to fish that out with a net after Shiteater swam repeatedly over the spot where it rested, like Flipper the dolphin from that old TV show, trying to explain something to the stupid humans. Shiteater ate almost everything Graydon threw him. Graydon intentionally threw in a few things with no connection to Alton—a used paperback he'd picked up at a yard sale for a dime, a salt shaker that came with the house, a handful of change. Shiteater ignored those things, and nothing came back in return. After an hour of casting in and receiving back, Graydon sat by a pile of returned objects, all of them things lost for years before.

"Did you eat my brother, you fuck?" Graydon asked, but knew it was absurd. Alton had died in a body of water that was little more than a creek, miles from here. The connection between his brother and Shiteater was stranger than that, more complicated, more mysterious. Perhaps it would prove too mysterious for Graydon to understand. When it grew dark, Graydon started to gather the objects Shiteater had given him, or allowed the pond to give him, or whatever. But why would he want to keep those things? They were just lost things, some with a charge of sentimental value, most lacking even that. Graydon began tossing the objects into the water, as he'd thrown back the helmet that first day, and Shiteater rose up again and swallowed it all, wolfing the things down as quickly as Graydon could throw them in.

It was hard to tell in the dark, but Shiteater seemed larger than he had been before. Nothing new came floating out of the pond after Graydon finished throwing everything in, and Shiteater didn't break the surface of the black water again once he finished eating. Graydon kept only the dreamcatcher—he suspected he might need it, as nightmares seemed inevitable— and trudged back to his house, thinking.

In psychoanalysis, "fishing" refers to a process whereby subconscious thoughts, feelings, and motivations are drawn up randomly, without any attempt to order or explain them until later. The process is poorly named, since it is more like dredging or using a dragnet than the precise efforts of an angler—it pulls up everything, garbage and treasure alike. It's a technique that only a catfish could love.

A good fisherman, on the other hand, knows just what sort of bait to use, and where to cast his line.

Graydon woke early on Friday morning and decided to continue his experiments.

He threw in one of his mother's good china cups and received a small jar, labeled with a piece of masking tape, that contained the gallstones she'd had surgically removed when Graydon was fifteen. He remembered visiting her in the hospital, remembered her telling him that the doctors were going to give her the gallstones, how she planned to throw them into the ocean next time they went to the coast. She was already starting to lose it, then, her mind beginning its slow unraveling, but it had seemed like simple eccentricity in those days, not the full-blown dementia it would become.

Graydon looked at the jar for a while. This was a valuable discovery. This meant the fish didn't have anything to do with Alton, not specifically. Graydon threw the gallstones back into the water. Shiteater was—was—

He didn't know what Shiteater was. Something to do with the dead, maybe. Or memory, or loss, or grief, or hope, or closure. Graydon couldn't figure it out. It wasn't like in stories, where things were neatly explained, where the mystery had a function, however obscure, where the operations of the supernatural could be explained. This was something else. Something magical, but incomprehensible, which was perhaps the nature of real magic. But Graydon couldn't ignore it, couldn't turn his back and go on living, forget about the pond, and the creature that lived in it.

There was a story about a magical salmon. Rebekah had told him about it, after her trip to Ireland, where she met Lorrie. There once was a wise salmon that lived in a pool, and ate magic nuts, and some great Irish hero caught the fish, and roasted it, and that was a pretty good deal, because whoever ate the fish would gain its wisdom.

What would happen if Graydon ate Shiteater? Would he gain wisdom? Or magic? The ability to call the dead, speak to the dead? Or the ability to *forget* the dead? There was supposed to be a river in Hell whose waters made you forget, and Graydon suspected that, if such a river were real, it would be inhabited by fat brown channel cats, just like Shiteater. What better fish to have the flesh of forgetfulness than a bland catfish, fed on garbage?

Hadn't Rebekah said the fish was also called Sineater?

It didn't matter. He'd never catch it anyway.

Graydon lay under the willow tree, and looked up at the sky, and after a while he fell asleep.

Someone nudged Graydon in the ribs. He opened his eyes, and there was his brother Alton, standing over him, wearing his motorcycle jacket, boots, and jeans. His hair was wet, even his stupid little goatee. "You're more full of shit than that fish, bro," he said.

"Alton?" Graydon said. The tree was making a low noise, like weeping, and the branches were moving despite the lack of wind.

Alton squatted down beside Graydon. "Oh, don't get up," he said ironically. "I'm not offended. I'm dead, after all. But *you're* not."

"Alton, I don't understand," Graydon said. That was the simple truth, and it almost made him burst out crying—he didn't understand why his mother had lost her mind, why Rebekah had fallen in love with a woman, why his brother had died, why grad school had been so difficult, why Shiteater was eating the physical reminders of his loss without taking the memories themselves away.

"Nobody understands," Alton said. "Maybe that's for the best. Listen. You don't want to eat that fish. I don't know what would happen if you did, but it's a big monster that eats dead things, it's not shiny and silver and full of magic nuts. Let it go. Quit wallowing. Get your life back together, while you still have one."

Alton had never been so blunt in life—he'd always been very live-and-let-live, but maybe death had changed that. "Shit, Alton, it's *hard*, you don't know what it's like."

"Nobody knows what it's like. And just because it hurts your feelings when I say you're wallowing, that doesn't mean it isn't *true*. You can't go on like this." The tree was moaning more loudly now, and night was falling quickly. "I have to go," Alton said. "It's getting late."

"Alton, no, I still don't—"

Someone nudged Graydon in the ribs. He opened his eyes. Rebekah stood over him, the sun behind her and a bottle of wine in her hand, looking down at him with a grin. "Have a nice nap? Shall I assume dinner isn't ready?"

Graydon groaned and sat up. "I had a dream..."

"I bet," Rebekah said. "Did it involve me and Lorrie and warm oil?"

Graydon grimaced. "Lorrie isn't my type."

"I thought all you guys got off on the idea of two women together."

"I like it better when the women are interested in me, too."

"Well, hey, it's your dream," she said. "Come on. I brought steaks."

"I was supposed to cook for *you!*"

"Knock yourself out. I don't mind if you do the cooking. I just brought the food."

"Does Lorrie know you're eating steak?"

"What Lorrie doesn't know..." Rebekah said airily, and Graydon wondered what *that* meant, if Rebekah had other things in mind for tonight, more things Lorrie didn't need to know about.

He went back to the house with her, and for the first time in days, he didn't think about Shiteater at all.

Graydon made steaks while Rebekah good-naturedly insulted his housekeeping.

"You never used to care so much about tidiness," Graydon said, standing at the stove, sautéing mushrooms.

"You try living with Lorrie, you'll start to care about tidy, too. One of us has to, and it's not going to be her."

"Sounds like you guys are going through a tough time."

"Yeah, but I don't think Lorrie realizes it. She can be pretty clueless sometimes." Rebekah had opened the wine right away, and now she sipped from a full glass. "Her newest thing? She says I drink too much. I have a few beers on the weekends, maybe a glass of wine at night, and she says I'm an 'incipient alcoholic.'"

"Sounds like she's worrying about all the wrong things," Graydon said.

"I didn't come here to talk about Lorrie, Gray," Rebekah said. "No offense, but it's a subject I'm a little tired of, having to live with it every day."

"Sorry. What *did* you come here to talk about?"

"Honestly? I'd hoped we could talk a little bit about you, Gray."

He kept cooking, unsure how to take that. Rebekah always favored the direct approach—she would just ask, in his position—but Graydon was not so comfortable. So he said, "I've been trying to catch that fish. I see it, all the time, but I can't get it."

"Try a speargun," she said. "They're pretty accurate over short distances. If you really see it that often, you can probably get it."

"Yeah? Nothing I've read suggested a speargun."

She shrugged. "Well, you could try dynamite, but I figure you want to get the fish out in one piece. Should I take this change of subject to mean you don't want to talk about you? Because I'm worried about you, Gray. I think you're sinking here, and I'm trying to throw you a rope."

Graydon turned off the heat under the mushrooms. "Oh," he said. "And here I'd hoped you were planning to confess your love." He said it lightly, but he could tell from her expression that she saw past that. She'd always been able to look straight through him.

"I wish I could, Gray. I know you've carried a candle for me all this time, but..." She shook her head. "I've got to stick things out with Lorrie. We've been in it too long to just give up."

"But if things don't work out..."

Rebekah looked into her wine, then shook her head, her braids swaying. "No, Gray."

"I thought you always said you were bisexual?"

She half-smiled. "It's not about the sex. It's... I don't know. I just don't see you that way anymore. Romantically. I'm not sure I did even when we were dating. You were the nicest guy I knew—you still are—and that's what attracted me, but as for any real spark, chemistry... I don't think it was there. I wanted it to be."

Graydon poured a glass of wine for himself, trying to keep his hands steady. "That's great, Rebekah," he said. "Telling me you never loved me at all."

"I always loved you. I still do. Just... not that way. And I think you needed to hear that, so you'd stop holding out hope, if that's what you've been doing. The way you look when I tell you I'm having problems with Lorrie, you try to hide how happy it makes you, but I can see it, and I don't like it. Maybe it's my own fault, for not saying this before."

"Understood," Graydon said, turning back to the stove. "I'm going to make salad."

"Do you want me to leave?" she said.

Graydon stood stiffly for a moment, then slumped. He sighed. "No. I like having you here. Obviously. You can't blame a guy for hoping, can you?"

"I guess not," she said.

Dinner was subdued, but after a few more glasses of wine Graydon began to relax. He felt oddly burned-out inside, hollow, but not tense. The reason for the tension was gone. Besides, maybe Rebekah was just fooling herself, maybe in time she'd see how good he was for her... He thought of his dream of Alton, his dead brother telling him to move on. But he wanted to move on with *Rebekah*. What else did he have left?

Midnight came, and went, as they talked about books, movies, old memories. They didn't talk about Lorrie, and Rebekah didn't bring up whatever she'd wanted to say about Graydon wasting his life and his time. Finally Rebekah stretched and said, "So where do I sleep?"

"You can take my bed. I'll take the couch."

She nodded, then looked down at her hands in her lap, uncharacteristically shy. "Listen, Gray, I know you must be feeling very isolated and cut off... if you wanted, you could come to bed with me. I know how hard it is to be alone, to crave intimacy and not find it. Things haven't exactly been warm between me and Lorrie lately, and I could use some comfort, too. It wouldn't mean anything, except that you're my friend and I love you, but, if you want..."

In that moment, Graydon realized that Rebekah didn't know him, not really; or if she did, she was deluding herself now, or just using him for her own needs. If Graydon made love to Rebekah, he *wanted* it to mean something. He wanted it to mean that she was coming back to him, that they would be lovers, that they would be together. To have sex together, without any of that... it would be a killing thing. He would hate himself tomorrow, and this hollow feeling might never go away. He should say no.

But how could he say no to the chance to make love to Rebekah?

"Yes," he said. "I'd like that."

Here is the reason the salmon of wisdom laughed when it thought of being eaten:

It was prophesied that the hero Finegas would catch the salmon, and cook it, and eat it, and gain all knowledge, and thus become a greater hero. Finegas caught the salmon, but, being a hero, he was not accustomed to doing his own cooking, and so he had his apprentice Fionn roast the fish instead. The apprentice would not have dreamed of eating his master's meal, but he accidentally burned his thumb while turning the fish on the fire. Without thinking, Fionn stuck his burned thumb into his mouth and sucked it.

Thus tasting the fish. Thus gaining all its knowledge, and leaving his master, the hero, no wiser than before.

That is why the salmon laughed.

The morning after he slept with Rebekah, Graydon was perfectly charming, cooking breakfast, laughing with her, kissing her cheek. Inside, his heart was a cinder. He bid her farewell, promising to get together with her later in the week.

When she was gone, he took four bottles of wine to the pond. He drank two, and poured the other two into the water. "Have a drink with me, Shiteater!" he shouted. "You're my only friend!"

The catfish did not surface.

On Sunday, Graydon didn't fish. During his research he'd learned that it was bad luck to fish on Sundays, and it seemed like a good time to be superstitious. Besides, he was hungover, and didn't wake up until midafternoon. He thought about going to Atlanta, but the stores would be closed already—nothing stayed open very late in the South on Sundays.

On Monday he went into the city and spent most of his remaining money on a speargun. He practiced in the yard with it all afternoon, shooting his sofa cushions for practice. There was no reason to rush. He wanted to do this right.

Tuesday he rose before dawn, took the speargun and a bag of his most precious things to the pond, and waded into the water. He scattered his bait, and called for Shiteater as it began to rain.

The catfish came out of the water and began to eat the things Graydon had scattered. Graydon watched, not moving, rain soaking his hair and filling the pond with ripples. As Shiteater swallowed the last floating thing—Rebekah's braid—Graydon pointed the speargun at its head and fired.

The spear sank deep into Shiteater's head, and the fish spasmed, tail flailing against the water. Graydon wrapped both hands around the shaft of the spear and began pulling Shiteater toward the bank. It was easier than he'd expected, because the water buoyed the dead fish up. Graydon climbed onto the muddy, slick bank and wrestled Shiteater's vast body onto the grass. He went back to the house and returned with a wheelbarrow and some scrap boards. After bracing the wheelbarrow's wheel with a brick, he leaned the boards against the wheelbarrow, creating a makeshift ramp. Graydon shoved Shiteater's heavy corpse up the boards until it flopped into the wheelbarrow, then wheeled it to the concrete patio behind his house. As he pushed, the rain stopped, just a brief summer shower, there and gone.

Graydon dumped Shiteater onto the concrete and stood looking down at it, expecting some thrill of triumph, but he was still all cinders and stones inside, and felt nothing. He went inside for his knives, then set about gutting and cleaning the catfish, referring often to a book he'd bought that explained the process.

After a while Graydon examined the contents of Shiteater's stomach, but found little of interest, not even the things he'd most recently fed the fish—just weeds and mud. That was a disappointment. Graydon had hoped there would be... something inside. Something special.

Well. He could still eat the catfish. That was the main thing. And it would cause something to happen—kill him, give him transcendent wisdom, make him forget, give him oblivion. Something.

While Graydon cleaned the fish, the phone rang, but he ignored it, and eventually the caller gave up.

Graydon was covered in blood and fishguts by the time he finished cleaning Shiteater. He wrapped the edible parts in plastic bags to keep the bugs from getting at them, then went to clean out the fireplace—Shiteater was too big for the oven, and Graydon wanted to cook him all at once.

When the fireplace was clean, Graydon put charcoal and lighter fluid under the grate and started a fire. Once it was burning well, he put Shiteater on the grate. Soon, the fish began to roast. The smoke was strangely odorless.

Graydon went into the bathroom and took a shower, letting the blood and guts cascade into the tub, letting the hot water pound on his over-strained muscles. After a while, afraid the fish would burn, he got out and wrapped a towel around himself.

Rebekah was in the living room, kneeling before the fire, looking at the fish. "Hey, naked guy," she said. "I tried to call, but you didn't pick up. I figured you were out fishing. I guess I was right. This thing's enormous."

"What are you doing here?" he said, thoroughly derailed. He hadn't expected to see Rebekah again so soon, and he wasn't sure what to do—as if, having successfully captured Shiteater, he had no further inner resources, and could make no more plans.

"God, Lorrie and I had the worst fight, you wouldn't believe it," she said. "I had to get out of there for a while." She leaned closer to the fire. "I think your fish is starting to crumble and fall apart," she said, and reached out to nudge the flesh more securely onto the grate.

"No!" Graydon shouted, stepping toward her.

Rebekah hissed and said "Shit! I burned myself." She stuck her thumb in her mouth and sucked.

Graydon watched her, holding his breath.

After a long moment, Rebekah took her thumb out of her mouth. A string of glistening saliva still connected the ball of her thumb to her lips.

She looked up at Graydon, into his face. The string of saliva broke.

Rebekah's eyes went wide.

THE TYRANT IN LOVE

The tyrant reclined on his mound of sticky pillows, staring up at the arched ceiling. A pig's head, ragged at the neck, dangled above him on a chain. The tyrant stuck out his tongue to catch a drop of falling blood. He licked his lips, sighed, and rang a silver bell.

Two virgins from the provinces cowered in a corner, dressed only in honey, their hair shorn to the skin. They clutched one another and watched the tyrant, who had already forgotten them, who had found their degradation routine, who would eventually feed them to the moat-beasts or give them to the guards.

The harlequin arrived, summoned by the bell. He led an ape larger than himself on a leash. The ape wore rainbow leggings and a jester's cap-and-bells. The harlequin, club-footed and grinning (his eyes were the color of jaundice), came dressed only in his pale, hairy skin. A faded pink ribbon dangled, wrapped around his purple erection. The ape swayed, eyes drooping, evidently drugged. "Your majesty," the harlequin said, bowing low. He smacked the ape across the head, and it bowed in imitation. The harlequin slipped behind the ape and mimed buggering it, an exaggerated look of ecstasy on his face.

The tyrant did not laugh, or even shift on his pillows.

The harlequin frowned and unwrapped the pink ribbon. He draped it around the ape's neck, then removed the cap-and-bells and hung it from his penis. "His majesty seems morose and pale as a ghost," the harlequin sang. "What troubles him?"

"I am bored," the tyrant said.

The jester clasped his hands together. "Then you must be entertained! We have a cannibal chef from the south. Do you care to dine?"

"It does not suit my palate," the tyrant said.

"Then the artist, Vassini. Shall we buy his new canvases and burn them in the courtyard? His weeping always cheers you."

"It has been done too often. I seek novelty."

"There is a captured mermaid in Madame Pizarra's brothel. I understand she is a genius with her tongue. You would not find her a cold fish." The harlequin hopped, and the bells on his cap jingled.

The tyrant waved a lazy hand. "Not novel enough. I had the snakewoman a month ago, and all scales seem the same."

The harlequin frowned. "Impalements on the vinegar-spike?"

"No."

"The cripples' street race?"

"No."

"A decree of nudity, save studded collars, for all the citizens?"

"Trite."

"A human cockfight, with bound hands and spiked helmets, with merchants fighting for a purse?"

"Overdone."

"A feast of hearts? A war of stregas? An orgy of lepers?"

"It all seems so *pale*," the tyrant said angrily, sitting up on his pillows, pulling at the front of his bloodstained tunic. He frowned.

The harlequin jeered at the (formerly) virgins and threw hollowed-out eggs full of itching powder at them.

"Harlequin," the tyrant said suddenly. "You have served me fifteen years, ever trusted."

"Yes, my lord, my only friend," the harlequin said.

"As my advisors died, as my friends transgressed, you remained."

"As it pleases you."

"I will give you this confidence," the tyrant said. "I have conceived of a new entertainment."

"Sir?" the harlequin said greedily, thinking: knives, knives, knives.

"I will go into the city tomorrow, in secret," the tyrant said, "and I will do *good*."

The harlequin's erection shriveled like a salted snail. His cap-and-bells fell to the tile with a clatter. "Glorious, sir," he said.

The tyrant wore merchant's clothes, a gold-embroidered shirt, tight leggings, and shiny black boots. A sword swung on his hip and a pouch of coins dangled from a chain around his neck. He went unrecognized, for few had seen the tyrant, and the portraits were all wrong.

He helped an old woman cross a busy street, with carts and coaches rattling dangerously by. She gave him a copper penny.

He came upon a merchant beating his slave, bought the boy, and set him free. The boy offered certain sexual services, which the tyrant politely agreed to collect another time. He thought not. The boy was ill-made, all elbows and knees.

In an alley, a foul-smelling mugger with stringy limbs attacked him. After disarming and holding the mugger at sword-point, the tyrant spared his life.

He threw pennies to the ghouls in the graveyard (no one knew what they did with the money) and they clung to the iron gates, shouting a thousand conflicting predictions of his death.

He killed a red-haired strega suspected of boiling local pets and souring mother's milk. He hung her head on her door in the middle of a poison-ivy wreath. The neighborhood cheered.

He purchased an hour with the oldest, ugliest prostitute he could find and spent it amusing her with sleight-of-hand and massaging her bunion-covered feet. His fingers smelled like rancid cheese for the rest of the day.

The tyrant swelled with charity. A lightness grew in his head, not unlike the euphoria he felt when smoking the apothecary's special herbs. He discovered unfeigned smiles and good will and they pleased him. This was new. This was a novelty.

Near day's end, the tyrant began the trek back to the palace. He would free a few prisoners, release his new bed-slave with her sanity still intact, and halve his mother's nightly allotment of lashes. Then he would sleep with the ugly serving girl (in a straightforward fashion, without implements) and turn in early. Doing good exhausted him almost as much as doing otherwise.

In a small square, he saw her. She leaned over a well, drawing water. The wind, wheezing through the alleys, lifted her copper-colored hair. Her shapeless gray dress blew around her, pressing against her breasts and hips. Her dark eyes seemed preoccupied beneath her heavy brows. The sight of her gave the tyrant wonderful pains in his chest.

The tyrant sat on a doorstep next to an old man. The man grimaced soundlessly, revealing diseased red gums.

"Who is she?" the tyrant asked, nodding his head toward the woman.

"Lucrezia, the goldsmith's widow," the man said, his no-color eyes unfocused.

"Widow?" the tyrant said, gaily colored butterflies breaking loose in his chest. "What became of her husband?"

"The tyrant commissioned him to make a necklace, and the tyrant" (the man tried to spit but came up dry) "didn't like his work. The bastard. He cut her husband open with a hatchet and fed his entrails to the ravens. Lucrezia's had to start washing and mending clothes to get by. She has a boy, too, a good lad."

"You shouldn't call the tyrant a bastard," the tyrant said. "He might hear."

The man spat again. This time a little moisture hit the cobblestones. "The tyrant kills when he will, whether he's insulted or not. I'm old, and don't fear death. Lucrezia curses the tyrant when she wakes and before bed, she doesn't care who hears."

The tyrant gave the old man a small silver coin. The man bit it suspiciously. The tyrant didn't remember killing a goldsmith, but it seemed likely he had. He thought of having Lucrezia brought to the palace, but that didn't seem right. He didn't want to force her affections; he wanted to win them. The prospect seemed something more than a new diversion.

He went to the palace, his noble face crouched in thought.

The next evening the tyrant rang a crystal bell, and the poet came. The poet, a pale effeminate youth with a lazy eye and a feather cap, hailed from the north. He bowed, trembling.

"Tell me," the tyrant demanded, "what is love?"

The poet seemed surprised. His left eye looked off to the side, at nothing. "Love is a wondrous and vexing thing, my lord."

"How does it feel?"

The poet mused, but only for a moment, because hesitations could kill. "Like a warmth, sir. Like sliding naked between silk sheets. Like a thirst that cannot be slaked, no matter how you fill your eyes and arms." The poet warmed to his subject. "Love makes men whisper promises to the stars. It gives them wings, and yet chains their hearts."

Well, thought the tyrant, then I am in love. "How long does it last?"

Now the poet looked confused. "Forever, sir. An evening, sir."

"You are not a very good poet," said the tyrant. "But I am pleased. You will be rewarded." The poet's drifting eyes brightened eagerly. The tyrant looked around the room. "Would you like a bald, honey-covered virgin? Or two?" he asked politely.

"I have found a new entertainment," the tyrant said.

The harlequin, who stood only four and a half feet tall, rode a naked serving boy with a bridle in his mouth. The harlequin wore black boots that reached his thighs, a broad straw hat, and nothing else. He held a shiny black crop in his left hand. Knives, knives, knives, he thought. "Yes, lord?"

"I have found love," the tyrant said.

The harlequin managed a brittle smile. "Lovely, my lord," he said. The tyrant dismissed him, and the harlequin spurred the serving boy onward. He went to his apartment and, in a fit of pique, killed his ape with a fire poker. Then he ate bananas until he got sick, and went to sleep alone.

The tyrant obtained a small apartment (he sent the inhabitants to the platinum mines) near Lucrezia's. He posed as a spice-dealer and began his courtship. In the past, he had never sought more than mastery over a woman's body. The novelty of pursuing a heart delighted him.

At first, Lucrezia rebuffed him. The tyrant persisted, buying her flowers, nutmeg cakes, and small jeweled bracelets. He developed an affection for her quick-witted son Giorgio, bouncing the copper-haired boy on his knee, teaching him to read and do sums. Giorgio called him "Uncle Tyrus" (for that was the name he assumed) and brought him drawings of goats and lions. The tyrant hung them on his apartment's walls.

Lucrezia loved Giorgio more than her own life, and said he had her husband's face. She watched the tyrant play with the boy, and her practical heart softened. Lucrezia gave in to his courtship and let him take her to bed. The tyrant touched her gently. He discovered the joys of giving pleasure. Such a wonder, he thought; new delights nestled in the old.

Meanwhile the harlequin ruled in his absence. Everyone at the palace believed the tyrant had shut himself in his rooms. No one suspected that he lived among the people. The harlequin committed daily atrocities in the tyrant's name, but nothing worse than the tyrant had done himself. The tyrant discussed the horrors with Lucrezia. She denounced the tyrant tirelessly: monster, demon, killer, fiend. Her husband's death stung her daily. She told the tyrant that her first husband could never be replaced in her heart.

The tyrant marveled at the rigors of her grief. Such tears! Such furies!

Lucrezia preferred to make love sitting up, face to face. She kissed the tyrant on the eyelids and forehead, murmuring promises. One night, over a fine dinner of shellfish in the tyrant's new apartment, Giorgio asked, "Will you be my father, Tyrus?" Lucrezia shushed him without blushing (she never blushed). The tyrant wiped his mouth, put down his napkin, and drew a golden ring from his pocket. He offered it to Lucrezia as the symbol of a promise. She kissed him fiercely, her tongue sweet on his, and they became engaged. Giorgio laughed like bells ringing and clapped his hands.

The night before the wedding the tyrant returned to the palace and had Lucrezia brought to him. The guards dragged her in. She struggled like a wet cat until they threw her to the floor. The tyrant dismissed the guards, and Lucrezia stood. She did not run to his arms; she did not do such things. "Tyrus! Have they captured you, too?"

The harlequin had stayed in the tyrant's rooms while his master lived in the city. He'd left a dead maid and a headless goat in the reflecting pool. The rooms stank worse than ever. "Lucrezia, I must tell you something." Now that the moment of drama had arrived, he wanted only to rush through it. "I am not what you think. I am not a spice merchant. I am the tyrant."

"That isn't funny, Tyrus," she said, lower lip trembling.

"No," he said. "It isn't."

Lucrezia took off the gold ring and threw it at him. She leapt, fingernails outstretched, seeking his eyes. The tyrant slapped her from the air. She hit her head on the tiles, and lay, dazed. He bound her with leather cords.

He kissed her forehead, her eyelids, and her cheeks. She snapped wolfishly at him with her teeth. "I love you," he murmured, "I love you, I have loved you, I will love you so." She screamed and cursed him, but did not cry, because she cried only for the memory of her husband.

He listened to her for a time, nodding. Then he killed her, not with knives, but with small hammers made of gold.

"Harlequin," said the tyrant some days later, his voice heavy as a sack of meat. "I have discovered a new entertainment." Thick dust choked the air in his darkened rooms.

"Oh, lord?" said the harlequin. He wore great black wings, feathered by dead crows. He'd painted his face white, in the semblance of a skull. His genitals were exposed. He had once trysted with the tyrant, and sought always to arouse him again.

"I have discovered grief and guilt," said the tyrant, who had not eaten or gone out for days.

Grief and guilt, like love, were unknown to the harlequin. "Shall I fetch the poet?" he said doubtfully.

"No," said the tyrant, "I know how grief feels."

The harlequin shifted from foot to foot. If the tyrant enjoyed his grief, the harlequin shouldn't try to lighten his mood. He said, "The boy, Giorgio, seems well. But he does not understand that you have made him heir. He does not understand what it means."

"He will understand many things in time," the tyrant said. "I will teach him." He straightened slightly, sitting among his pillows. "Harlequin, we have been together so long. I know I can count on you always." He reached out and stroked the harlequin's cheek. The harlequin shivered and sighed with pleasure. "I have a gift for you," the tyrant said, and took a small, brightly wrapped box from under his robe.

The harlequin's eyes lit. He tore open the box, pulled tissue paper aside, and drew out the morsel within.

"It's a rare truffle from the Sinking Forest," the tyrant said. "Worth your weight in gold, harlequin, and tasted only by the very wealthy. Enjoy it."

The harlequin gulped the truffle greedily and chewed. Genuine ecstasy filled his crabbed features.

"I understand nothing surpasses its taste," the tyrant said.

The harlequin only nodded, his eyes closed, trying to hold the already-fading flavor.

"It is all the more precious," the tyrant said, "because it can be eaten only once. I have never tasted one. I must enjoy it vicariously through you."

"Why only once, my lord?" the harlequin asked, absently stroking his testicles.

"The truffle is poisonous," the tyrant said.

The harlequin wretched his death throes through the room, tumbling into the bloody reflecting pool and finally floating. The tyrant watched, and savored his sorrow, and nursed it in his breast.

"That was good," he said aloud. "Not as good as Lucrezia, but good." He rang a small iron bell, and bearers came to take the harlequin's body away.

The tyrant nestled into his filthy blankets and wept.

IMPOSSIBLE DREAMS

Pete was walking home from the revival movie house, where he'd caught an evening showing of *To Have and Have Not*, when he first saw the video store.

He stopped on the sidewalk, head cocked, frowning at the narrow shop squeezed between a kitschy gift shop and a bakery. He stepped toward the door, peered inside, and saw racks of DVDs and VHS tapes, old movie posters on the walls, and a big screen TV against one wall. The lettering on the door read "Impossible Dreams Video," and the smudges on the glass suggested it had been in business for a while.

Except it *hadn't* been. Pete knew every video place in the county, from the big chains to the tiny place staffed by film students by the university to the little porno shop downtown that sometimes also sold classic Italian horror flicks and bootleg Asian movies. He'd never even heard of this place, and he walked this way at least twice a week. Pete believed in movies like other people believed in God, and he couldn't understand how he'd overlooked a store just three blocks from his own apartment. He pushed open the door, and a bell rang. The shop was small, just three aisles of DVDs and a wall of VHS tapes, and there were no customers. The clerk said, "Let me know if you need any help," and Pete nodded, barely noticing her beyond the fact that she was female, somewhere south of thirty, and had short pale hair that stuck up like the fluff on a baby chick.

Pete headed toward the classics section. He was a cinematic omnivore, but you could judge a video store by the quality of its classics shelf the same way you could judge a civilization by the state of its prisons. He looked along the row of familiar titles—and stopped at a DVD turned face-out, with a foil "New Release" sticker on the front.

Pete picked it up with trembling hands. The box purported to be the director's cut of *The Magnificent Ambersons* by Orson Welles.

155

"Is this a joke?" he said, holding up the box, almost angry.

"What?" the clerk said.

He approached her, brandishing the box, and he could tell by her arched eyebrows and guarded posture that she thought he was going to be a problem. "Sorry," he said. "This says it's the director's cut of *The Magnificent Ambersons*, with the missing footage restored."

"Yeah," she said, brightening. "That came out a few weeks ago. You didn't know? Before, you could only get the original theatrical version, the one the studio butchered—"

"But the missing footage," he interrupted, "it was lost, destroyed, and the only record of the last fifty minutes was the continuity notes from the production."

She frowned. "Well, yeah, the footage *was* lost, and everyone assumed it was destroyed, but they found the film last year in the back corner of some warehouse."

How had this news passed Pete by? The forums he visited online should have been *buzzing* with this, a film buff's wet dream. "How did they find the footage?"

"It's an interesting story, actually. Welles talks about it on the commentary track. I mean, it's a little scattered, but the guy's in his nineties, what do you expect? He—"

"You're mistaken," Pete said. "Unless Welles is speaking from beyond the grave. He died in the 1980s."

She opened her mouth, closed it, then smiled falsely. Pete could practically hear her repeating mental customer service mantras: the customer is always right, even when he's wrong. "Sure, whatever you say. Do you want to rent the DVD?"

"Yeah," he said. "But I don't have an account here."

"You local? We just need a phone number and ID, and some proof of address."

"I think I've got my last pay stub," Pete said, rooting through his wallet and passing over his papers. She gave him a form to fill out, then typed his information into her computer. While she worked he said "Look, I don't mean to be a jerk, it's just—I'd *know*. I know a lot about movies."

"You don't have to believe me," she said, tapping the DVD case with her finger. "Total's $3.18."

He took out his wallet again, but though it bulged with unsorted receipts and scraps of paper with notes to himself, there was no cash. "Take a credit card?"

She grimaced. "There's a five buck minimum on credit card purchases, sorry—house rules."

"I'll get a couple of other movies," he said.

She glanced at the clock on the wall. It was almost 10:00.

"I know you're about to close, I'll hurry," he said.

She shrugged. "Sure."

He went to the Sci-Fi shelf—and had another shock. *I, Robot* was there, but *not* the forgettable action movie with Will Smith—this was older, and the credits said "written by Harlan Ellison." But Ellison's adaptation of the Isaac Asimov book had never been produced, though it *had* been published in book form. "Must be some bootleg student production," he muttered, and he didn't recognize the name of the production company. But—but—it said "winner of the Academy Award for Best Adapted Screenplay." That *had* to be a student director's little joke, straight-facedly absurd box copy, as if this were a film from some alternate reality. Worth watching, certainly, though again, he couldn't imagine how he'd never heard of this. Maybe it had been done by someone local. He took it to the counter and offered his credit card.

She looked at the card dubiously. "Visa? Sorry, we only take Weber and FosterCard."

Pete stared at her, and took back the card she held out to him. "This is a major credit card," he said, speaking slowly, as if to a child. "I've never even heard of—"

Shrugging, she looked at the clock again, more pointedly this time. "Sorry, I don't make the rules."

He *had* to see these movies. In matters of film—new film! strange film!—Pete had little patience, though in other areas of his life he was easygoing to a fault. But movies *mattered*. "Please, I live right around the corner, just let me go grab some cash and come back, ten minutes, please?"

Her lips were set in a hard line. He gestured at *The Magnificent Ambersons*. "I just want to see it, as it was meant to be seen. You're into movies, right? *You* understand."

Her expression softened. "Okay. Ten minutes, but that's it. I want to get home, too."

Pete thanked her profusely and all but ran out of the store. He *did* run when he got outside, three mostly-uphill blocks to his apartment in a stucco duplex, fumbling the keys and cursing, finally getting into his sock drawer where he kept a slim roll of emergency cash. He raced back to Impossible Dreams, breathing so hard he could feel every exhalation burning through his body, a stitch of pain in his side. Pete hadn't run, *really* run, since gym class in high school, a decade earlier.

He reached the bakery, and the gift shop, but there was no door to Impossible Dreams Video between them—there was no *between* at all. The stores stood side by side, without even an alleyway dividing them.

Pete put his hand against the brick wall. He tried to convince himself he was on the wrong block, that he'd gotten turned around while running, but he knew it wasn't true. He walked back home, slowly, and when he got to his apartment, he went into his living room, with its floor-to-ceiling metal shelves of tapes and DVDs. He took a disc down and loaded it into his high-end, region-free player, then took his remote in hand and turned on the vast plasma flat-screen TV. The surround-sound speakers hummed to life, and Pete sank into the exquisitely contoured leather chair in the center of the room. Pete owned a rusty four-door Honda with 200,000 miles on the engine, he lived mostly on cheap macaroni and cheese, and he saved money on toilet paper by stealing rolls from the bathrooms in the university's Admissions Office, where he worked. He lived simply in almost every way, so that he could live extravagantly in the world of film.

He pressed play. Pete owned the entire *Twilight Zone* television series on DVD, and now the narrator's eminently reasonable voice spoke from the speakers, introducing the tale of a man who finds a dusty little magic shop, full of wonders.

As he watched, Pete began to nod his head, and whispered, "Yes."

Pete checked in the morning; he checked at lunch; he checked after leaving his job in the Admissions Office in the evening; but Impossible Dreams did not reappear. He grabbed dinner at a little sandwich shop, then paced up and down the few blocks at the far end of the commercial street near his apartment. At 8:30 he leaned against a light pole, and stared at the place where Impossible Dreams had been. He'd arrived at, what, 9:45 last night? But who knew if time had anything to do with the miraculous video store's manifestation? What if it had been a one-time only appearance?

Around 8:45, the door was suddenly there. Pete had blinked, that was all, but between blinkings, something had *happened*, and the store was present again.

Pete shivered, a strange exultance filling him, and he wondered if this was how people who witnessed miraculous healings or bleeding statues felt. He took a deep breath and went into the store.

The same clerk was there, and she glared at him. "I waited for you last night."

"I'm sorry," Pete said, trying not to stare at her. Did she know this was a shop of wonders? She certainly didn't *act* as though she did. He thought she was *of* the miracle, not outside it, and to her, a world with *The Magnificent Ambersons* complete and uncut was nothing special. "I couldn't find any cash at home, but I brought plenty tonight."

"I held the videos for you," she said. "You really should see the Welles, it'll change your whole opinion of his career."

"That's really nice of you. I'm going to browse a little, maybe pick up a few things."

"Take your time. It's been really slow tonight, even for a Tuesday."

Pete's curiosity about her—the proprietor (or at least clerk) of a magic shop!—warred with his desire to ransack the shelves. "Do you work here every night?"

"Lately, yeah. I'm working as much as I can, double shifts some days. I need the money. I can't even afford to eat lately, beyond like an apple at lunch time and noodles for dinner. My roommate bailed on me, and I've had to pay twice the usual rent while I look for a new roommate, it sucks. I just—ah, sorry, I didn't mean to dump all over you."

"No, it's fine," Pete said. While she spoke, he was able to look straight at her openly, and he'd noticed that, in addition to being a purveyor of miracles, she was pretty, in a frayed-at-the-edges ex-punk sort of way. Not his type at all—except that she obviously loved movies.

"Browse on," she said, and leaned on the counter, where she had a heavy textbook open.

Pete didn't need any more encouragement than that. Last night he'd developed a theory, and everything he saw now supported it. He thought this store belonged to some parallel universe, a world much like his own, but with subtle changes, like different names for the major credit cards. But even small differences could lead to huge divergences when it came to movies. Every film depended on so many variables—a director's capricious enthusiasm, a studio's faith in a script, a big star's availability, which starlet a producer happened to be sleeping with—*any* of those factors could irrevocably alter the course of a film, and Hollywood history was littered with the corpses of films that *almost* got made. Here, in this world, some of them *were* made, and Pete would go without sleeping for a week, if necessary, to see as many as possible.

The shelves yielded miracle after miracle. Here was *The Death of Superman*, directed by Tim Burton, starring Nicolas Cage; in Pete's universe, Burton and Cage had both dropped the project early on. Here was *Total Recall*, but directed and written by David Cronenberg, not Paul Verhoeven. Here was *The Terminator*, but starring O.J. Simpson rather than Arnold Schwarzenegger—though Schwarzenegger was still in the film, as Kyle Reese. Here was *Raiders of the Lost Ark*, but starring Tom Selleck instead of Harrison Ford—and there was no sign of any later *Indiana Jones* films, which was sad. Pete's hands were already full of DVDs, and he juggled them awkwardly while pulling more movies from the shelves. Here was *Casablanca* starring George Raft instead of Bogart, and maybe it had one of the alternate endings, too! Here a John Wayne World War II movie he'd never heard of, but the box copy said it was about the *ground invasion* of the Japanese islands, and called it a "riveting historical drama." A quick scan of the shelves revealed no sign of Stanley Kubrick's *Dr. Strangelove*, and those two things together suggested that in *this* world, the atomic bomb was never dropped on Japan. The implications of that were potentially vast... but Pete dismissed broader speculations from his mind as another film caught his eye. In this world, Kubrick had lived long enough to complete *Artificial Intelligence* on his own, and Pete *had* to see that, without Steven Spielberg's sentimental touch turning the movie into Pinocchio.

"You only get them for three days," the clerk said, amused, and Pete blinked at her, feeling like a man in a dream. "You going to have time to watch all those?"

"I'm having a little film festival," Pete said, and he was—he planned to call in sick to work and watch *all* these movies, and copy any of them he could; who knew what kind of bizarre copy protection technology existed in this world?

"Well, my boss won't want to rent twenty movies to a brand new member, you know? Could you maybe cut it down to four or five, to save me the hassle of dealing with him? You live near here, right? So you can always bring them back and rent more when you're done."

"Sure," Pete said. He didn't like it, but he was afraid she'd insist if he pushed her. He selected four movies—*The Magnificent Ambersons*, *The Death of Superman*, *I, Robot*, and *Casablanca*—and put the others away. Once he'd rented a few times, maybe she'd let him take ten or twenty movies at once. Pete would have to see how much sick time he had saved up. This was a good time to get a nasty flu and miss a couple of weeks of work.

The clerk scanned the boxes, tapped her keyboard, and told him the total, $12.72. He handed over two fives, two ones, two quarters, a dime, two nickels, and couple of pennies—he'd brought *lots* of cash this time.

The clerk looked at the money on the counter, then up at him with an expression caught between amusement and wariness. She tapped the bills. "I know you aren't a counterfeiter, because then you'd at least try to make the fake money look real. What is this, from a game or something? It's not foreign, because I recognize our presidents, except the guy on, what's this, a dime?"

Pete suppressed a groan. The *money* was different, he'd never even thought of that. He began to contemplate the logistics of armed robbery.

"Wait, you've got a couple of nickels mixed in with the fake money," she said, and pulled the two nickels aside. "So that's only $12.62 you still owe me."

"I feel really dumb," Pete said. "Yeah, it's money from a game I was playing yesterday, I must have picked it up by mistake." He swept up his bills and coins.

"You're a weird guy, Pete. I hope you don't mind me saying."

Nodding dolefully, he pulled a fistful of change from his pockets. "I guess I am." He had a lot of nickels, which were real—or close enough—in this world, and he counted them out on the counter, $3.35 worth, enough for one movie. He'd go to the bank tomorrow and change his cash for *sacks* of nickels, as much as he could carry, and he would rent all these movies, five cents at a time. Sure, he could just snatch all four movies and run now, but then he'd never be able to come *back*, and there were shelves upon shelves of movies he wanted to see here. For tonight, he'd settle for just *The Magnificent Ambersons*. "This one," he said, and she took his nickels, shaking her head in amusement. She passed him a translucent plastic case and pennies in change, odd little octagonal coins.

"I'll put these away, Mr. Nickels," she said, taking the other movies he'd brought to the counter. "Enjoy, and let me know what you think of it."

Pete mumbled some pleasantry as he hurried out the door, disc clutched tight to his chest, and he alternated walking and running back to his apartment. Once inside, he turned on his humming stack of A/V components and opened the tray on the DVD player. He popped open the plastic case and removed the disc—simple, black with the title in silver letters—and put it in the tray. The disc was a little smaller than DVDs in this world, but it seemed to fit okay. The disc spun, hummed, and the display on the DVD flashed a few times before going blank. The television screen read "No disc." Pete swore and tried loading the disc again, but it didn't work. He sat in his leather chair and held his head in his hands. Money wasn't the only thing that was different in that other world. DVD encryption was, too. Even his region-free player, which could play discs form all over the world, couldn't read this version of *The Magnificent Ambersons*. The videotapes would be similarly useless—he'd noticed they were different than the tapes he knew from this world, some format that didn't exist here, smaller than VHS, larger than Betamax.

But all was not lost. Pete went out the door, carrying *The Magnificent Ambersons* with him, since he couldn't bear to let it go. He raced back to Impossible Dreams. "Do you rent DVD players?" he gasped, out of breath. "Mine's broken."

"We do, Pete," she said, "but there's a $300 deposit. You planning to pay that in nickels?"

"Of course not," he said. "I got some real money from home. Can I see the player?" To hell with being reasonable. He'd snatch the player and run. She had his address, but this wasn't *her* world, and in a few more minutes the shop would disappear again. He could come back tomorrow night with a toy gun and steal all the DVDs he could carry, he would bring a *suitcase* to load them all in, he'd—

She set the DVD player on the counter with the cord curled on top. The electrical plug's two posts were oddly angled, one perpendicular to the other, and Pete remembered that electrical standards weren't even the same in Europe and North America, so it was ridiculous to assume his own outlets would be compatible with devices from another universe. He rather doubted he'd be able to find an adapter at the local Radio Shack, and even if he could rig something, the amount of voltage carried in his wires at home could be all wrong, and he might destroy the DVD player, the way some American computers got fried if you plugged them into a European power outlet.

"Never mind," he said, defeated. He made a desultory show of patting his pockets and said, "I forgot my wallet."

"You okay, Pete?" she asked.

"Sure, I was just really excited about seeing it." He expected some contemptuous reply, something like "It's just a movie," the sort of thing he'd been hearing from friends and relatives his entire life.

Instead she said, "Hey, I get that. Don't worry, we'll have it in stock when you get your player fixed. Old Orson isn't such a hot seller anymore."

"Sure," Pete said. He pushed the DVD back across the counter at her.

"Want a refund? You only had it for twenty minutes."

"Keep it," Pete said. He hung around outside and watched from across the street as the clerk locked up. About ten minutes past 10:00, he blinked, and the store disappeared in the moment his eyes were closed. He trudged away.

That night, at home, he watched his own DVD of *The Magnificent*

Ambersons, with its butchered continuity, its studio-mandated happy ending, tacked-on so as not to depress wartime audiences, and afterward he couldn't sleep for wondering what might have been.

Pete didn't think Impossible Dreams was going to reappear, and it was 9:00 before it did. He wondered if the window was closing, if the store would appear later and later each night until it never reappeared at all, gone forever in a week or a day. Pete pushed open the door, a heavy plastic bag in his hand. The clerk leaned on the counter, eating crackers from little plastic packages, the kind that came with soup in a restaurant. "Hi."

"Mr. Nickels," she said. "You're the only customer I get after 9:00 lately."

"You, ah, said you didn't have money for dinner lately, and I wanted to apologize for being so much trouble and everything... anyway, I brought some food, if you want some." He'd debated all day about what to bring. Fast food was out—what if her world didn't *have* McDonald's, what would she make of the packaging? He worried about other things, too—should he avoid beef, in case mad cow disease was rampant in her world? What if bird flu had made chicken into a rare delicacy? What if her culture was exclusively vegetarian? He'd finally settled on vegetarian egg rolls and rice noodles and hot and sour soup. He'd seen Hong Kong action movies in the store, so he knew Chinese culture still existed in her world, at least, and it was a safe bet that the food would be mostly the same.

"You are a *god*, Pete," she said, opening a paper container of noodles and wielding her chopsticks like a pro. "You know what I had for lunch today? A *pear*, and I had to steal it off my neighbor's tree. I got the crackers off a tray in the dining hall. You saved my life."

"Don't mention it. I'm really sorry I was so annoying the last couple of nights."

She waved her hand dismissively, mouth crammed with egg roll, and in her presence, Pete realized his new plan was impossible. He'd hoped to endear himself to her, and convince her to let him hang around until after closing, so he could... *stow away*, and travel to her world, where he could see *all* the movies, and maybe become the clerk's new roommate. It had all made sense at 3:00 in the morning the night before, and he'd spent most of the day thinking about nothing else, but now that he'd set his plan in motion he realized it was more theatrical than practical. It might work in a *movie*, but in life he didn't even know this woman's name, she wouldn't welcome him into her life, and even if she *did*, what would he do in her world? He spent all day processing applications, ordering transcripts, massaging a database, and filing things, but what would he do in her world? What if the computers there had totally different programming languages? What would he do for money, once his hypothetical giant sack of nickels ran out?

"I'm sorry, I never asked your name," he said.

"I'm Ally," she said. "Eat an egg roll, I feel like a pig."

Pete complied, and Ally came around the counter. "I've got something for you." She went to the big screen TV and switched it on. "We don't have time to watch the whole thing, but there's just enough time to see the last fifty minutes, the restored footage, before I have to close up." She turned on the DVD player, and *The Magnificent Ambersons* began.

"Oh, Ally, thanks," he said.

"Hey, your DVD player's busted, and you really *should* see this."

For the next fifty minutes, Pete watched. The cast was similar, with only one different actor that he noticed, and from everything he'd read, this was substantially the same as the lost footage he'd heard about in his world. Welles's genius was apparent even in the butchered RKO release, but here it was undiluted, a clarity of vision that was almost overwhelming, and this version was *sad*, profoundly so, a tale of glory and inevitable decline.

When it ended, Pete felt physically drained, and sublimely happy.

"Closing time, Pete," Ally said. "Thanks again for dinner. I'm a fiend for Chinese." She gently herded him toward the door as he thanked her, again and again. "Glad you liked it," she said. "We can talk about it tomorrow." She closed and locked the door, and Pete watched from a doorway across the street until the shop disappeared, just a few minutes after 10:00. The window *was* closing, the shop appearing for less time each night.

He'd just have to enjoy it while it lasted. You couldn't ask more of a miracle than it was willing to give.

The next night he brought kung pao chicken and asked what her favorite movies were. She led him to the Employee Picks shelf and showed him her selections. "It's mostly nostalgia, but I still love *The Lunch Bunch*—you know, the sequel to *The Breakfast Club*, set ten years later? Molly Ringwald's awesome in it. And *Return of the Jedi*, I know a lot of people hate it, but it's one of the best movies David Lynch ever directed, I thought *Dune* was a muddle, but he really got to the heart of the *Star Wars* universe, it's so much darker than *The Empire Strikes Back*. *Jason and the Argonauts* by Orson Welles, of course, that's on *everybody's* list..."

Pete found himself looking at her while she talked, instead of at the boxes of the movies she enthused over. He wanted to see them, of course, every one, but he wouldn't be able to, and really, he was talking to a woman from *another universe*, and that was as remarkable as anything he'd ever seen on a screen. She was smart, funny, and knew as much about movies as he did. He'd never dated much—he was more comfortable alone in the dark in front of a screen than he was sitting across from a woman at dinner, and his relationships seldom lasted more than a few dates when the women realized movies were his main mode of recreation. But with Ally—he could talk to her. Their obsessions were congruent and complementary.

Or maybe he was just trying to turn this miracle into some kind of theatrical romance.

"You look really beautiful when you talk about movies," he said.

"You're sweet, Mr. Nickels."

Pete came the next three nights, a few minutes later each time, as the door appeared for shorter periods of time. Ally talked to him about movies, incredulous at the bizarre gaps in his knowledge—"You've never heard of Sara Hansen? She's one of the greatest directors of all time!" (Pete wondered if she'd died young in his world, or never been born at all.) Ally had a fondness for bad science fiction movies, especially the many Ed Wood films starring Bela Lugosi, who had lived many years longer in Ally's world, rather than dying during the filming of *Plan 9 from Outer Space*. She liked good sci-fi movies, too, especially Ron Howard's *Ender's Game*. Pete regretted that he'd never see any of those films, beyond the snippets she showed him to illustrate her points, and he regretted even more that he'd soon be unable to see Ally at all, when the shop ceased to appear, as seemed inevitable. She understood character arcs, the use of color, the underappreciated skills of silent film actors, the bizarre audacity of pre-Hayes-Code-era films, the perils of voiceover, why an extended single-camera continuous scene was worth becoming rapturous about, why the animation of Ray Harryhausen was in some ways infinitely more satisfying than the slickest CGI. She was his *people*.

"Why do you like movies so much?" he asked on that third night, over a meal of Szechwan shrimp, her leaning on her side of the counter, he on his.

She chewed, thinking. "Somebody described the experience of reading great fiction as being caught up in a vivid, continuous dream. Someone else said comics were the perfect medium, because they're words and pictures, and you can do *anything* with words and pictures. I think movies are the most immediate and immersive form of fiction, and they do comics one better. People say movies are passive, or that the best movie isn't as good as the best book, and I say they're not watching the right movies, or else they're not watching them *right*. My life doesn't make a lot of sense to me, I'm hungry and lonely and cold a lot of the time. My parents are shit, I can't afford tuition for next semester, I don't know what I want to do when I graduate anyway. But when I see a great film, I feel like I understand life a little better, and when I see a not-so-great film, it at least makes me forget the shitty parts of my life for a couple of hours. Movies taught me to be brave, to be romantic, to stand up for myself, to not be treacherous, and those were all things my parents never taught me. Movies showed me there was more to the world than chores and whippings when I didn't do the chores good enough. I didn't have church or loving parents, but I had *movies*, cheap matinees when I cut school, videos after I worked and saved up enough to buy a TV and player of my own. I didn't have a mentor, but I had Obi-Wan Kenobi, and Jimmy Stewart in *It's a Wonderful Life*. Sometimes, sure, movies are a way to hide from life, but shit, sometimes you need to hide from life, to see a better life on the screen, or a life that makes your life not seem so bad. Movies taught me not to settle for less." She took a swig from her water bottle. "That's why I love movies."

"Wow," Pete said. "That's... wow."

"So," she said, looking at him oddly. "Why do you pretend to like movies?"

Pete frowned. "What? Pretend?"

"Hey, it's okay. You came in and said you were a big movie buff, but you don't even know who Sara Hansen is, you've never seen *Jason and the Argonauts*, you talk about actors starring in movies they didn't appear in... I mean, I figured you liked me, you didn't know how else to flirt with me or something, but I *like* you, and if you want to ask me out, you can, you don't have to be a movie trivia expert to impress me."

"I *do* like you," Pete said. "But I *love* movies. I really do."

"Pete... you thought Clark Gable was in *Gone with the Wind*." She shrugged. "Need I say more?"

Pete looked at the clock. He had fifteen minutes. "Wait here," he said. "I want to show you something."

He ran home. The run was getting easier. Maybe exercise wasn't such a bad idea. He filled a backpack with books from his reference shelves—*The*

Encyclopedia of Science Fiction Movies, the *AFI Film Guide*, the previous year's *Video and DVD Guide*, others—then ran back. Panting, he set the heavy bag on the counter. "Books," he gasped. "Read," gasp. "See you," gasp, "tomorrow."

"Okay, Pete," Ally said, raising her eyebrow in that way she had. "Whatever you say."

Pete lurched out of the store, still breathing hard, and when he turned to look back, the door had already disappeared. It wasn't even 10:00 yet. Time was running out, and even though Ally would soon leave his life forever, he couldn't let her think he was ignorant about their shared passion. The books might not be enough to convince her. Tomorrow, he'd show her something more.

Pete went in as soon as the door appeared, at nearly 9:30. Ally didn't waste time with pleasantries. She slammed down his copy of the *AFI Desk Reference* and said, "What the *hell* is going on?"

Pete took the bag off his shoulder, opened it, and withdrew his slim silver laptop, along with a CD wallet full of DVDs. "*Gone with the Wind*," he said, inserting a disc into the laptop, calling up the DVD controls, and fast forwarding to the first scene with Clark Gable.

Ally stared at the LCD screen, and Pete watched the reflected colors move against her face. Gable's voice, though tinny through the small speakers, was resonant as always.

Pete closed the laptop gently. "I *do* know movies," he said. "Just not exactly the same ones you do."

"This, those books, *you*... you're from another world. It's like... like..."

"Something out of the *Twilight Zone*, I know. But actually, *you're* from another world. Every night, for an hour or so—less, lately—the door to Impossible Dreams appears on my street.

"What? I don't understand."

"Come on," he said, and held out his hand. She took it, and he led her out the door. "Look," he said, gesturing to the bakery next door, the gift shop on the other side, the bike repair place across the street."

Ally sagged back against the door, half-retreating back inside the shop. "This isn't right. This isn't what's supposed to be here."

"Go on back in," he said. "The store has been appearing later and vanishing sooner every night, and I'd hate for you to get stranded here."

"Why is this happening?" Ally said, still holding his hand.

"I don't know," Pete said. "Maybe there's no reason. Maybe in a movie there would be, but..."

"Some movies reassure us that life makes sense," Ally said. "And some movies remind us that life doesn't make any sense at all." She exhaled roughly. "And some things don't have anything to do with movies."

"Bite your tongue," Pete said. "Listen, keep the laptop. The battery should run for a couple of hours. There's a spare in the bag, all charged up, which should be good for a couple more hours. Watching movies really sucks up the power, I'm afraid. I don't know if you'll be able to find an adapter to charge the laptop in your world—the standards are different. But you can see a couple of movies at least. I gave you all my favorite DVDs, great stuff by Hayao Miyazaki, Beat Takeshi, Wes Anderson, some classics... take your pick."

"Pete..."

He leaned over and kissed her cheek. "It's been great talking to you these past few nights." He tried to think of what he'd say if this was the last scene in a movie, his *Casablanca* farewell moment, and a dozen appropriate quotes sprang to mind. He dismissed all of them. "I'm going to miss you, Ally."

"Thank you, Pete," she said, and went, reluctantly, back into Impossible Dreams. She looked at him from the other side of the glass, and he raised his hand to wave just as the door disappeared.

Pete didn't let himself go back the next night, because he knew the temptation to go into the store would be too great, and it might only be open for ten minutes this time. But after pacing around his living room for hours, he finally went out after 10:00 and walked to the place the store had been, thinking maybe she'd left a note, wishing for some closure, some final-reel gesture, a rose on the doorstep, something.

But there was nothing, no door, no note, no rose, and Pete sat on the sidewalk, wishing he'd thought to photograph Ally, wondering which movies she'd decided to watch, and what she'd thought of them.

"Hey, Mr. Nickels."

Pete looked up. Ally stood there, wearing a red coat, his laptop bag hanging from her shoulder. She sat down beside him. "I didn't think you'd show, and I did *not* relish the prospect of wandering in a strange city all night with only fifty dollars in nickels to keep me warm. Some of the street names are the same as where I'm from, but not enough of them for me to figure out where you lived."

"Ally! What are you doing here?"

"You gave me those *books*," she said, "and they all talk about *Citizen*

Kane by Orson Welles, how it transformed cinema." She punched him gently in the shoulder. "But you didn't give me the DVD!"

"But... Everyone's seen *Citizen Kane!*"

"Not where I'm from. The print was destroyed. Hearst knew the movie was based on his life, and he made a deal with the studio, the guards looked the other way, and someone destroyed the film. Welles had to start over from nothing, and he made *Jason and the Argonauts* instead. But you've got *Citizen Kane!* How could I *not* come see it?"

"But Ally... you might not be able to go back."

She laughed, then leaned her head on his shoulder. "I don't plan to go back. There's nothing for me there."

Pete felt a fist of panic clench in his chest. "This isn't a movie," he said.

"No," Ally said. "It's better than that. It's my life."

"I just don't know—"

Ally patted his leg. "Relax, Pete. I'm not asking you to take me in. Unlike Blanche DuBois—played by Jessica Tandy, not Vivien Leigh, where I'm from—I don't depend on the kindness of strangers. I ran away from home when I was fifteen, and never looked back. I've started from nothing before, with no friends or prospects or ID, and I can do it again."

"You're not starting from nothing," Pete said, putting his arm around her. "Definitely not." The lights weren't going to come up, the curtain wasn't coming down; this wasn't the end of a movie. For once, Pete liked his life better than the vivid continuous dream of the screen. "Come on. Let's go watch *Citizen Kane.*"

They stood and walked together. "Just out of curiosity," he said. "Which movies did you watch on the laptop?"

"Oh, none of them. I thought it would be more fun watching them with you."

Pete laughed. "Ally, I think this could be the beginning of a beautiful friendship."

She cocked her head and raised her eyebrows. "You sound like you're quoting something," she said, "but I don't know what."

"We've got a lot of watching to do," he said.

"We've got a lot of *everything* to do," Ally replied.

LACHRYMOSE AND THE GOLDEN EGG

The woman in the wood was fair-skinned, white-gowned, and altogether lovely, but I didn't let her beauty lull me. In the Forest of Intangibles, things are seldom what they seem. That might be the fundamental truth of doing Vision, of coming to this place—you're lying on a couch somewhere, dying, but in your mind you live life richly in peril and beauty.

The woman stepped from the shadows onto that winding, redwood-crowded path, close enough for me to see the iridescence of her eyes and to smell the roses on her breath, which made me suspicious, because what kind of woman eats roses? She looked fuzzy, like a soft-focus photograph. She had red hair. They often do.

"Foul temptress?" I said, stepping back, clanking in my armor. A suit of plate mail often appears when I'm startled. I wished the armor away and replaced it with soft green leggings and a deerskin shirt. "Wily seductress?"

"Damsel in distress." She leaned against a tree, hands clasped before her.

I clutched my stick and looked around. "Immediate distress, or general distress?" I worried about ogres, or killbots. They often menace damsels, and when the wind's wrong, you can't smell them coming, neither rotten meat nor engine oil. It's hard to hurt an ogre or a killbot with a staff, but I'm useless with a sword. I used a blade on my first few outings, but after chopping off my feet six times, I switched to a stick.

"General distress. I seek an artifact. If I do not find it, I will die."

"What sort of artifact?" I'd just finished a war, so a quest sounded fun. "A heavy one, I bet, and you need me to carry it for you."

She glared, straightening. Her image sharpened. Women here come in two varieties: Princess Beautiful and Hag Ugly. Only hair color and the number of warts vary. My damsel fell into the first category.

"I seek the golden egg. I am *quite* capable of carrying it myself. I hoped to enlist your aid as a warrior."

"Rogue warrior and occasional thief, actually," I said. "My name is Lachrymose."

She covered her mouth in surprise. "Lachrymose! *The* Lachrymose?"

I bowed. "None other. And I will gladly join you, my fair—"

"Get up, Larry!" my sister Franny said, slapping my face. Back to the real world, I blinked and groaned. She put down the hypodermic she'd just used to inject me with anti-Vision, neutralizing my drug, my therapy, my escape.

"What? I just started a new thread!"

"You've been under for two days. It's almost time for your appointment." She took the IV needle from my elbow.

I covered my eyes. The dingy walls, the pebbly plaster, and the misshapen hook-rugs depressed me after the glories of the Forest of Intangibles. "I can miss it this time. I'll go next week."

"You're nearabout out of money," she said.

My stomach rumbled. I uncovered my eyes. Franny handed me a tube of vitamin-packed protein mush. "All right," I said. "I'll go. What've you been doing?"

"Nothing." Franny's in her twenties, but she can pass for fifteen, and she gave me an innocent blue-eyed look. "Sitting around. Anything interesting happen this outing?"

"There's always something interesting. You should try it."

She shook her head. "No thanks. I value my brain cells."

"I defeated the Barbarian Chieftain of the Plains of Squalor. His people call me 'He Who Lacks Remorse.' I had just met up with a sexy damsel when you woke me."

She giggled. "I looked up 'lachrymose' in the dictionary this weekend. It means 'weepy.' 'Given to shedding tears.' Lachrymose, rogue crybaby."

I sighed. "Yeah, I know what it means. I must've read it years ago, without knowing what it meant, and my subconscious thought it would make a good name. It doesn't mean weepy when I'm out, though. It's just my name, striking fear into the hearts and all that."

She ignored me. "Eat your mush and get to your appointment on time, or I'll get fired."

"I won't fire you."

"They randomly monitor us, you know. Dr. Hammond can dismiss me, get my license revoked, and you couldn't do anything about it."

"Yeah yeah yeah." I stood, unkinking my muscles. "I shouldn't have given you this job."

"No other nurse would let you go out on Vision so much."

"True. I guess I'll keep you." I did a few jumping jacks, then started jogging in place.

"What's this?" Franny said. She lifted a long wooden staff, like a dowel, from the corner.

I stopped jogging. "A quarterstaff. How'd it get here? I use one when I'm out, it's Lachrymose's weapon." I took it, feeling the heft. I'd never held one before, really.

"Are there gaps in your memory?" Franny asked, suddenly nurse-professional.

I laughed, uneasy, and looked at the floor. "Don't know. Can't remember. I guess so, since I don't remember getting this." I leaned the stick in the corner.

"I don't remember seeing it before," she said.

I shrugged. "I'll get a regenerative shot today, grow some new brain cells. Don't worry."

"Maybe you shouldn't do so much Vision," she said. "The deterioration wouldn't happen so fast if you didn't compound it—"

I held up my hand. I didn't say anything, but she stopped talking. I got my jacket and left for the clinic. I could sense Franny watching me with worried eyes.

"How's the leech business, Doc?" I asked.

Dr. Montressor laughed dutifully and hung the blood bag on a hook. He gave me a rubber ball to squeeze while my blood (worth more, per ounce, than gold) dripped out.

"Relax," he said. "You always get so tense." He went to his desk and sat down. "We lost two producers over the weekend, so the market rate's gone up. You'll get a bigger check than usual."

"Great news," I said, fake-smiling. I don't know why he tells me when another producer dies. Reminders of impending death can't be good for my mental health.

"You won't last much longer yourself if you keep using Vision," he said.

Doc's built like a side of beef, only flabbier. He probably played football when the world was young. Now he runs the Hammond's Disease Research Institute, a Very Important Man. He'd never let Vision or any other pollutant into his bloodstream. But he doesn't need to escape reality like we producers do.

"I don't have much longer either way," I said. "I'm thirty-three." In five or six more years, Hammond's would get to my involuntary functions, and I'd forget how to breathe. Not something I liked to think about. "How goes the quest for a cure?"

"We're making progress." He wrote something on a clipboard.

"How about the synthetic Serum?"

"Lots of promising work being done."

The usual answers. Some say the Institute isn't looking for a cure at all, or that they've found one and won't release it until they can synthesize the Serum. I don't know. Doc's not friendly, but I can't believe he'd watch us die just to keep the Serum supply coming.

"Tell me—"

"Let me ask the questions. Have you had any symptoms?"

I thought about the mysterious quarterstaff. "Forgetting stuff, maybe, losing time. I'm not sure."

He grunted. "The Vision does that. Memory loss is only a symptom in late-stage Hammond's. You might have hallucinations at this point, but anything else is due to Vision. You should stop using it. People depend on you."

"People depend on the Serum." I wiggled the tube in my arm. "Other people have Hammond's, they're churning out super-antibodies. Let them stay sober." I looked away. Normally I'm easygoing, but finding the quarterstaff made me edgy. I hadn't suffered any symptoms before, of Hammond's disease *or* Vision killing my brain cells. I thought I'd adjusted years ago to the idea of dying young, but maybe I just avoided thinking about it. Going out on Vision helps you avoid thinking about things. "Stop bugging me. Vision gets me through."

"Your entire life is ruled by chemicals, Larry. The one we get from your blood, that saves lives, and the one you shoot into your arm, to help hide you from life. It's funny."

"Yeah, hilarious. I should take my show on the road."

Doc withdrew the needle and put the blood bag in his silver refrigeration unit. They do something to the blood, extract the Serum from it, and send it to save the world. The Serum cures Parkinson's disease and, with regular administration, stops epilepsy. It halts a dozen different cancers and speeds up human metabolism. They're still finding uses for it.

My jacked-up immune system works almost flawlessly. I don't get colds or infections or anything. Just Hammond's disease, gradually turning my gray matter to mush. Having Hammond's is like finding the fountain of youth and realizing it's running through lead pipes, poisoned.

I took my money and walked home, ready for another Vision-shot. *That's* the wonder drug if you ask me, and it comes from Colombian laboratories, not some guy's bloodstream. It doesn't keep me alive, but it keeps me from wanting to die.

Back in the Forest, with the damsel. The background wavered for a moment, then came into focus. I've used Vision for a long time, and believing in the world comes naturally. Vision induces a prolonged dream state, but the dreams are lucid and more vivid than opium fantasies. I can exercise some control over the environment, but not much. My subconscious crafts the world. I read fantasy and horror stories to get material, but sometimes unexpected stuff rises from memory-depths I can't consciously access.

"—lady, in your quest," I finished.

"There are many travails ahead, Lachrymose."

"I have a stout stick and a strong heart. Let's begin." She nodded, and we walked. "Why do you require the egg? Are you under a curse only its touch can cure? Will you be killed by a bad fairy if you don't find it?"

"No, no. The golden egg bestows immortality, and without that, I will surely die."

I stopped twirling my stick. "What do you mean?"

Patiently, as if explaining to a child, "If I do not obtain immortality, my life is forfeit, for eventually I will die."

"But not anytime soon. So you aren't a damsel in distress after all."

"Not *immediate* distress, no."

So. A very forward-thinking damsel.

A day later, after a few typical altercations with monsters and brigands, we came to a castle. Normally reality doesn't intrude when I'm on an outing (Lachrymose the Rogue acts in the moment), but I wished I could achieve immortality as easily in the real world as I could here.

"This is the home of Montrose, the evil Ninja King," she said.

I tried not to giggle. This wasn't the first time my subconscious had mixed together incompatible elements. Once I'd fought dinosaurs and aliens in the same outing, and another time I'd battled Electrified Robots and the Slime God, working together for my destruction. Now I faced a Ninja King in a black gothic castle. "He has the egg?"

"Yes, but surely hidden away."

"Then we'll have to find it." I twirled my staff.

"You will have to kill him first. And, having the golden egg, he may be immortal."

"We'll figure it out." I went to the massive iron doors and banged on them with my quarterstaff. The door rang like a gong. "Montrose! Let us in, villain, and face your death!" I waited.

The doors didn't open, but a black, hairy man jumped from a high window. He landed in a crouch and grinned at me, yellow teeth in a furred face. He snarled, half-gorilla, half-werewolf. He whipped out a wickedly sharp katana. He wore a red headband, and his eyes wept pus.

"Montrose!" I shouted, lifting my staff to a defensive position.

"No," my damsel said. "That is Griffonious, the Ninja King's bodyguard and chief lieutenant."

The big ape came at me with his sword, and I whipped my staff down across his—

"Your timing sucks!" I shouted at Franny when I woke.

"Wasn't me." She didn't look up from her magazine. "It wore off naturally. I think your new supplier cut this batch with something, you were only under for about thirty hours."

I buy Vision in unusually (illegally) strong doses, and I'd hooked up with a new dealer for this batch. It was sufficiently strong, cutting out bleed-through from the real world, but it lasted only half as long as usual. I'd have to go back to my old supplier.

"Were you about to get lucky with your damsel?"

"No. I was fighting a ninja were-gorilla."

"Mmm. You hear about this 'Applied Psychomechanics' stuff?"

"No."

She flipped to a page in her magazine. "Some researchers think Hammond's disease activates latent psychic powers. That people who have the disease or use the Serum can be telepathic, telekinetic, stuff like that."

"Jesus. I've got enough trouble inside my own head. Why would I want to see into someone else's?"

Franny grunted. "Could you go to the store and get some milk, since you're up? The walk would do you good."

I grumbled. "Nurse's orders," she said. "You don't exercise enough."

"Last time I try to help out somebody in the family. I could pay a regular nurse to leave me alone."

"You wish."

We Serum-producers, being so valuable to the medical community, have to be attended by a live-in nurse. The doc pays for it, and I pulled some strings to get Franny hired. It's nice having a friendly face around, even if she does get weepy sometimes, thinking how I'm going to die.

I walked two blocks and stopped. When I'd passed by a few days ago, an empty lot bordered this street. Now a big black castle filled the space. The castle, only half-complete, resembled Montrose's, from my outing. Workers on scaffolding mortared stones. "What the hell's this?" I called.

"Some rich doctor's new house!" a stonemason called back. "Ain't it the damnedest thing?"

I went to the store, got the milk, and came back by a different route. First the quarterstaff shows up, and now the castle. Hallucinations? But other people saw this stuff, too. Unless I was hallucinating their reactions.

Time to take more Vision. I couldn't handle the real world in large doses, especially when reality wasn't behaving like it should.

—blade, spinning it from his hands. Griffonious growled and somersaulted toward me. I threw my staff, jumped over him, and did a handspring. I landed perfectly. As he stood, I snatched up my staff and struck him behind the knees, producing a nice crack, and he fell face-down.

The damsel lifted the hem of her dress and stepped on Griffonious's head. She drove his face into the dirt, which suddenly turned to mud. Griffonious struggled and grunted, but she held him down, seemingly without effort, until he stopped moving.

Impressive. "Nice trick with the mud."

"You're not the only one with magic, Lachrymose." She cocked her head. "I've always wondered, how did you get your name? You don't strike me as the crying type."

Before I could invent a suitably apocryphal answer, someone bellowed from the castle. A black-clad ninja stood on the ramparts. "Who dares attack my keep?" he shouted. His voice was muffled by his mask, but still seemed familiar. I couldn't place it.

"Lachrymose the Rogue and, uh..." I looked to the damsel for her name, but she didn't say anything, just put her hands on her hips and glared.

"We've come for the egg, Montrose," she said.

He put his hands on his belly and laughed. *He's pretty pudgy for a ninja,* I thought. "You'll never have it! I've hidden it below my castle, in the Cellar of Icy Madness! You can't possibly breach my gates!"

I glanced at Griffonious and wrinkled my nose. Were-apes rot fast. I'd forgotten that. "Maybe the ape has a key in his pocket," I said hopefully.

"Not necessary," she said. "We'll fly."

She touched my elbow and we rose from the ground, slowly at first, then faster. We rushed toward Montrose. He stumbled back. Only his shocked, wide eyes showed above his mask. He hadn't expected such a direct approach.

I held on to my stick and tried not to get queasy. Most damsels don't do much besides get kidnapped and look pretty. I preferred my damsel to the standard variety. She was the sort of woman I'd like to get involved with in the *real* world, if I wasn't going to die in a year or three.

Thoughts of reality don't belong in an outing, so I let them go. I put my foot on the rampart and leapt for Montrose. He escaped down a trapdoor before I could reach him.

My damsel led the way down, through dim rooms filled with hags and ghosts and, yes, ninjas. She dispelled the supernatural creatures with her spells and I dispatched the others with my staff. We reached the bottom floor and found Montrose standing before the entrance to the Cellar of Icy Madness. Frosty air blew from the recessed doorway. He cackled and drew down his mask.

Revealing Dr. Montressor. His image, anyway. I must've had a lot of repressed bitterness and suspicion for my subconscious to cast my doctor in this role. "Follow me, if you dare!" He ran down the cellar stairs.

I lifted my staff with a snarl and started for the frigid entrance. The damsel put her hand on my arm. "Wait," she said, "before we go I want to—"

Franny again, with the anti-Vision. I sighed. "You know, once upon a time I could finish a thread and wake up between storylines. Not anymore."

"Time for your appointment. You want me to walk with you?"

I didn't look forward to going into the world, but I didn't want Franny to worry. "No, it's only a few blocks. I'll be fine."

I got to the office and sat in the waiting room. Brass lamps, bland landscapes on the wall, white carpet. All very tasteful and not at all homey. The nurse apologized for making me wait. "Dr. Monstressor's with another patient."

I twiddled my thumbs and read a fishing magazine. I heard Doc's voice and looked up.

My damsel walked at his side. I recognized her instantly. She had frizzier hair than she did on the outings, and shadows bagged under her eyes. Even so, she looked good. She thanked the doctor and went toward the exit. She paused with her hand on the doorknob, frowning at me, then shook her head and went on.

I swallowed. "Hey, Doc," I said. "Who was that?"

"Hmm? A new producer, just got diagnosed a few months ago. This was her third or fourth draining. She says she's been hallucinating, and she was worried about the accelerated strain of Hammond's disease, but she does Vision, so it's probably just that." He grunted. "'Just that.' As if that isn't enough."

I didn't talk as he drained me. I thought about Vision, the collective unconscious, the Serum, and telepathy. I wondered if Doc was having a new house built, a big ostentatious Gothic folly, but I didn't ask. I thought about all sorts of crazy shit, to be honest, but I couldn't make it fit together.

When the doc put my blood bag in his metal refrigerator, I thought I saw a golden gleam on one of the shelves. But I wasn't sure, and I didn't want to ask about it.

"— kiss you. We've fought together this far, and I've come to care for you, rogue."

"And I for you, damsel." She was definitely the woman I'd seen at Doc's office. Had I seen her before, and subconsciously cast her in this role? That seemed more likely than the possibility of us somehow Visioning *together*. This wasn't a massively multiplayer RPG—this was the territory inside my mind. Besides, if she was the woman from the office, why hadn't she recognized me?

As I thought about it, I realized that she couldn't have recognized me. Lachrymose doesn't look much like Larry, the *real* me. Lachrymose looks like the guy who played Robin Hood in the old movies, with a thin mustache and a twinkle in his eye. The real me is a normal brown-haired brown-eyed average-height sort. "Before you kiss me," I said, "I must reveal my true face. I have traveled in disguise for years, but you deserve to see me as I am."

I wanted to know if I'd lost my mind. I concentrated and changed my appearance to match the guy I saw in the mirror every few days, when I wasn't out on Vision.

Her eyes widened. She opened her mouth, but no sounds emerged. It's hard to talk about reality from inside an outing, almost impossible, but she recognized me.

That, or my subconscious created the illusion that this Vision-construct recognized me. Multilevel mental breakdown and nested hallucinations can be pretty confusing.

Before she spoke, a dozen ninjas burst literally from the walls, bricks and mortar exploding outward as they came. They screeched and whirled various nasty weapons. I grabbed the damsel's hand and we raced down the cellar stairs. The door slammed shut behind us, cutting off the ninja pursuit.

Those ninjas came at a convenient time, I thought. My subconscious must have been trying to protect me from an awkward moment. I glanced at the damsel. *Or maybe her subconscious was protecting her.*

The Cellar of Icy Madness was cold, the kind of cold that makes the outer layer of your skin feel like chapped leather. We shivered and hurried down the stairs. "So this egg," I said, "is there enough for two?"

"Would you share immortality with me?"

"I wouldn't turn it down."

"I don't know exactly how it works. The tales vary. Some believe it is the rare Phoenix egg, and can be used only once. Others say it can be used to decant the elixir vitae, the elixir of eternal life. I suspect it can be used only once, and I don't think Montrose has used it."

"Why do you say that?"

"If he were immortal, why would he flee and send his minions after us?"

I wanted to say, "Because this is an outing, a Vision-trip, and it's more exciting that way." Instead I said, "You're right. But why wouldn't he use it?"

"Another legend says the golden egg can only be used by one with a love-filled heart. Montrose's heart is cold. The egg would poison him."

"Right you are." Montrose stood at the bottom of the stairs. We'd reached the lowest level of the Cellar of Icy Madness. He held the golden egg, a gleaming ellipsoid bigger than a baseball, in one hand. "But if I cannot have immortality, no one will!" He lifted the egg high overhead, as if to dash it to the floor.

"No!" the damsel and I shouted, and Montrose flung the egg—

"Already?" I shivered.

"Yeah." Franny put down the needle.

"How long was I out?"

"A week. That must've been some super-strong Vision."

I rubbed my forehead. The golden egg, immortality, flung to the Cellar's floor—I couldn't stand to think about it.

I went to the doc's office for the blood-drain. I sneaked glances at his specimen refrigerator the whole time. When he put away the blood bag, I distinctly saw gold inside. "I'm out of anti-Vision, Doc. Want to give me some, take it out of my payment?"

He made a face. "Sure." He left the room.

I opened his refrigerator. Icy wind blew into my face. There it was, the golden egg, nestled among beakers and racks of test tubes. *It can't be real*, I thought. *I'm hallucinating.* I picked up the egg, and found it fragile and lighter than I'd expected. I slipped it into my jacket pocket. Doc probably wouldn't notice the bulge. He might not even know about the egg. He wasn't really the ninja king—just a guy making a living on my death.

The doc didn't suspect anything. I took the anti-Vision and the money and left.

When I got home, Franny said, "Going under again? Or I could make a meatloaf, if you want some real food."

"I'd like that." I put the golden egg in the refrigerator, in the vegetable drawer under some broccoli.

"Really?"

"Yeah. I think I'm going to lay off the Vision for a while."

After dinner I stood in the living room and twirled my staff. I dropped it a lot, but I had fun. I went to bed, to ordinary sleep, for the first time in ages. I had dreams, not Visions. Montrose was there, and the damsel, and Franny, and the were-ape, and a cast of thousands. I dreamed of golden fruit, a rising Phoenix, and men in star-patterned robes boiling lion's blood in beakers.

I woke early and went to the kitchen. I poured a glass of milk. Franny sat reading the paper at the table. She looked irritated at my intrusion. She usually had the run of the house, aside from emptying my piss-bag. She'd have to get used to me staying awake. I didn't want to go on another outing anytime soon, not if it meant seeing the egg smashed and Montrose triumphant. Could the damsel, if she was really the woman I'd seen in Doc's office, go to the Cellar of Icy Madness without me? I hoped not. I hoped the egg survived, whole, in both worlds.

Someone knocked on the door. I answered before Franny could.

The damsel stood in the hallway. She wore yellow stretchpants, and I couldn't look at her enough. "You don't know me," she said. "I got your name and address from Dr.—"

"Franny!" I shouted, startling the damsel and my sister both. I made a shooing motion toward the door. "Out, Franny, out, take a walk, go, go, go."

"Larry, what are you—" She saw the damsel and lifted an eyebrow. "Hey there."

"Go!"

She took her purse and kissed me on the cheek. "Be good, brother," she said, and slipped out.

"I've got the egg," I said when the damsel came in.

She leaned against the kitchen counter as if she couldn't support her own weight. "It's real?"

"I hope so. If you can see it, too, then I'll believe it."

I took down a frying pan and turned on the stove. My hands were shaking

"Wait." She stepped toward me. "We never had a chance to kiss. The ninjas came."

"I remember." I put my arms around her, not too awkwardly. Her breath didn't smell of roses, but it was nice. After the kiss broke I said, "This is really stupid. We've both got Hammond's. I don't have much longer to live. You're younger, but..."

"There's the egg."

I shook my head. "It's crazy. We've got to be hallucinating, we're Vision-heads."

"Maybe we're only seeing the truth in a different way."

I opened my mouth, then closed it. Was it a golden egg, or did I just see it that way? "You think it might be the cure. The cure that isn't supposed to exist. That we read the doc's mind somehow, and found out about it."

"I don't think anything. I've never been in this situation before. I haven't even seen the egg, if it is an egg."

"I'll show you." I opened the refrigerator, dug under the broccoli, and lifted out the egg. I held it wordlessly.

"That's a lovely potato," she said. "Where's the egg?"

I relaxed my hands and let the egg fall. A potato. I wanted to cry.

She shouted and dove, catching the egg before it hit the floor. She looked up at me, and I saw the woman who'd propelled us through the air, the woman who'd shoved a were-ape's face in the mud. "Crazy! I was kidding! I thought you could take a joke! Yes, it's the golden egg, I see it!"

I closed my eyes. I could react in one of two ways. One involved shouting and anger. I chose the other. "You're too much. You really had me going."

She grunted and handed me the egg. "I like them scrambled."

I felt its roundness. If it looks like a golden egg, and it feels like a golden egg, let it be a golden egg. "A woman after my own heart."

I lifted the egg over the pan and suddenly everything shifted. The cold air of the Cellar of Icy Madness chilled me. I held my quarterstaff, with the damsel at my side. Montrose cackled and flung the egg down before we could reach him, before we could possibly reach him, and the egg struck—

—and broke into the pan, where it sizzled. The enormous yolk gleamed, brass-colored. I set the shell fragments aside reverently. When Franny got home, would she see pieces of golden shell, or the shards of a glass test tube?

The damsel, whose name I still didn't know, looked into the pan with me.

"Maybe we should have it sunny-side up," I said. "We can share the yolk."

"Sure." She took my hand and squeezed it. "And tomorrow, I'll make breakfast."

DREAM ENGINE

The Stolen State, The Magpie City, The Nex, The Ax—this is the place where I live, and hover, and chafe in my service; the place where I take my small bodiless pleasures where I may. Nexington-on-Axis is the proper name, the one the Regent uses in his infrequent public addresses, but most of the residents call it other things, and my—prisoner? partner? charge? trust?—my *associate*, Howlaa Moor, calls it The Cage, at least when zie is feeling sorry for zimself.

The day the fat man began his killing spree, I woke early, while Howlaa slept on, in a human form that snored. I looked down on the streets of our neighborhood, home to low-level government servants and the wretchedly poor. The sky was bleak, and rain filled the potholes. The royal orphans had snatched a storm from somewhere, which was good, as the district's roof gardens needed rain.

I saw a messenger approach through the cratered street. I didn't recognize his species—he was bipedal, with a tail, and his skin glistened like a salamander's, though his gait was birdlike—but I recognized the red plume jutting from his headband, which allowed him to go unmolested through this rough quarter.

"Howlaa," I said. "Wake. A messenger approaches."

Howlaa stirred on zir heaped bedding, furs and silks piled indiscriminately with burlap and canvas and even coarser fabrics, because Howlaa's kind enjoy having as much tactile variety as possible. And, I suspect, because zie likes to taunt me with reminders of the physical sensations I can not experience.

"Shushit, Wisp," zie said. My name is not Wisp, but that is what zie calls me, and I have long since given up on changing the habit. "The messenger could be coming for anyone. There are four score civil servants on this block alone. Let me sleep." Zie picked up a piece of half-eaten globe-fruit and hurled it at me. It passed through me without effect, of course, but

185

it annoyed me, which was Howlaa's intent.

"The messenger has a *red plume*, skinshifter," I said, making my voice resonate, making it creep and rattle in zir tissues and bones, making sleep or shutting me out impossible.

"Ah. Blood business, then." Howlaa threw off furs, rose, and stretched, zir arms growing more joints and bends as zie moved, unfolding like origami in flesh. I could not help a little subvocal gasp of wonder as zir skin rippled and shifted and settled into Howlaa's chosen morning shape. I have no body, and am filled with wonder at Howlaa's mastery of zir own.

Howlaa settled into the form of a male Nagalinda, a biped with long limbs, a broad face with opalescent eyes, and a lipless mouth full of triangular teeth. Nagalinda are fearsome creatures with a reputation for viciousness, though I have found them no more uniformly monstrous than any other species; their cultural penchant for devouring their enemies has earned them a certain amount of notoriety even in the Ax, though. Howlaa liked to take on such forms to terrify government messengers if zie could. Such behavior was insubordinate, but it was such a small rebellion that the Regent didn't even bother to reprimand Howlaa for it—and having zir rude behavior so completely disregarded only served to annoy Howlaa further.

The Regent knew how to control us, which levers to tug and which leads to jerk, which is why he was the Regent, and we were in his employ. I often think that the Regent controls the city as skillfully as Howlaa controls zir own form, and it is a pretty analogy, for the Ax is in its way as mutable as Howlaa's body.

The buzzer buzzed. "Why don't you get that?" Howlaa said, grinning. "Oh, yes, right, no hands, makes opening the door tricky. I'll get it, then."

Howlaa opened the door to the messenger, who didn't find zim especially terrifying. The messenger was too busy being frightened of the fat man for Howlaa to scare him.

I floated. Howlaa ambled. The messenger hurried ahead, hurried back, hurried ahead again, like an anxious pet. Howlaa could not be rushed, and I went at the pace Howlaa chose, of necessity, but I sympathized with the messenger's discomfort. Being bound so closely to the Regent's will made even tardiness cause for bone-deep anxiety.

"He's a fat human, with no shirt on, carrying a giant battle-axe, and he chopped up a brace of Beetleboys armed with dung-muskets?"

Howlaa's voice was blandly curious, but I knew zie was incredulous, just as I was.

"So the messenger reports," I said.

"And then he disappeared, in full view of everyone in Moth Moon Market?"

"Why do you repeat things?" I asked.

"I just wondered if it would sound more plausible coming from my own mouth. But even my vast reserves of personal conviction fail to lend the story weight. Perhaps the Regent made it up, and plans to execute me when I arrive." Howlaa sounded almost hopeful. "Would you tell me, little Wisp, if that were his plan?"

Howlaa imagines I have a closer relationship with the Regent than zie does zimself, and zie has always believed that I willingly became a civil servant. Zie does not know that I am bound to community service for my past crimes, just as Howlaa zimself is, and I let zim persist in this misapprehension because it allows me to act superior and, on occasion, even condescend, which is one of the small pleasures available to we bodiless ones. "I think you are still too valuable and tractable for the Regent to kill," I said.

"Perhaps. But I find the whole tale rather unlikely."

Howlaa walked along with zir mouth open, letting the rain fall into zir mouth, tasting the weather of other worlds, looking at the clouds.

I looked everywhere at once, because it is my duty and burden to look, and record, and, when called upon, to bear witness. I never sleep, but every day I go into a small dark closet and look at the darkness for hours, to escape my own senses. So I saw everything in the streets we passed, for the thousandth time, and though details were changed, the essential nature of the neighborhood was the same. The buildings were mostly brute and functional, structures stolen from dockyards, ghettoes, and public housing projects, taken from the worst parts of the thousand thousand worlds that grind around and above Nexington-on-Axis in the complicated gearwork that supports the structure of all the universes. We live in the pivot, and all times and places turn past us eventually, and we residents of the Ax grab what we can from those worlds in the moment of their passing—and so our city grows, and our traders trade, and our government prospers.

But sometimes we grasp too hastily, and the great snatch-engines tended by the Regent's brood of royal orphans become overzealous in their cross-dimensional thieving, and we take things we didn't want after all, things the other worlds must be glad to be rid of. Unfortunate imports of that sort can be a problem, because they sometimes disrupt the profitable chaos of the city, which the Regent cannot allow. Solving such problems is Howlaa's job.

We passed out of our neighborhood into a more flamboyant one, filled with emptied crypts, tombs, and other oddments of necropoleis, from chipped marble angels to fragments of ornamental wrought iron. To counteract this funereal air, the residents had decorated their few square blocks as brightly and ostentatiously as possible, so that great papier-mâché birds clung to railings, and tombs were painted yellow and red and blue. In the central plaza, where the pavement was made of ancient headstones laid flat, a midday market was well underway. The pale vendors sold the usual trinkets, obtained with privately owned, low-yield snatch-engines, along with the district's sole specialty, the exotic mushrooms grown in cadaver-earth deep in the underground catacombs. Citizens shied away from the red-plumed messenger, bearer of bloody news, and shied further away at the sight of Howlaa, because Nagalinda seldom strayed from their own part of the city, except on errands of menace.

As we neared the edge of the plaza there was a great crack and whoosh, and a wind whipped through the square, eddying the weakly linked charged particles that made up my barely physical form.

A naked man appeared in the center of the square. He did not rise from a hidden trapdoor, did not drop from a passing airship, did not slip in from an adjoining alley. Anyone else might have thought he'd arrived by such an avenue, but I see in all directions, to the limits of vision, and the man was simply *there.*

Such magics were not unheard of, but they were never associated with someone like this. He appeared human, about six feet tall, bare-chested, and obese, pale skin smeared with blood. He was bald, and his features were brutish, almost like a child's clay figure of a man.

He held an absurd sword in his right hand, the blade as long as he was tall, but curved like a scimitar in a theatrical production about air-pirates, and it appeared to be made of *gold*, an impractical metal for weaponry. When he smiled, his lips peeled back to show an amazing array of yellow stump-teeth. He reared back his right arm and swung the sword, striking a merrow-woman swaddled all over in wet towels, nearly severing her arm. The square plunged into chaos, with vendors, customers, and passers-by screaming and fleeing in all directions, while the fat man kept swinging his sword, moving no more than a step or two in any direction, chopping people down as they ran.

"The reports were accurate after all," Howlaa said. "I'll go sort this." The messenger stood behind zim, whimpering, tugging at zir arm, trying to get zim to leave.

"*No*," I said. "We were ordered to report to the Regent, and that's what we'll do."

Howlaa spoke with exaggerated patience. "The Regent will only tell me to find and kill this man. Why not spare myself the walk, and kill him *now*? Or do you think the Regent would prefer that I let him kill more of the city's residents?"

We both knew the Regent was uninterested in the well-being of individual citizens—more residents were just a snatch-and-grab away, after all—but I could tell Howlaa would not be swayed. I considered invoking my sole real power over zim, but I was under orders to take that extreme step only in the event that Howlaa tried to escape the Ax or harm one of the royal orphans. "I do not condone this," I said.

"I don't care." Howlaa strode into the still-flurrying mass of people. In a few moments he was within range of the fat man's swinging sword. Howlaa ducked under the man's wild swings, and reached up with a long arm to grab the man's wrist. By now most of the people able to escape the square had done so, and I had a clear view of the action.

The fat man looked down at Howlaa as if zie were a minor annoyance, then shook his arm as if to displace a biting fly.

Howlaa flew through the air and struck a red-and-white striped crypt headfirst, landing in a heap.

The fat man caught sight of the messenger—who was now rather pointlessly trying to cower behind *me*—and sauntered over. The fat man was extraordinarily bowlegged, his chest hair was gray, and his genitals were entirely hidden under the generous flop of his belly-rolls.

As always in these situations, I wondered what it would be like to fear for my physical existence, and regretted that I would never know.

Behind the fat man, Howlaa rose, rippled, and transformed, taking on zir most fearsome shape, a creature I had never otherwise encountered, that Howlaa called a Rendigo. It was reptilian, armored in sharpened bony plates, with a long snout reminiscent of the were-crocodiles that lived in the sewer labyrinths below the Regent's palace. The Rendigo's four arms were useless for anything but killing, paws gauntleted in razor scales, with claws that dripped blinding toxins, and its four legs were capable of great speed and leaps. Howlaa seldom resorted to this form, because it came with a heavy freight of biochemical killing rage that could be hard to shake off afterward. Howlaa leapt at the fat man, landing on his back with unimaginable force, poison-wet claws flashing.

The fat man swiveled at the waist and flung Howlaa off his back, not even breaking stride, raising his sword over the messenger. The fat man was uninjured; all the blood and nastiness that streaked his body came from his victims. His sword passed through me and cleaved the messenger nearly in two.

The fat man smiled, looking at his work, then frowned, and blinked. His body flickered, becoming transparent in places, and he moaned before disappearing.

Howlaa, back in zir Nagalinda form, crouched and vomited out a sizzling stream of Rendigo venom and biochemical rage-agents.

Zie wiped zir mouth on zir arm, then stood up, glancing at the dead messenger. "Let's try it your way, Wisp," zie said. "On to the Regent's palace. Perhaps he has an idea for... another approach to the problem."

I thought about saying, "I told you so." I couldn't think of any reason to refrain. "I told you so," I said.

"Shushit," Howlaa said, but zie was preoccupied, thinking, doing what zie did best, assessing complex problems and trying to figure out the easiest way to kill the source of those problems, so I let zim be, and didn't taunt zim further.

Before we entered the palace, Howlaa took on one of zir common working shapes, that of a human woman with a trim assassin-athlete's body, short dark hair, and deceptively innocent-looking brown eyes. The Regent—who had begun his life as human, though long contact with the royal orphans had wrought certain changes in him physiologically and otherwise—found this form attractive, as I had often sensed from fluctuations in his body heat. I'd made the mistake of sharing that information with Howlaa once, and now Howlaa wore this shape every time zie met with the Regent, in hopes of discomforting him. I thought it was a wasted effort, as the Regent simply looked, and enjoyed, and was untroubled by Howlaa's unavailability.

We went up the cloudy white stone steps of the palace, which had been a great king's residence in some world far away, and was unlike any other architecture in Nexington-on-Axis. Some said the palace was alive, a growing thing, which seemed borne out by the ever-shifting arrangement of minarets and spires, the way the hallways meandered organically, and walls that appeared and disappeared. Others said it was not alive but simply magical. I had been reliably informed that the palace, unable to grow *out* because of the press of other government buildings on all sides, was growing *down*, adding a new subbasement every five years or so. No one knew where the excavated dirt went, or where the building materials came from—no one; that is, except possibly the royal orphans, who were not likely to share the knowledge with anyone.

Two armored Nagalinda guards escorted us into the palace. That was a better reason for Howlaa to change shape—Nagalinda didn't like seeing skinshifters wearing their forms, because it meant that at some point the skinshifter had ingested some portion of a Nagalinda's body, and while their species enjoyed eating their enemies, they didn't tolerate being eaten by others.

We were escorted, not to the audience room, but into one of the sub-basements. We were working members of the government, and received no pomp or ceremony. As we walked, the Nagalinda guards muttered to one another, complaining of bad dreams that had kept them up all night. I hadn't even realized that Nagalinda *could* dream.

We reached the underground heart of the palace, where the Regent stood at a railing looking down into the great pit that held the royal snatch-engines. He was tall, dressed in simple linen, white-haired, old but not elderly. We joined him, waiting to be spoken to, and as always I was staggered at the scale of the machinery that brought new buildings and land and large flora and fauna to the Ax.

The snatch-engines were towering coils of copper and silver and gleaming adamant, baroque machines that wheezed and rumbled and squealed, with huge gears turning, stacks venting steam, and catwalks crisscrossing down to the unseen bottom of the engine-shaft. The royal orphans scuttled along the catwalks and on the machinery itself, their bodies feathered and insectlike, scaled and horned, multilegged, some winged, all of them chittering and squeaking to one another, making subtle and gross refinements to the engines their long-dead parents, the Queen and Kings of Nexington-on-Axis, had built so many centuries ago. The orphans all had the inherent ability to steal things from passing worlds, but the engines augmented their powers by many orders of magnitude. The Queen and Kings had been able to communicate with other species, it was said, though they'd seldom bothered to do so; their orphans, each unlike its siblings except for the bizarre chimera-like make-up of their bodies, communicated with no one except the Regent.

"I understand you attempted to stop the killer on your way here," the Regent said, turning to face us. While his eyes were alert, his bearing was less upright than usual. He looked tired. "That was profoundly stupid."

"I've never encountered anything my Rendigo form couldn't kill," Howlaa said.

"I don't think *that's* a true statement anymore. You should have come to me first. I have something that might help you." The Regent stifled a yawn, then snapped his fingers. One of the royal orphans—a trundling thing with translucent skin through which deep blue organs could be seen—scrambled up to the railing, carrying a smoked-glass vial in one tiny hand. The Regent bowed formally, took the vial, and shooed the orphan away. "This is the blood of a questing beast. You may drink it."

"A questing beast!" I said. "How did you ever capture one?"

"We have our secrets," the Regent said.

Howlaa snorted. "Even questing beasts die sometime, Wisp. The snatch-engines probably grabbed the corpse of one." Zie was pretending to be unimpressed, but I saw zir hands shake as zie took the vial.

Questing beasts were near-legendary apex predators, the only creatures able to hunt extra-dimensional creatures. They could pursue prey across dimensions, grasping their victims with tendrils of math and magic, and pursuing them forever, even across branching worlds.

"Wherever the killer disappears to, you'll be able to follow him, once you shift into the skin of a questing beast," the Regent said.

"Yes, I've grasped the implications," Howlaa said.

"Then you've also grasped the possible avenues of escape this skin will provide you," the Regent said. "But if you think of leaving this world for frivolous reasons, or of not returning when your mission is complete, there will be... consequences."

"I know," Howlaa said, squeezing the vial in zir hand. "That's what my little Wisp is for."

"I will be vigilant, Regent," I said.

"Oh, indeed, I'm sure," the Regent said. "Away, then. Go into the city. The killer seems to favor marketplaces and restaurants, places where there is a high concentration of victims—he has appeared in five such locations since yesterday. Take this." He passed Howlaa a misshapen sapphire, cloudy and cracked, dangling on a thin metal chain. "If any civil servant sees the killer, they will notify you through this, and, once you drink the blood of the questing beast, you will be able to 'port yourself to the location instantly."

Howlaa nodded. I would go wherever Howlaa did, for my particulate substance was inextricably entangled with zir gross anatomy. Howlaa uncapped the vial and drank the blood. Zir body, through the arcane processes of zir kind, sequenced the genetic information of the questing beast, the macro-in-the-micro implicit in the blood, and incorporated the properties of the beast. Howlaa shivered, closed zir eyes, swallowed, and whined deep in zir throat. Then, with a little sigh of pleasure, Howlaa opened zir eyes and said, voice only slightly trembling, "Let's go, Wisp. On with the hunt."

The killer did not reappear that day. Howlaa and I went to the Western Outskirts, one of the few safe open spaces in the Ax, so zie could practice being the questing beast. It's dangerous to loiter in empty lots in the city proper, because the royal snatch-engines are configured to look for buildings that can fill available gaps. Thus, a space that is at one moment a weed-filled lot can in another instant be occupied by an apartment building full of bewildered humans, or a plaster-hive of angrily jostled buzz-men, or stranger things—and anyone who happened to be standing in the empty lot when the building appeared would be flattened. But the Western Outskirts are set aside for outdoor recreations, acre upon acre of playing fields, ramshackle wooden sky-diving platforms, lakes of various liquids for swimming or bathing or dueling, obstacle courses, consensual-cannibalism hunting grounds, and similar public spaces. Howlaa chose an empty field marked off with white lines for some unknown game, and transformed into the questing beast.

As one of the bodiless, dedicated to observation, it shames me to admit that I could make little sense of Howlaa's new form; too much of zir body occupied non-visible dimensions. I saw limbs, golden fur, the impression of claws, something flickering that might have been a tail, pendulum-swinging in and out of phase, but nothing my vision could settle on or hold. Looking at Howlaa in this form agitated me. If I had a stomach, I might have found it nauseating.

Howlaa flickered back to zir female human form and spent some minutes curled on the ground, moaning. "Coming back to this body is a bit of a shock," zie said after a while. "But I think I get the general idea. I can go anywhere just by finding the right trail of scent."

"But you *won't* go anywhere. You won't try to escape."

Howlaa threw a clod of dirt at me. "Correct, Wisp, I won't. But not because you'd try to stop me—"

"I *would* stop you."

"— only because I don't like being tossed aside in a fight. I'm going to follow this fat bastard, and I'm going to *chew* on him. You can't lose a questing beast once it gets its claws in you."

"So... now we wait."

"Now *you* wait. I'm going to drink," Howlaa said. "One of the advantages of wearing a human skin is that something as cheap and plentiful as alcohol provides such a fine buzz."

"Is this the best time to become intoxicated?" We bodiless have a reputation for being prudish and judgmental, which is not unwarranted. I can never get drunk, can never pleasantly impair my own faculties, and I am resentful of (and confused by) those bodied creatures that can.

"Which time? This time, when I might be killed by a fat man with a golden sword tomorrow? Yes, I'd say that's the best time for intoxication."

The next morning, we went to a den of vile iniquity near the palace. While Howlaa drank, I observed, and listened. I learned that a plague of nightmares was troubling the city center, and many of the bar's patrons had gone to stay with relatives in more far-flung districts in order to get some sleep. At least Howlaa and I wouldn't be called upon to deal with *that* crisis—bad dreams were rather too metaphysical a problem for Howlaa's methods to solve.

After a morning of Howlaa's hard drinking, the sing-charm the Regent had given us began to sound. Howlaa was underneath a table, talking to zimself, and seemed oblivious to the gem's keening, though everyone else in the bar heard, and went silent.

"Howlaa," I said, rumbling my voice in zir bones, making zim sit up. Zie scowled, then skinshifted into a Nagalinda form, becoming instantly sober. Nagalinda process alcohol as easily as humans process water.

"Off we go," Howlaa said, and rushed into the street, transforming into the questing beast once zie was far enough away to avoid inadvertently snagging any of the bar patrons with extra-dimensional tendrils.

We *traveled*, the city folding and flickering around us, buildings bleeding light, darkness pressing in from odd angles until I was hopelessly disoriented. Seconds later we were in the middle of the Landlock Sea, on a floating wooden platform so large that it barely seemed to move. The sea-market nearby was in chaos, fishermen and hunters of various species—Manipogos, Hydrans, Mhorags, others—running wildly for boats and bridges or diving into the water to get away from the fat man, who was now armed with a golden trident. He speared people, laughing, and Howlaa went for him and grappled, flashing tendrils wrapping around the fat man's bulk, barely seen limbs knocking aside his weapon. The fat man stumbled, staggered, and fell to his knees. Howlaa's ferocious lashings didn't penetrate the man's impossibly durable flesh, but at least he'd been prevented from doing further murder.

Then the man vanished, and Howlaa with him, and I was pulled along in their wake, on my way to wherever the fat man went when he wasn't killing residents of the Ax for sport.

For a moment, I looked down on the Ax, which spun as sedately as a gear in a great machine, and other universes flashed past, their edges blue- and red-shifting as they went by at tremendous speeds, briefly touching the Ax, sparks flying at the contact, the royal snatch-engines making their cross-dimensional depredations. Then we plummeted into an oncoming blur of blue-green-white, and after a period of blackness, I found myself in another world.

"*Wisp*," Howlaa hissed as I came back into focus. I had never been unconscious before—even my "sleep" is just a blessed respite from sensory input, not a loss of consciousness—and I did not like the sensation. Our passage from the Ax to this other plane had agitated my particles so severely that I'd lost cohesion, and, thus, awareness.

Now that my faculties were in control of me again, I saw a star-flecked night sky above, and Howlaa in zir human-female form, crouching by bushes beside a brick wall. I did not see the fat man anywhere.

"What—" I began.

"Quiet," Howlaa whispered, looking around nervously. I looked, but saw nothing to worry about. Grass, flowerbeds, and beside us a single-story brick house of a sort sometimes seen in the blander sections of the Middling Residential District. "The fat man got away," Howlaa said. "Only he actually *melted* away, or misted away, or... My tentacles didn't slip. He didn't slip through them. He just *disappeared*. Nothing can escape a questing beast."

"Perhaps the legends exaggerate the beast's powers," I said.

"Perhaps you'd best shushit and *listen*, Wisp. There's an open window just over there, and I can *almost* hear..."

I did not have to settle for almost. I floated above the bushes a few feet to the window, which opened onto a bedroom occupied by two humans, neither of them the fat man. The man and woman were both in bed, illuminated by a single bedside lamp. The man, who was pigeon-chested and had thinning hair, gestured excitedly, and the woman, an exhausted-looking blonde, lay propped on one elbow, looking at him through half-closed eyelids.

I listened, and because Howlaa is (I grudgingly admit) better at data analysis than I am, I let zir listen, too, by extending a portion of my attenuated substance down toward zim, a probing presence that zie sensed and accepted. My vision blurred, and sounds took on strange echoes, but then I found my focus and stopped picking up residuals of Howlaa's sensory input—but zie would see and hear everything as clearly as I did.

"It's amazing," the man was saying. "They get more real all the time. I know you think it's stupid, but lucid dreaming is *amazing*, I'm so glad I took that seminar. It's like living a whole other life while I'm asleep!"

"What did you do this time?" She leaned back and closed her eyes.

The man hesitated. "I was in a sort of fish-market. There were fish-people, mermaids, selkies, things like that, and ordinary people, too, all buying and selling things. There was a lake, or an inland sea, and we were all on a wooden platform floating on the water..."

"You get seasick just stepping over a puddle," she said.

He looked at her, mouth a tense line, eyes narrowed, and I think if she had seen his expression she would have leapt from the bed in fear for her life. Unless long association with this man had dulled her awareness to the dark currents in him I saw so clearly.

"My dream body doesn't get sick," he said. "It's part of my positive visualization technique. My dream body is impervious to harm."

"And I bet you look like a movie star, too."

Another hesitation, this one accompanied by a troubled frown. "Something like that."

I wondered what his dream-self *really* looked like—his father? An old enemy? A figure from a childhood nightmare that he could not escape, but was eventually able to embody?

He continued. "The only problem is, I can't seem to control where I *go*. The teacher at the seminar said that was the best part, being able to go to the mountains or the beach or outer space as easily as thinking it. But I just find myself in this city full of strange people and creatures, and..."

"Do you fuck any of those strange people?" she asked.

"No. It's not like that."

"What good's having control of your dreams if you can't wish yourself into a sex dream? Seems like *that* would be the best part."

"I want to go back to sleep," he said. "I want to try again."

"You don't have to ask my permission. I was sleeping fine until you sat up and started yelling. Doesn't sound like lucid dreaming is doing you much good—you're still having nightmares."

"The nightmares are different now," he said. "I'm in control." But she just turned over and pulled the sheet up to her neck.

"He's the fat man," Howlaa said, speaking silently into me, able to share thoughts as easily as we shared senses. "He goes to the Ax in his dreams, and he kills us for pleasure. That's why the questing beast couldn't hold the killer, why he melted away, because he has no substance beyond the borders of the Ax."

"Madness," I said, though Howlaa's intuitive leaps had proven right more often than my resultant skepticism.

"No, I think I've figured it. The Regent has consulted with many onei-romancers, lucid dreamers, and archetype-hunters over the years—I know, because I was sent to kidnap many of them and press-gang them into civil service. I never knew why he wanted them before. I think that, with the Regent's help, the royal orphans have constructed a machine to steal dreams. A *dream* engine, that grabs mental figments and makes them real. But they locked on to this madman's dream, and now his dream-self will keep coming, and killing, until this world spirals too far from the Ax for the engine to reach, which could take years."

"A dream engine," I repeated. "The activity of such a machine might explain the plague of nightmares in the city center."

"I doubt the Regent would worry overmuch about properly shielding any strange radiations," Howlaa said. "This is a new low for him. It's not enough that he grows rich through the orphans' thefts—now he wants to pillage our dreams, too."

The man lay on his back, staring at the ceiling. Despite his words, he did not seem eager to sleep again. If Howlaa was right, the man had just been chased out of his fantasy of infinite strength by the monstrous questing beast, which would be enough to give any dreamer pause.

"If you're right, we have to kill him," I said.

"Or not," Howlaa said.

Howlaa severed our connection, swirling my motes, and so it took me a moment to realize zie was transforming into the questing beast again—and I knew why. To jump away from this world, to another plane, adjacent to this one but not necessarily adjacent to the Ax. A few dimensional leaps, a little time, and zie would be far beyond the Ax's influence, beyond the grasp of even the greatest snatch-engines.

But I still had a chance, this brief moment between transformations, to strike, and I did. I performed the one act that Howlaa could not resist, the power I was given permission to use only in circumstances as extreme as these.

I took possession of Howlaa's body.

Zie fought, and I batted zir efforts aside, then simply reveled in having a body, especially a body as sensitive as the questing beast's, seeing into higher dimensions, seeing colors that only exist between worlds. I wanted to fly through suns, roll across jagged stones, immerse myself in lava, *feel feel feel* this forever.

Howlaa was laughing at me, a tinny internal sound. "Shushit," I said, not speaking aloud. I didn't even know if this body had vocal cords. "You didn't escape. You failed. We're going to kill this man, and then return to the Ax."

"Go on then," Howlaa said. "Best of luck."

I attempted to take a step forward, and everything blurred. My head rang with odd chimes, and bizarre scents assailed me. I had never been in a body so sensitive to smell—each scent was like a line attached to me, tugging me in one direction or another. I paused, and the chaos of sensory input lessened. I took another step toward the dream-killer's window, and this time a whole new set of sensations struck me, making me fall to the ground.

"This form will not do," I said.

"Why not? Because you have no finesse, Wisp? Because you can control gross motor functions, but the intricacies are lost to you? In the questing beast's form, even the most trivial movement is intricate. Then why not take another form, a simpler one?"

I felt rage—glandular rage, pumping up from somewhere in this body, a biological response to a mental state. I never get used to that, the feedback loop of mind and body that the corporeal undergo constantly, and I tried to dismiss its effects. I couldn't shift into another form. That was far too intricate a task for my understanding of how to control a body. If Howlaa had been in a human form, I could have broken into the man's house, stabbed him with a knife, and walked out again—such simple physical manipulation was within my powers. But as the questing beast...

"We have reached an impasse," I said.

"And what do you propose?"

"Kill this man," I said. "And I will not report your attempt to escape."

Howlaa laughed. "Oh, please, don't report me. What will they do? Sentence me to another lifetime of servitude?"

"Just kill him! That's why we came."

"I came to kill an invulnerable fat man with the golden weapons, Wisp, not a mentally disturbed human in his bed."

"They are the same!"

"They are not the same. This man is mad, but he is not the killer—he simply dreams of killing."

"But... his dreams are evil..."

"You would hold us responsible for our dreams now? If so, I am a regicide a thousand times over, for in my dreams, I rip the Regent and his orphans to wet bits every night. The Regent is the guilty party in this—he has made a machine that steals dreams, and he brought the killer to our city."

"What do you recommend?" I said.

"Fixing this problem at the source. Which is what I was trying to do when you so rudely possessed me."

"You were trying to escape." I said.

"No, Wisp, I was trying to return to Nexington-on-Axis. Sorry I didn't consult you—my understanding was that you're an observer, here to lend me support."

"I am here to make sure you serve your duty," I replied, wondering if zie was telling the truth.

"I will. But my duty is not to the Regent. I serve the welfare of Nexington-on-Axis. Come, Wisp, and I'll show you I do have a sense of responsibility. Such a strong one, in fact, that I won't kill an innocent madman for the Regent's crimes."

With more shifting, we returned to the Ax.

We appeared in the Regent's private chambers, which should have been impossible, as there were safeguards against teleportation there. The Regent sat in a wingback chair, holding a ledger in his lap, and he raised his eyebrows when we appeared.

Howlaa shifted to zir female human form, only swaying a bit on zir feet in the aftermath of being the beast. "Huh," zie said. "I wondered if that would work. It's said nothing can stop a questing beast from coming and going as it pleases."

"Mmm," the Regent said. "I trust you solved our problem, and disposed of the fat man? I'll see you get something extra in your next pay allotment. Now, go away. I'm busy." He looked back down at his ledger.

Howlaa cleared zir throat. "Regent. I require your assistance in the fulfillment of my duties."

The Regent looked up. "You didn't kill the fat man?"

"My investigation is ongoing. I need to see the new snatch-engine, the one that steals dreams, and I may have some questions regarding its operation."

The Regent set his ledger aside and stared at Howlaa for a long moment. "Well," he said. "You are not famed for your powers of deduction,

Howlaa Moor, but for your powers of destruction. I had not expected you to make inquiries, and I did not ask you to. You are dismissed from this case. I will assign someone else to deal with the fat man."

"Respectfully, sir, you may not interfere with any legitimate inquiries I care to make in an ongoing investigation. My contract prohibits such interference. Again, please have me escorted to the new snatch-engine, and provide someone knowledgeable to answer any questions I might have. Or do you believe this line of inquiry is without cause? If so, I would be happy to bring my evidence before the magisters." Howlaa smiled.

I was in awe at zir audacity. To confront the Regent this way! And zie had no evidence, just intuition and inference. If the Regent called zir bluff... But no. He didn't want any evidence Howlaa might possess brought before the magisters and, indirectly, the citizens of the Ax.

"I am the Regent, Moor. You take orders from me."

"Indeed. But my contract states that I serve the city, and not the ruler. You may not lawfully inhibit me. Break my contract, if you like, and I'll not trouble you again. Otherwise, you are obliged to cooperate."

"I could have you executed for treason."

Howlaa bowed. "You are welcome to try, sir." Skinshifters *could* be executed, but it was difficult, since a long-lived member of the species would have forms resistant to most obvious methods of execution. "But if you choose not to execute me or break my contract, then I must ask, for the third time, that you take me to the dream engine and provide —"

"Yes," the Regent snapped. "Fine."

I was astonished. Howlaa's bluff had succeeded. Zie was too valuable for the Regent to dismiss from duty or kill, and his own laws prevented any other action.

The Regent couldn't simply disregard these laws, for they were the source of his power. Without his laws, there would be no city of Nexington-on-Axis, just a giant junkheap full of things snatched at random by the orphans, indiscriminate slaves to their magpie impulses. "But I am about to show you a state secret."

"That's fine," Howlaa said. "My contract gives me any necessary clearances to fulfill my duties—"

"I *know* what your contract says, Moor. I wrote it myself, so you would be forced to serve the city in perpetuity, even in the event of my death. Now shut up about it. I'm taking you where you want to go. If you speak a word about this device to anyone, you *will* be executed for treason. We have methods designed for your kind. There's a special chamber in one of the basements for disposing of skinshifters."

"I serve the state," Howlaa said. "I will not betray it."

I wondered what kind of execution chamber the Regent had that could hold a questing beast, since the safeguards on his private chambers had been insufficient to keep the beast *out*. I didn't think the Regent realized what kind of power he was giving Howlaa by letting zim drink the questing beast's blood.

We set off down the shifting opalescent corridors of the palace, and the walls groaned around us as they moved.

"You think the killer is a dream-being, snatched here by the experimental engine," the Regent said as we walked.

"I'll submit my report when my investigation is complete," Howlaa said. "Along with my recommendations for how to rectify the problem."

The Regent scowled, but kept walking. Finally we reached a door of black iron. The stone around it was discolored and cracked—the substance of the palace apparently had an allergy to iron, but the heavy metal had certain magic-resistant properties that made its use necessary on occasion. The Regent knocked, a complex rhythm, his unbreakable adamant signet ring clanging against the metal with each rap.

The door swung open silently, and the Regent ushered us into the dimly lit place beyond.

"This is the dream engine," the Regent said. "Not what you expected, I wager."

"No," Howlaa murmured. "It's not."

Unlike the snatch-engines, there were no gears here, no oiled pistons, no sparking ladders of electricity, no bell-shaped domes of glass, no miles of copper pipes for coolant. There was only a throbbing organic mass in a web of wires, a red-and-green slick thing with no visible eyes or limbs, though it did have vestigial wings, prismatic like a dragonfly's, which drooped to the floor. A royal orphan, pinned in a web of wires.

Howlaa crossed zir arms. "So it's psychic, then," zie said.

The Regent smiled. "In a way. It sees dreams. More importantly, it *covets* dreams. And what the royal orphans covet, they get. Much of the process of governing Nexington-on-Axis is making sure the orphans want things the city *needs*. They don't care what happens to the things they snatch. They simply live for the process of snatching. This one is no different, except for the sorts of thing it snatches."

"You haven't been successful making this one want things the city needs, since it pulled a madman's murderous dream to this world."

"You're certain of that?" the Regent said.

Howlaa just nodded, and the Regent sighed. "I'll have to spend some time tuning the process. It's still experimental. I trust you found and killed the dreamer, to prevent another incident?"

"I did not," Howlaa said. "If I had known for certain about the existence of this dream engine, I would have tried, but I only had suspicions. When I grabbed the fat man, I was carried to another world, surrounded by houses filled with sleeping humans, with no sign of the fat man anywhere. That's when I began to suspect that I'd grabbed a dream-figment—I remembered your studies with various experts on dreaming, Platonic ideals, the collective unconscious, things of that nature."

"You have quite a memory," the Regent said.

"I drank the blood of an elephant once," Howlaa said, and I almost laughed. "Since I wasn't *sure* the killer was a dream-thing, I came back here to inquire further."

"We should talk in the hall," the Regent said abruptly. "Vibrations disturb the engine." Indeed, the vestigial wings were flickering, weakly, and we left the room. Once in the hall, the Regent said, "How do you intend to proceed?"

"When the killer appears again, I'll grab him, and when he sweeps me back to the human world with him again... well, I think it's safe to assume that the dangerous dreamer will be somewhere in the general vicinity of the place where I land. I'll simply kill everyone within a mile or so. It will take time, but I have some forms that are suited to the task."

I was stunned. I knew Howlaa was lying. Zie knew very well who the dreamer was, and had shown no inclination to kill him. So what *was* zie planning?

"Very good," the Regent said. "But if you mention a *word* about the contents of that room, I'll have you flayed into your component atoms. Understood?"

"The authorities appreciate your cooperation," Howlaa said. The Regent sniffed and walked away.

"Come, Wisp. Back to our eternal vigilance."

"Back to the bar, you mean."

"Just so." Howlaa grimaced, touching zir stomach. "Shit," zie said. "I've got a pain in my gut."

"Are you all right?"

"Probably something I ate in another form, that doesn't agree with this one. I'll be all right." Zie shivered, stretched, and became the questing beast. We traveled.

I tried to get some sense out of Howlaa at the bar, before zie drank too many red bulldozers, primal screams, and gravity wells to maintain a coherent conversation. I slipped a tendril into zir mind and said, "What is your plan?"

"Assume what I told the Regent is true," Howlaa said, smiling at the human bartender, who looked appreciatively at zir human breasts as she mixed drinks. "If things work out, it won't matter, but if things go badly, you'll need all the plausible deniability you can get. No reason for you to go down with me if I fail. This way you can honestly claim ignorance of my plans."

"You want to protect me from getting in trouble with the Regent?" I said, almost touched.

Zie laughed aloud and gulped a fizzing reddish concoction. "No, Wisp. But on the off chance that they imprison me instead of putting me to death, I don't want to be stuck in a cell with you forever."

After that, zie wouldn't talk to me at all, but had fun as only Howlaa on the eve of zir potential death can.

Zie vomited more often than usual, though.

A day passed, and Howlaa was sober and bored at home, playing five-deck solitaire while I made desultory suggestions, before the fat man reappeared. The singing gem keened at midday. Howlaa cocked zir head, taking information from the gem.

Zie became the questing beast, and we were away.

This time we landed in the city center. The fat man sat on the obsidian steps of the Courthouse of Lesser Infractions, face turned up to the sun, smiling up at the light. He held a golden scythe across his knees, and blood and bodies lay strewn all over the steps around him, many wearing the star-patterned robes of magisters.

Howlaa did not hesitate, but traveled again, this time appearing directly in front of the fat man. Zie lashed out with barely visible hooked appendages and grasped the fat man. Then Howlaa traveled again. We reappeared in the racing precinct, startling the spectators and scattering the thoroughbred chimeras. The fat man struggled in the hoof-churned mud, his weapon gone.

I had barely overcome my disorientation before Howlaa traveled again. I knew it was Howlaa controlling the movement, for the sensation was quite different from the swirling transcendence that came when the fat man dragged us to that other world. This time we appeared in another populated area, the vaulted gray halls of the Chapel of Blessed Increase in the monastic quarter. We flickered again, Howlaa and the fat man still locked in struggle, and flashed briefly through another dozen places around the city, all filled with startled citizens—in the adder's pit, the ladder to the stars, the moss forest, the monster farm, the glass park, the burning island. We even passed through the Regent's inner chamber, briefly, though he was not there, and through other rooms in the palace, courtrooms, dungeons, and chambers of government. There was a fair amount of incidental damage in many of these instances, as the fat man rolled around, kicked, and thrashed.

Then we appeared in the dream engine's chamber, and everything in my full-circle visual field wobbled and ran, either as an aftereffect of all that spatial violation, or because bringing a dream into such proximity with the dream engine set up unstable resonances.

Howlaa and the fat man thrashed right into the pulsing royal orphan in its tangle of wires. The orphan's wings fluttered as it broke free from the mountings, and the ovoid body fell to the floor with a sick, liquid sound, like a piece of rotten fruit dropping onto pavement. The fat man broke free of Howlaa—though that wasn't possible, so Howlaa must have *let* him go. He attacked Howlaa, who flickered and reappeared on the far side of the weakly pulsing royal orphan. The fat man roared and strode forward, a new weapon suddenly in his hand, a six-foot polearm covered in barbs and hooks. He tread on the royal orphan, which popped and deflated, a wet, ripe odor filling the room. The fat man swung at the unmoving Howlaa, but the weapon disappeared in mid-arc. The fat man stumbled, falling to one knee, then moaned and came apart. It was like seeing a shadow-sculpture dissolve at the wave of an artist's hand, his substance darkening, becoming transparent, and finally melting away.

Howlaa became human, fell to zir knees, and shivered. "Feel sick," zie said, grimacing.

I was terrified. The Regent might kill us for this. We'd stopped the fat man, yes, but at the cost of a royal orphan's life. "We have to go, Howlaa," I said. "Become the questing beast. I won't try to stop you—let's flee across the worlds. We have to get away."

But Howlaa did not hear, for zie was vomiting now, violently, zir whole body heaving, red and milky white and translucent syrupy stuff coming from zir mouth, mingling with the ichor from the dead orphan on the floor.

The door opened. The Regent and two Nagalinda guards entered. "No!" the Regent cried. "No, no, no!" The guards seized Howlaa, who was still vomiting, and dragged zim away. I floated along inexorably behind. The

Regent stayed, kneeling by the dead orphan, gently touching its unmoving rainbow wings.

"Feeling better, traitor?," the Regent said. Howlaa sat, pale and still unwell, on a hard wooden bench before the Regent's desk.

"A bit," Howlaa said.

The Regent smiled. "You didn't think I'd let you be the questing beast forever, did you? I couldn't risk your escape. Wisp is one line of defense against that, but I felt another was needed, so I laced the blood with poison and bound their substances together. When the poison activated, your body expelled it, along with all the questing beast's genetic material. You've lost the power to take that form."

"I've never vomited up an entire shape before," Howlaa said. "It was an unpleasant experience."

"The first of many, for a traitor like you."

"Regent," I said. "As Howlaa's witness, I must inform you that you are incorrect. Howlaa did not mean to harm the orphan. The fat man appeared and disappeared, and Howlaa and I were simply carried along with him. Surely there are others who can attest to that, testify that we appeared all over the city, fighting? Howlaa held on, hoping the fat man would fade and we would be taken to the world of the dreamer, but before that could happen... well. The dream engine was damaged."

"The *orphan* was *killed*," the Regent said. "You expect me to believe that, by coincidence, the last place Howlaa and the killer appeared was in that room?"

"We could hardly appear anywhere after that, Regent, since the dream engine was destroyed, dissolving the fat man in the process." I spoke respectfully. "Had that not happened, I cannot tell you where the fat man might have traveled next."

"He was a lucid dreamer," Howlaa said. "He'd learned to move around at will. He was trying to shake me off, bouncing all over the city."

The Regent stared at Howlaa. "That orphan was the result of decades of research, cloning, cross-breeding—the pinnacle of the bloodline. With a bit of practice, it would have been the most powerful of the orphans, and this city would have flourished as never before. We would have entered an age of dreams."

"It is a great loss, Regent," Howlaa said. "And we certainly deserve no honor or glory for our work—I failed to kill the dreamer. He killed himself. But I did not kill the orphan, either. The fat man tread upon it."

"Wisp," the Regent said. "You affirm, on your honor as a witness, that this is true?"

My honor as a witness. My honor demanded that I respect Howlaa's elegant solution, which had saved the city further murder and also destroyed the Regent's wicked dream engine. I think the Regent misunderstood the oath he requested. "Yes," I said.

"Get out of here, both of you," he said. "There will be no bonus pay for this farce. No pay at all, in fact, until I decide to reinstate you to active duty."

"As you say, Regent," Howlaa and I said together, and took our leave.

"You lied for me, Wisp," Howlaa said that night, reclining on zir heap of soft furs and coarse fabrics.

"I provided an interpretation that fit the objectively available facts," I said.

"You knew I was the one dragging the killer around the city, not vice-versa."

"So it seemed to me subjectively," I said. "But if the Regent chose to access my memory and see things as I had seen them, there would be no such subjectivity, so it hardly seemed relevant to the discussion."

"I owe you one, Wisp," Howlaa said.

"I did what I thought best. We are partners."

"No, you misunderstand. I owe you one, and I want you to take it, right now." Zie held out zir hand.

After a moment, I understood. I drifted down to Howlaa's body, and into it, taking over zir body. Howlaa did not resist, and the sensation was utterly different from the other times I had taken possession, when most of my attention went to fighting zir for control. I sank back in the furs and fabrics, shivering in ecstasy at the sensations on zir—on *my*—skin.

"The body is yours for the night," Howlaa said in my—our—mind. "Do with it what you will."

"Thank you."

"You had the right of it," Howlaa said. "We are partners. Finally, and for the first time, partners."

I buried myself in furs, and reveled in the tactile experience until the exquisite, never-before-experienced sensation of drowsiness overtook me. I fell asleep in that body, and in sleep I dreamed my own dreams, the first dreams of my life. They were beautiful, and lush, and could not be stolen.

STORY NOTES

Story notes are self-indulgent, I know, but I've always loved back-and-front matter, introductions and conclusions and author's notes, so it's an indulgence I allow myself. I hope you find some pleasure in them too.

Hart and Boot

I've always been fascinated by the Old West, especially the way it was mythologized even as it was happening—people were living in a real, dirty, dangerous, lawless frontier, and those same people were writing dime novels set in the Wild West, telling idealized stories about justice, heroism, villainy, and revenge! "Hart and Boot" is a magical secret history in that same spirit. Pearl Hart and John (or Joe) Boot were real stagecoach robbers, and they were captured and imprisoned much as the story describes. I didn't intentionally violate any known facts about their history, though I did streamline things a bit and take some liberties with chronology—Pearl's backstory, in particular, is rather more complex than the way I described it, and I encourage interested readers to research her further. The fact that there are conflicting histories about Pearl Hart made my work easier, because faced with two or three versions of the same story, I chose whichever best served the story's needs. My version of John Boot is a tulpa—a being created from imagination and willpower—though that word never appears in the story, since it's not a term Pearl would have been likely to know. This story was chosen to appear in *The Best American Short Stories: 2005*. I thank editor Michael Chabon for selecting the story (and significantly raising my writerly profile in the process).

Life in Stone

I have an acknowledged but conflicted fascination with badasses in literature. My friend Dawson (himself something of a badass) and I used

207

to stage mental contests between our favorite literary, comic book, and cinematic badasses: Elric, Lan Mandragoran, Jules Winnfield, the Corinthian, Storm Shadow, Hap Collins & Leonard Pine, Hannibal Lecter... you get the idea. Not all heroes, not all villains, just "people with which you would not wish to fuck," as we used to say. I'm frequently tempted to write about badasses of my own, but I try to be careful not to oversimplify, or to make them one-dimensional. Mr. Zealand is one such badass, and one of my own favorite characters. I like his weariness, his capability, his tragedy, his potential for redemption.

I wrote this story at the Hidden City writing workshop in Lake Tahoe, in 2004, a week-long retreat organized by the writers Susan Fry and Jae Brim. The first draft came out in a single afternoon, quite fast for me, which freed up the rest of the week for drinking, eating gourmet meals, hiking, and almost drowning after passing out in the hot tub. It is probably not necessary to note that I am, personally, not much of a badass.

Cup and Table

"Cup and Table" is one of those stories I thought about for years, though it was the characters, more than their journey, that I found most fascinating. Sigmund the addicted visionary; Carlsbad the reluctant monster; Carlotta and Ray, the despicable duo; and the enigmatic New Doctor. I always thought I would write a novel about those characters, or possibly a series of novels, but I could never get a handle on what the *story* should be, except that I knew it should be vast, and involve interlocking conspiracies, and secret societies, and physical and moral decay, and possibly my characters running through a booby-trapped temple full of poison arrows and flaming boulders. I wrote several scenes about them over the years, but none of them added up to anything substantial. When David Moles and Susan Marie Groppi put out the call for their *Twenty Epics* anthology—they wanted epic fantasy stories without the epic length—my thoughts immediately turned back to those characters. I realized that I *could* write a novel about them, and have it compressed into under 5,000 words, if I just left out most of the connective tissue. What I wound up with was an epic contemporary fantasy novel, smashed with a hammer, with only the brightest fragments picked up and made into a mosaic. I might return to these characters at greater length another time, though of necessity I'd have to set any stories about them *before* the events of "Cup and Table." Because, since it's an epic, at the end of the story the world is forever changed.

In a Glass Casket

I love writing about kids, and I try to do so without condescension, drawing as much as possible on my own memories of childhood. This story isn't autobiographical in any literal sense, but it seems almost like autobiography in *spirit*—I see a lot of myself in Billy Cates, just trying to do the right thing, and afraid of everything going wrong.

Terrible Ones

I'm wary of writing about figures from Greek mythology—I wrote a *lot* of stories based on Greek myths when I was younger, and lately I've tried to diversify—but this story idea was irresistible, and the images of doddering old Furies and a Greek Chorus in bedsheet-togas were too tempting to pass up. Those ideas combined with some thoughts I was having about various permutations of the sex trade. My wife is a book buyer for an erotica catalogue, and San Francisco (just across the bay from where I live) has a boisterous and sprawling sex-positive and kinky community, so I've met various people in the business. There's a certain kind of customer who has trouble ascertaining the dividing line between fantasy and reality, and that seemed like the sort of fatal flaw from which Greek tragedies are made. I tossed in a little *Medea*, stirred the pot, and out came "Terrible Ones." My thanks to the members of the 2003 Rio Hondo Writers Workshop for their comments and critiques on this piece.

Romanticore

This is one of the stories I'm most proud of, and one of the most difficult to write. There are some stories where there's so much to say that it's better to say nothing at all, so I leave this one to speak for itself.

Living with the Harpy

Some people complain that the protagonist of this story is an idiot for choosing a mundane life over a magical one. I respectfully disagree. This story isn't about the choice between the magical and the ordinary; it's a story about being brave enough to let yourself get hurt in the pursuit of something potentially wonderful. But, mostly, it's about how weird it would be to live with a harpy.

This story was one of my early experiments with telling a story solely through the use of connective tissue—showing the moments *between* dramatic scenes, rather than the dramatic scenes themselves, and letting the quiet interstitial moments resonate with things left unsaid. I used something of the same approach in "Cup and Table," though in both instances there are *some* moments of real drama, because, at the end of the day, I love a good spectacle.

Komodo

I like tough female protagonists. I don't know why; maybe because I was raised by tough women. The heroine of "Komodo" is probably too tough for her own good, though, and so this is a story about letting yourself be helped by your community. It's also about Komodo dragons and guys who are cavalier assholes.

Bottom Feeding

I always liked those salmon of wisdom stories, but I grew up in the South, where the local fish of legend and story is the catfish (mudcats, channel cats, etc.). I thought how neat it would be to write a salmon of wisdom story wrapped in Southern trappings, sort of the way Howard Waldrop recast the story of Hercules as a Southern epic in *A Dozen Tough Jobs*. But the more I thought about it, the more I began to feel that catfish were fundamentally different from salmon—being bottom-feeders with bellies full of garbage, eating indiscriminately. So the story became something far stranger—and, I hope, far better—than a simple retelling of an Irish legend in a Georgia setting.

Like many of my stories, this one is about grief, and love, and how one can be the antidote for the other.

The Tyrant in Love

I think "The Tyrant in Love" is the oldest story in this collection. I wrote it in college, probably in 1997 or 1998, though it's been revised since then, to clean up the clunky language. I won't comment on the story, except to say that, shortly after it was written, I read it aloud to a woman who admired my writing, and whom I hoped to seduce. In retrospect, that was probably one of my stupider ideas.

Impossible Dreams

"Impossible Dreams" is my long-talked-about alternate-universe-video-store story. I've been gathering material for this for *years*. It's light, and certainly a little silly, but it's also sweet, which is exactly what it's supposed to be. Sweet love stories are underrated. Romance makes me happy, and so do movies, and so does movie trivia, and all those things are present here. My thanks go to my friend Brian Auton for first telling me about much of the movie trivia I used here, and to the generous readers of my online journal, who contributed other tidbits. Most of the alternate-universe movies described are at least remotely plausible; at the very least they're firmly rooted in specious Hollywood apocrypha.

Lachrymose and the Golden Egg

"Lachrymose and the Golden Egg" is another romance, almost a romantic comedy, except for the whole dying-of-a-terminal-illness thing. It is, despite the obvious fantasy trappings, arguably a pure science fiction story, which makes it a rarity for me. I wrote it because I wanted to do a Virtual Reality story without the goggles-and-gloves, sensory-deprivation-tank trappings of most VR stories, and because opium dreams are at *least* as interesting as immersive video games, and definitely have better graphics.

Dream Engine

I never, ever, ever start a story with nothing in mind but a title. Except this one time. I'd wanted to write something called "Dream Engine" for years (and I still expect to someday write a story called "Meme Engine"), but never found the story that belonged to the title. I finally put that title, and the weird steampunk imagery it conjured, together with an old idea about a man who becomes a murderer in his dreams. I'd also been thinking a lot about the structure of the Sherlock Holmes stories and similar tales, where the narrator is not the obvious protagonist of the story (Watson tells the stories, but Holmes is the hero)—it's an odd structure, with both advantages and disadvantages, but at its best, it can serve to illuminate the character of both the narrator and his subject. Then, somehow, in one of those occasional gifts from the gods of story, I started scribbling, and out came Wisp's voice, and his opening complaint about the city where he lives, at the center of all universes, and about his unreasonable partner/prisoner/whatever, Howlaa Moor. This story is dear to me, and it was a pleasure to write from start to finish, from setting to character to plot. The hardest thing about the story was keeping the pronouns straight when Howlaa constantly switched genders, so I finally decided to go with gender-neutral pronouns, which adds a nice touch of up-front weirdness to the tale. I think I'll return to the city of royal orphans and their voracious snatch-engines another time. Wisp has other stories to tell about Howlaa.

Night Shade Books Is an Independent Publisher of Quality SF, Fantasy and Horror

Night Shade Books Is an Independent Publisher of Quality SF, Fantasy and Horror

Tim Pratt's stories have appeared in *The Best American Short Stories*, *The Year's Best Fantasy and Horror*, and lots of other nice places. His first novel, *The Strange Adventures of Rangergirl*, debuted in 2005, and his new urban fantasy series will begin with *Blood Engines*, due in Fall 2007. He lives in Oakland California with his wife, writer Heather Shaw.